No. 1 SECRET STREET

A NOVEL

CHARLES McDONALD

For information about this title or to order other books and/or electronic media, contact the publisher:
Deaniemac
P.O. Box 987
Freeport, FL 32439
charles@deaniemac.com

ISBN: 978-0-9987981-0-3 (Hardback)
        978-0-9987981-4-1 (Paperback)
        978-0-9987981-7-2 (eBook)

Printed in the United States of America
Cover and Interior design: 1106 Design

Dedicated to Deanie and Judy
for your encouragement and understanding
during my life.

Chapter 1
BREAKFAST

Duncan and Nellie Kent woke up exactly ten minutes before sunrise in their twenty thousand-square-foot beachfront home in Destin, Florida. The home had three stories, but only their guests used the upper floors. There was plenty of room on the first floor for just two people.

The coffeepot timer was set with an outside light sensor that "talked" to their digitized home-management system. By the time they had slipped on their usual beach attire, the coffee was brewed and ready on the patio. Early-morning coffee on the patio was warming and good. The coffee provided a slow and tasty awakening, especially with Duncan's coffee-mix recipe of two packs of Splenda and one teaspoon each of the chocolate, vanilla, and original flavor Coffeemate creamers per cup. Duncan and Nellie enjoyed quietly sipping on their coffee until the caffeine kicked in. The sound and smell of the soft surf provided a sense of relaxation, comfort, and peace.

Duncan would check the *Wall Street Journal* while Nellie read the emails that came in over night.

After the coffee, and as the sun began to rise over the Sandestin resort area, Duncan walked into the kitchen to cook breakfast, leaving Nellie to enjoy the breeze and continue with her emails. He liked to cook breakfast. Today he prepared bacon, over-easy eggs, and biscuits that would give a good start to the big day ahead. After twenty minutes in the kitchen, he carried the meal onto the patio, including a small jar of pink May Haw jelly from Louisiana and butter. Duncan buttered the biscuits to allow the butter to soak into them. The jelly would give a great finishing touch. Although she ate some of everything, Nellie never finished all of her breakfast. Perhaps that was why she maintained her trim figure. As they finished their breakfast, Duncan walked over to one of the other patio lounge chairs and pulled out from under its cushion a small box in gold wrapping paper and a beautiful green bow.

"Happy Birthday, Nellie. I hope you like it," said Duncan.

Nellie smiled and said, "Duncan, you are such a wonderful husband. You've given me everything I could possibly want. Thank you for thinking of me. I love you, sweetheart."

Nellie proceeded to unwrap the package and looked inside. She reached in, pulled out a ring box, and opened it slowly. Inside was a beautiful gold dinner ring that had a large cream-colored pearl with an intricately cut emerald inlay in the shape of a kiwi bird on top of the beautiful pearl. The bird was standing on a small strip inlay of 24-karat gold.

"I love it! It's perfect!" exclaimed Nellie.

"I had it custom made for you, my dear. And it will fit perfectly into our upcoming plans," said Duncan.

They watched a few early-rising beach walkers stroll down the sugar-sand beaches. The water this morning was that beautiful, clear, emerald-green color that caused the area to be known as "The Emerald Coast of Florida." The breeze was from the north, making the waves less than a foot high. A few fishing boats were trolling for mackerel about two hundred yards offshore.

In his younger days, Duncan's hair had been black. Now, at sixty-five, strands of gray added a sophisticated salt-and-pepper air about him. Duncan was tall, at six foot three, and muscular, at 225 pounds. He worked out almost every day, but today he would not have the time. His mostly wrinkle-free olive complexion was likely a genetic gift from his Italian mother. His curiosity about his own genetics was the initial driving force that had started him on his lifelong career.

At an early age Duncan realized his main interest was around biology. By twenty-four, he had completed a PhD in genetics, and after a few years at a California genetics company, he started his own company. His company, Grainteck Incorporated, was very successful, primarily because of Duncan's knowledge in developing many genetic improvements in plant food sources. He developed strains of vegetables that would last substantially longer during shipment, and genetic strains of grains that improved yields by almost 50 percent and were also resistant to drought and disease.

Over time, those patented genetic grain improvements became the standard for genetically modified wheat, corn and rice seeds worldwide. Through licensing programs with other growers of genetically modified seeds, Grainteck's patented genetics held 100 percent of the genetically modified market share for those three primary grains. Since his genetically modified seed would not reproduce naturally, the seeds had to be specially grown each year and shipped to farmers around the world. Each year, millions of tons of genetically modified Grainteck seeds were grown and sold. He was proud of his contribution to fighting world hunger and it was paying off handsomely.

Five years earlier, on his sixtieth birthday, Duncan had hand selected a company president, John Earnest. John kept Duncan's business going strong. Remaining as CEO, Duncan could keep an eye on his empire but not have to be at the office. Although he had some up-and-coming seed geneticists in the company, he personally directed any modifications to his patented genetic formulas. With modern computer technology it was easy for him to work from home. It was his passion and he wasn't ready to give that up, at least not yet.

Duncan owned 100 percent of the company, and the Kent personal fortune had grown and continued to grow rapidly. It was now in excess of $26 billion in personal investments plus the intrinsic value of his company, and that didn't include the billions of dollars spent in the previous ten years on special personal projects and charities.

Since Grainteck was not a public company, no one knew Duncan and Nellie's personal net worth and that was just fine with them. Their investments were reasonably secure, and their investment manager was instructed to buy only decent dividend-paying stocks and bonds. Those investments were currently paying an average of 5.5 percent, and that amounted to more than a billion dollars a year in excess of their already colossal company income. They had more money than they would ever need. Philanthropy made sense to them both. They preferred to fly under the radar of the government, politicians, charities and anyone else with their hand out, so most of their charity work was anonymous. Most of their recent contributions had been to aid American soldiers returning from fighting in useless wars in the Middle East after having been sent by stupid politicians with nothing personally to lose.

The first five years of semi-retirement had been good and gave Duncan and Nellie an opportunity to consider what "giving back" really meant. They often discussed which charities were a good fit, and which weren't. With some research, they had discovered dishonest people were running several charities. Those people took most of the contributions as salaries for themselves, their families, and cronies.

Having just celebrated his sixty-fifth birthday, they decided it was time to start giving back beyond his and Nellie's normal charity contributions. They had decided to do something really big. Something that would make a real difference and have a true impact on mankind.

Although the typical summer humidity was high, there was no rain in the forecast. They had anticipated an easy ten-mile drive over Mid-Bay Bridge to the town of Niceville to see their lawyer, Joe Hawkins. This meeting was perhaps one of the most important steps in their lives.

The ten o'clock appointment would be the beginning of a very long meeting. Joe had been their personal lawyer for the past thirty-five years, and Duncan and Nellie trusted him—unlike most practicing lawyers. They thought that all of the lawyer jokes had to have some degree of validity to them, but they had never found that issue to be the case with Joe.

Duncan quickly read the headlines from the morning paper as he finished his jelly biscuit.

"Nellie, this goddamn world is just a mess. People are being killed everywhere in the wars being fought in the name of religion in Iraq, Syria, Libya, Afghanistan, Palestine, Israel, Ukraine, and Nigeria, just to mention a few! They are either religious wars or egotistical political leaders' wars. There are drugs, gangs, crime, and disease everywhere! Air and water pollution are accelerating. Clean, fresh water is in short supply. People are afraid to fly, take a cruise, or attend any large events. All governments are failing to protect and defend their citizens! Excessive taxation and free handouts from government have broken down the whole system.

"Poverty is rampant throughout the world, and people are starving despite all of the hard work that I and other people have done to improve food supplies. And yet, the population continues to grow every year, with no end in sight! Everyone acts like the earth's resources are unlimited. They say that we have global warming caused by any number of issues from coal to oil to cows farting. They never consider the fact that it might be people farting! Besides, there would not need to be so many cows and cars and power plants if people would stop breeding like rats! None of those self-serving politicians have the balls to address the real issues and fix this mess. They all have to be politically correct to ensure they keep their taxpayer-funded jobs!" He could feel his blood pressure rising. Was it the coffee or his anger over the mess the world was in?

Nellie, in her normal easygoing tone replied, "So . . . hotshot, what are you going to do about it?" A quick glance and a big smile came to Duncan's scowling, reddened face. She had a way to calm him when his temper got the best of him. Nellie also knew that these issues were Duncan's pet peeves. He had worked his whole life to improve the well-being of mankind but had seen mankind's place in the world deteriorating rapidly. Nellie did not disagree, having seen the same negative evolution, but she didn't want to encourage his building anger.

Nellie was a beautiful woman. Her short black hair had to have just a little "color help" now at age sixty-four. Her blue eyes and light complexion made for an attractive combination. She'd earned a degree in math and had taught high school in Niceville for seven years.

She met Duncan when she was thirty at the Boathouse restaurant in Destin, while Duncan was on a summer vacation with his friends from California. It was his first night in Destin.

The Boathouse was a really fun and unique place. It was made from a large boat slip that somehow had earned city approval—or else was grandfathered in—to deck out a wooden floor just above the harbor water level and build walls and a tin roof over the deck. Food consisted mainly of raw oysters or burgers with fries. Their other specialty was an overpriced bowl of boiled peanuts that one could never seem to get filled up on. No air-conditioning existed, only a flow-through breeze. Music came from a small sixteen-square-foot area in one corner where typically a single singer with a guitar could play for tips.

The Boathouse tradition was simple and decidedly red-neck. Late at night or in the early morning hours, with drinks flowing and music playing, bras and other intimate items or signed dollar bills ended up stapled to the bare rafters and exposed stud walls. After several years of being in business, the wood of the support walls and ceiling were hardly visible. Duncan and Nellie had such a great time together that first night, they decided to go out every night that week.

After that week, they knew they were meant to be together. She had accepted his offer to move in with him in his San Diego apartment. After just three months, they got married. She never worked again. They were happy spending time dreaming of all the possibilities life could hold for their lifetime adventure. They had planned to have children, but Nellie's polycystic ovary syndrome prevented conception. Neither Duncan nor Nellie wanted to adopt.

Without children, happiness for the Kents was achieved with great vacations, good friends, and an uncommon agreement of views on almost everything.

Nellie had always dreamed of returning to the Gulf Coast, where she had grown up and first met Duncan. When he turned sixty, Duncan relinquished some control over his San Diego-based company to make Nellie's dream come true. It seemed as if their golden years would be a restful and happy time, filled with a pleasing lifestyle and good friends.

The old saying that "Old age is hell" didn't apply to Duncan and Nellie; they both were very active and energetic. They looked and felt more like they were in their late forties. Now in their mid-sixties they still enjoyed skiing every Christmas holiday in their favorite ski town of Steamboat Springs, Colorado. Hiking and bike riding kept their weight at optimal health levels on days when they didn't work out in their three thousand-square-foot spa and gym.

This fifth year of semi-retirement found Duncan and Nellie refreshed and re-energized with new thoughts, ideas and projects. And they were big projects.

He had been searching for direction over the past four years and now showed excitement and focus to his friends in Destin about some new challenge that he would not disclose. Duncan and Nellie had decided to keep their excitement to themselves until their ideas had a more solid foundation. They were making plans for their "new special project," which they named the ESCAPE Project.

ESCAPE was an acronym that they had thought up one night after a few glasses of wine. It stood for Environmentally Sustained Capacity and Peaceful Earth, even though it had the more obvious second meaning—escaping to a better place. Nellie was good at the work and enjoyed the additional challenges that Duncan would share with her. He was such a creative guy. They loved working as a team. She just loved him!

Duncan really loved Nellie, too. She was the perfect wife and partner. She could go into any social situation and charm everyone she met. She did have a valuable knack for spotting people they didn't want to associate with for any length of time. She would occasionally whisper in his ear during a meal about someone she had met, "That guy is an asshole" or "Wow, is she a slut—bless her little heart" in true southern fashion. He didn't know how she did it, but most of the time she was right. This had allowed Duncan to focus on business issues and Nellie to identify people issues. He called her his "people screener."

Chapter 2
WORLD TRAVELERS

When Duncan had first begun semi-retirement, he and Nellie were anxious to go and see the world. They began by traveling through Europe. It had been fun and enjoyable. They visited England, Scotland, Ireland, Portugal, Spain, France, Germany, Italy, Switzerland, Denmark, and Norway extensively over the first two years. Duncan kept in touch with his company through the Internet and cell phones.

During the third year, trips to the Middle East, India, Pakistan, and Africa had been shocking! After these trips, they wondered how such cultures could exist in modern times. The religious dogma that generated hate for other religions as well as the horrible treatment of women was just unbelievable; had they not seen it for themselves, they might not have believed that such places existed. The poverty and filthy conditions in many areas were havens for disease and death. Ebola, AIDS, malaria, and many other diseases were normal and common conditions. Malnutrition and starvation were growing. Education was pathetic.

They wondered why nothing was being done to stop the root cause of the problems. The primary cause was over-population relative to the capacity of the environment and the economic activity to support so many people. Instead of solutions, they saw futile attempts at "humanitarian efforts" to "save the children" without thought as to what they were being saved for! Was it really humanitarian to save a child *into* a future life of misery and horror? Was it really a "rescue," or was it an extension of a terribly torturous life? Or, was it just a guilt issue of the wealthy to help them feel better about their fortunes?

Even with Duncan's dramatic improvements in genetic crop yields, how many people could the earth really support? On one occasion, a friend had sent them a link to watch an Internet video on immigration relative to the population of the world poor. The video made the situation even clearer about the growing plight of overpopulation and how little anyone could really do to help stop the ultimate global disaster. No politician or world leader even talked about it, as it would be political suicide for the politicians running countries. They all had to be politically correct to keep their elected jobs. It was okay for the politicians to talk about global warming but not okay to talk about the real issues that are simply the result of demand from a growing world population.

If there were fewer people, there would be less demand for oil, gas, and chemicals, which would lead to fewer carbon dioxide emissions. Obviously the political and religious power struggles were all about the few and had never resulted in any real positive changes for the many. The situation they saw would forever impact their views and opinion of the world. It weighed heavily on Duncan and Nellie that they really couldn't fix it or make a dent in the problem, even with their wealth. They could see a sad end in the making and were somewhat relieved that they had not brought any children into this declining situation.

Chapter 3
THE CRUISE

Needing some level of recovery from the depressing and dismal third-world tour from the previous year, they began their fourth year of semi-retirement by taking a cruise in January from Long Beach, California, to Sydney, Australia. The cruise had lasted thirty-four days and was a blast. It was a smaller ship, with only about one hundred and sixty five suites. Room service and liquor were included in the price of the trip. The service was extraordinary—and tipping wasn't required.

The price wasn't cheap, but that didn't matter. Most everyone on board was financially well off. Most travelers were of the Kents' generation, and that presented opportunities for great conversations with people who had similar interests and ideas. Nellie, being the social butterfly, met many new people from around the world, several of whom remained their friends after the cruise. In particular, a medical doctor who had retired from the Baylor Medical Center and from teaching, Paul Stevens, and his wife, Mary Ellen, who now lived off the coast of Maine, north of Portland. Paul was seventy-nine and Mary Ellen was a few years younger. Mary Ellen was a firecracker. She was short, about five foot two, had been a lawyer and in a previous marriage had been a state attorney general's wife. After her first marriage, she had become a stunt pilot, and then moved to Belize, where she opened an Italian restaurant. It was while in Belize she had met Paul.

Duncan and Nellie hoped to visit them the following year in Maine. It would provide a great opportunity for the Kents to escape the tourists and humidity of Destin for a few weeks in August. They hoped to visit often to enjoy their companionship as well as some cool weather and a few great Maine lobster meals. Their mutual interest in medicine and genetics assured that conversations would always be interesting and enlightening.

Their stops on the thirty-four-day cruise had included four days in Hawaii, four in Polynesia, four in New Zealand, as well as the final destination of Sydney. Duncan had a big surprise for Nellie in Polynesia. He had planned for a tour to circle the round island of Mo'orea at 1 in the afternoon, but had insisted she leave the cruise ship with him at 8:30. They walked past rows of vendors hoping to sell the voyagers some souvenirs. Duncan rushed her past the vendors to prevent Nellie's time consuming desire to check out each one. He rushed her onto the parking lot, where cabs and shuttles would arrive for tours. Nellie was surprised that a shuttle was waiting for them to take them to Eva Pearles's shop about two miles away.

The shuttle driver was a French girl who worked for Eva. Five minutes later, they arrived and walked into the small, clean, modern shop. Duncan knew, from the 100 percent satisfaction from dozens of customers and a five-star rating, that this was the place to buy Tahitian black pearls. Eva was a trim French lady who had studied in Chicago and seventeen years earlier had moved to Mo'orea to start her own pearl business. Eva explained that most people don't know about Tahitian pearls. So she usually spent an hour or two explaining the differences and the value associated with those differences. She explained that the pearls weren't actually black. They were multicolored.

She told them the pearls in Tahiti were the result of a unique breed of oysters that live in the shallow areas around the islands. They were correctly known as black-lip pearl oysters, so named for the dark, black lips inside the oysters. She explained a lot about how the oysters were grown on farms and harvested and how the pearls were graded. She had cultivated her relationships with the growers to secure her ability to get priority selection for her custom jewelry.

At the end of the day, Duncan had bought Nellie a beautiful custom necklace, earrings, and a ring. They looked so nice on her. He hoped she would wear them. But Nellie had a tendency to fear losing her jewelry, so she would buy costume jewelry to wear and keep her "real" jewelry in a safe. It made no sense to Duncan at all. But then again, he had been told that 25 percent of the women in the United States were on some type of drugs for mental disorders. So, that meant to him that that 75 percent of American women were going around totally untreated. He would remind Nellie of that joke any time one of her "special" habits would pop up. She would always smile and say, "Look, this finger doesn't have a ring on it!" Then she would show him her right middle finger and laugh. Duncan would never win that one.

After the cruise ended in Sydney, they flew on to Phuket, Thailand, for two weeks at the JW Marriott Hotel. It was a superb hotel, and the service was first class. The people of Thailand were gracious and polite. The Kents couldn't help but notice the poverty that existed whenever they ventured away from the usual tourist traps.

Their favorite places of all of the ports-of-call were those in New Zealand. They enjoyed it so much they decided to fly back to Auckland for an additional three months, hoping to explore the north coast and enjoy some great New Zealand wines. With the exception of the inevitable creeping in of old age, it seemed as though their personal lives could not be better.

Duncan rented a black Mercedes SUV for their travels in New Zealand. It was waiting for them at the airport. Their chartered private jet landed at 6 in Auckland. After the porter loaded their luggage into the SUV, Duncan drove to the Hotel Sofitel and checked in. It was already dark when they arrived. The hotel was beautiful, with dazzling colors accented by strategically placed lights. They had reserved a penthouse suite for five days. The Viaduct Café provided a light dinner, and they settled in for the evening.

Duncan was up as the sun began to rise. After donning his favorite pair of worn white shorts and a red T-shirt, he opened the living room curtains wide to take in the view. He could see at least fifteen yachts in the adjoining harbor. People were already moving around the dock area and getting ready for a big day on the water. Nellie was still asleep. She would likely sleep until nine or later. She did not do well with jet lag.

They had ordered a pot of coffee, orange juice, and English muffins the night before, and the doorbell rang right on time at 6:30. Duncan opened the door, and the roomservice attendant entered and rolled his tray to the dining table. He was dressed in a black suit and was wearing white gloves. A white cotton tablecloth was spread over the round table in the dining area of the suite. The utensils were placed ever so properly. Duncan gave him a $40 tip, in US currency, as he hadn't had time to get any New Zealand money yet. The server smiled, thanked him, and left the room.

Duncan poured himself a cup of coffee and added his usual sweetener and creamer; then he walked to the balcony to sip on his first cup. He grabbed the morning paper the server had brought and took a seat on a patio chair. As he breathed in the fresh air and relaxed, he quickly scanned the front page of the Monday morning paper. More terror, more financial crises, more nations' political bullshit—a typical front page!

He couldn't help but wish he could hide from all that crap. New Zealand was such a beautiful country, without a lot of the crap, or at least it seemed that way. Surely there had to be something sinister brewing around this country somewhere. Duncan turned to the real estate section and looked under "Farms for Sale." His business with Grainteck had made him particularly fond of country farms and the peace and tranquility that seemed to exist there. Perhaps he should buy a farm here for Nellie and himself, he thought. Once he eventually sold Grainteck, what would keep his excitement going? He had questions, but answers were just not yet available.

In the "Land" section of the real estate page, Duncan saw an advertisement that caught his eye.

The advertisement read:

> For Sale: 10,000-acre farm 15 miles west of Tapora. Includes all livestock and equipment. Skilled resident farmhands to remain. $12,000,000.
>
> Contact Jonathan Collins of Whareshine Realty for detail information. Phone 919-777-3012.

The advertisement piqued Duncan's interest. *I wonder what it looks like? What would it be like to live there?* He had to see it!

Nellie awoke at 9:15. Wearing her favorite warm beige robe, she came out to the balcony to see Duncan. Duncan warmed up a cup of coffee for her. As usual Nellie's morning chatter was minimal. Duncan, however, had been up for three hours and was anxious to show Nellie the farm advertisement.

An hour passed, and Duncan opened up with a bang. "Nellie, what do you think about living on a farm? I found one advertised in the paper, and I want us to check it out. It's a ten thousand acre farm about a ninety-minute drive northwest of here. Here, see?" Duncan shoved the paper over Nellie's unfinished second cup of coffee, and she gave him a quick dirty look.

"You sure are pushy this morning. I thought we were going to take a few days to rest up from all of our travel," said Nellie.

"Yeah, you're right, dear; we did say that. But I saw the advertisement in the paper this morning, and it got my blood pumping," replied Duncan.

Nellie read the advertisement and handed the paper back to Duncan. He waited for her reply as she resumed sipping her coffee. She sat the cup down as Duncan realized he hadn't breathed during her apparently deliberately-delayed response. He took a deep breath and said, "Well?"

"Duncan, if we moved to a farm here in New Zealand, we would be totally without any of the friends we have known for so many years, and far away from what we are most familiar with," stated Nellie.

"Perhaps I could work that out to your satisfaction," Duncan said. "If I could do that, would you be open to at least giving it a chance?"

"I guess I would. Let's just check it out first," Nellie said, after finally finishing her coffee and moving on to her English muffin topped with butter and grape jelly. She knew Duncan would have his way. He was as stubborn as they came. But she also knew he would do nothing without her approval and cooperation.

Duncan called Jonathan Collins at eleven o'clock. Jonathan answered with a strong English accent. "Hello, mate, this is

Jonathan Collins, and whom do I have the pleasure of speaking with today?"

"This is Duncan Kent," Duncan replied. "I saw the advertisement in today's paper, and would like to see the ten thousand-acre farm. My wife and I are in Auckland. So how do you recommend that we do this?"

"Mate, since you're a ninety-minute drive away, I suggest you start out about 7:30 tomorrow morning and meet me here at my office in Whareshine at nine. From there, we can go in my Land Rover to the farm. It takes about fifteen minutes to get there from my office, and I can give you more details as we drive. It may take us about five or six hours to see it all. If you leave at 3, you'll be back in Auckland by four-thirty. There are no restaurants there, so I'll bring a picnic lunch and plenty of drinks. The mate who owned the land died about six months ago, and his family is quite anxious to sell."

"Okay, we'll see you tomorrow morning," responded Duncan.

The remainder of the day was spent relaxing in the hotel room. Duncan was writing and scribbling on paper like a madman most of the day. He had ideas and liked to write down his ideas on paper until he had a final idea or plan. He ordered a full package of copy paper and two rolls of clear tape from guest services for immediate delivery. Nellie could tell when he was in deep thought because his blue eyes would dart back and forth. Even though Nellie had told him about the darting before, he didn't want to believe it.

By the time they retired that night, Duncan had an entire wall of the penthouse covered with sheets of paper taped from floor to ceiling. Meals were ordered from room service. Duncan could hardly take time to eat. He would pace the floor, occasionally grab a bite, and then continue pacing. Nellie would occasionally check the wall of paper and try to figure out what he was doing. She said nothing. She would not interrupt Duncan's thought process.

Morning came quickly, and the Kents got up at 5:30, showered, and donned their blue jeans and long-sleeved light-blue shirts. They wanted to look somewhat like farm people, and that was the best they could do from their suitcases. A quick donut and coffee in the lobby, and they left the hotel promptly at 7:30. They could have left at least thirty minutes earlier, but Nellie always had to do her makeup thing. Duncan had long ago given up on trying to change her and now just accepted the minimum thirty- to sixty-minute makeup ritual.

The pinkish light of the sunrise slowly disappeared as they drove up Highway 1 over the Harbor Bridge and along the western side of Shoal Bay. They turned left on Highway 16 and continued on their planned ninety-minute drive.

Ten minutes after they left the city of Auckland, the trappings of a metropolitan city quickly ended. They were in farm country. They drove through expansive fields of grapevines and kiwi farms. Sheep grazed along the beautiful green hills adorned with fencerows of evergreen trees.

New Zealand vineyards had developed a substantial wine industry. The mild climate was similar to California's Napa

Valley, and the rich volcanic soil was perfect for growing grapevines. The numerous wineries were now shipping award-winning bottles of wine all over the world. Along the drive, Duncan outlined his plan to Nellie. She understood and was in full agreement, provided Duncan could actually make it all work. There were a lot of details that would have to be worked out, but she knew that if anyone could do it, Duncan could.

Chapter 4
THE FARM

They arrived right on time at Jonathan's small real estate office in Whareshine. Just above the front door was a large white sign with black letters that read "Whareshine Realty Company." Duncan dodged two water-filled potholes and parked in front of the office. It was an old, run-down brick gas station. The bricks had been painted white, but it was obviously a long time ago, as the paint was flaking off and falling on the gravel driveway. Landscaping didn't exist, and the grass along the sides of the building was more than a foot high. The gas pumps were long gone, but the elevated concrete bases still remained. The single front door was wood and was open halfway. The two front windows were covered with paper sheets of homes and land for sale. As they walked into the office, a gray-haired and brown-eyed man was getting up from behind an old wooden desk covered with paper. "Welcome, mates. I'm Jonathan." He was a small man, about five foot seven and weighed about 150 pounds. He appeared to be about sixty years old and had tried to dress up his well-worn clothes with a tan sport coat. Duncan and Nellie introduced themselves and shook hands with Jonathan. After a few brief exchanges, Jonathan said, "We should go now to be sure we get finished on time."

Driving to the farm, they passed a few scattered farms. They appeared to be dairy or cattle farms, but with the rolling hills, there could have been crops further from the road. Homes were few and far between. An occasional dirt road, with a mailbox on the corner, would head across the lush green grass-covered hills toward some likely distant homestead. Most side roads had steel fabricated cattle guards attached to old rusty barbed wire fences with leaning fence posts that lined the main roadsides. Even though the fences were in need of repair, the rustic country look that they gave the landscape was quite beautiful.

As they drove, Jonathan began sharing details of the farm. "There are a widow and three children who now own the land. They are all living in Auckland now, and their farm is being run by their foreman and several on-site farm families. The family has been bickering and arguing and want to get the land sold to settle the family's financial problems.

"Their land consists of ten thousand acres of various crops and pastureland. A large bay that almost surrounds the area known as the Tapora region makes the northern, western, and southern borders of the farm. There are three other large farms that make up Tapora, and those farms border the land on the east.

"The town of Tapora consists of about a dozen small homes, a small school and a milk processing plant. On the Kileney farm that we'll be seeing today, there are about seven hundred and fifty head of cattle, three hundred sheep and around two hundred and twenty hogs. Half of the cattle are dairy cattle. Hay production takes up about one thousand acres and there are about five thousand acres in pasture. Most of the three thousand acres of crops are corn, soybean, and wheat. They have about one thousand acres in orchards of apples, pears, peaches, oranges, lemons, grapes, and kiwis. Their profits, after all expenses and loan payments, were running about $20 per acre when the old man was alive. But this last year, I don't think they made any profit.

"I grew up here in Whareshine and know all of these people around here. They're good farmers, but are all getting older, and their kids want to leave the farm and start careers in the cities. The farmers' only chance of retiring is to sell the farm, but there just are not many buyers nowadays.

"The old man, Ted Kileney, who owned the farm, had me try selling it five years ago, but we couldn't find a buyer. Ted turned eighty last year; then he suddenly died a few months later. It really shook up the other farmers around here, since most of them are about the same age and grew up with Ted. They would probably want to sell too, but there just aren't any buyers.

"I sure hope you're serious about buying the Kileney place. It's really a beautiful farm and has been well taken care of."

As they approached Tapora Park, Jonathan began pointing out some of the features of the area. "Now, right here is where the Tapora Park starts up. The park is very beautiful but is mostly a set-aside for natural trees and wildlife preservation. There aren't many visitors to the park, and the roads are pretty rough."

Nellie asked Jonathan, "Do you mean even rougher than the road we're on now?"

"Oh, yes, Mrs. Kent. It's very hilly in there, and the roads are crooked, some have room for only one car at a time.

"The park is all on your right. There's a small branch of the bay that extends up close to the road on your left. If it weren't for this one-kilometer strip of hills on the west side of Tapora Park, this whole forty thousand-acre area ahead of us, including the Kileney farm, would be an island. Because of its isolation and no through roads, the area is very private and isolated."

Nellie asked, "Who takes care of the roads? It's suddenly become even more rough."

"I apologize for the rough road, Mrs. Kent. The road gets narrower the closer we get to the farm. That's because there's just not enough traffic to justify paving. It's a dead end, you know," responded Jonathan. "The government takes care of the road up to the park that we just passed. The farm families formed a joint venture and use their own equipment for road maintenance. As you can see, they're all gravel-covered dirt roads. The potholes can be a bit deep at times, especially during planting and harvesting seasons, when the equipment and people are all in the fields. Also, with Mr. Kileney passing away, the roads aren't getting much attention."

Jonathan had obviously wanted to talk about the area. Duncan and Nellie stayed quiet and were happy to let him do most of the talking. Jonathan wasn't really a good salesman; he was more of a friend to all of the landowners. That could work to Duncan's advantage.

The first part of the tour of the farm lasted about three hours. They visited the farmhouse, the barns, the warehouses, and the beach areas. They drove the farm edges and saw well-manicured orchards and crops. They could see sheep and cattle grazing along the distant, taller hills. There were several small lakes strategically located in the lower rolling hills to hold water for irrigation. Fresh water for the few houses on the farm was supplied by wells at each home.

At noon, they stopped at a picnic site that the farmhands had built on a high bluff. The bluff was on a point that was the westernmost part of the farm and the entire Tapora region. From the point, one could see the entrance to the bay nearly ten kilometers farther west. The hills of the Tapora region seemed to force the bay to divide into a north bay and a south bay. The point overlooked a small barren island about one hundred feet wide and a mile long that seemed to be placed there to protect the point from the waves that rolled in from the sea. The barren island was a natural haven for birds. Looking west past the island toward the sea was breathtaking. It looked much like San Francisco Bay as seen from Berkeley. Duncan expected to see large skyscrapers on the left side of the bay entrance. There was nothing.

Nellie commented, "Duncan, this looks like we've gone back in time and are seeing San Francisco Bay in the early

1800s. Isn't this beautiful and unspoiled? And the temperature is so mild, it must be around sixty-eight degrees!"

The point had large, shady, live-oak trees that appeared to have been planted long ago. Their long branches spread at least thirty feet in every direction. The point had been a military site during World War II, and the concrete bunkers and gun pads were still in place. It made a great place for a picnic. They picked one of the three covered picnic tables. Nellie felt the sea breeze drifting up on to the land and rustling the green tree leaves. Back to the east along the curvy road they had come in on were gently upward-sloping rolling hills with scattered trees. The grass appeared to have been mowed but surely was the work of roving herds of sheep or cattle. About a mile from the point was where the farming areas began. Nellie thought to herself, *This might be the most beautiful place I've ever seen. It's so pure, so tranquil, so peaceful. If we do buy this farm, this is where I'm going to build our home.*

Jonathan opened the lunch basket and brought out ham sandwiches and chips. A gallon jug held unsweetened tea, but no ice was supplied. As they began to eat their lunch, Jonathan asked, "What do you folks think so far? Is this something you can see yourselves buying?"

Duncan looked at Nellie. He could tell from the smile on her face and the twinkle in her eye that she had already fallen in love with the point if not the entire Tapora area. He responded, "Yes, I'm interested, but I have some questions. What's the situation with the three other farmers in Tapora? Would any or all of them be interested in selling their farms to us?"

"Why?" asked Jonathan. "Don't you like this farm?"

"Oh, I like it fine, but I would be interested in buying up all of the property on Tapora except for the national park, of course," stated Duncan.

Jonathan suddenly felt weak. If he could sell all four farms, he would come out with perhaps two or three million in commissions. "Wha . . . wha . . . what? That would be at least forty thousand acres and about $50 million. Can you do that, Duncan?"

Duncan responded without hesitation. "Not a problem, Jonathan. As a matter of fact, we've seen enough today already. I'll make you a special offer. I'll buy all four farms, but nothing less than all four, for $50 million. That would be everything from the park to the south and west. If you can do that, in addition to your commission from the sellers, I'll throw in a $2 million bonus for you. Do we have a deal?"

Jonathan was still in shock and turning quite pale. He stuttered, "D . . . de . . . deal!"

They shook on it, and the conversation quickly shifted to more details about the resources in the area, including deep-water portage areas along the bay, fishing, hunting, laborers, laws, and regulations. Nellie sat back and just smiled. Her mind drifted to how she would like the house designed on the point. The conversations continued as they finished lunch and drove back to Jonathan's office.

As the Kents got into their car to leave, Duncan instructed Jonathan, "You'd better get busy; I'd like to know something by the end of the day on Friday. Call me at my hotel."

As they drove away, they saw Jonathan jumping up and down as he headed toward his front door. "Nellie, I think we got his attention, don't you?"

Nellie responded, "Honey, we have to have this property. I want to build our home at the point. I'm in love with that place already." Duncan knew what that meant. He would need to get the property, no matter what the cost. That was okay, though. He liked it, too.

Friday came and, at 2:15 the phone in the Kents' room rang. It was Jonathan Collins. "Duncan, this is Jonathan Collins. I have good news and bad news; which do you want first?"

"Give me the good news," replied Duncan.

"All three of the other farms will sell," continued Jonathan. "But the bad news is that the final price for all four farms would be $57 million. Each of the farmers have set their sales prices and signed a contract with me today. They want a 10 percent deposit, too. Can you do it, Duncan?"

"Hell yes, Jonathan! I wanted it all, so bring your ass over here with those contracts, and Nellie and I will sign them today contingent upon legal review and discovery. Oh, and we want to close in two weeks; this will be a cash deal," answered Duncan. "I'll be there in two hours. Don't go any-where," said Jonathan.

Duncan and Nellie decided to celebrate their new farming venture with a fine dinner in the Omni Restaurant, over-looking downtown Auckland. Over dinner, they discussed how they would begin to transition the four farms into a single farm with one general foreman reporting to Duncan.

They would find and hire the most skilled individual in New Zealand with a PhD in agriculture and make him an offer he couldn't refuse.

Over the next week, Duncan threw out many new ideas to Nellie. She'd added a lot to his thinking process. He continued to remove papers from his "thinking" wall and add new ones. She liked the planning of this adventure just as much as Duncan, perhaps even more.

Although she had been involved in a small way with Duncan's Grainteck business, she was a true equal partner in the farm and in determining what it would eventually become. Nellie wanted to hire an architectural firm in Auckland to begin the design of their new home. There were a multitude of very expensive projects buzzing around in Duncan's head, as well. Being a multibillionaire definitely had its advantages. They were about to spend a lot of their fortune to set up a farm halfway around the world from their home in Destin. The task would be huge. He needed help and lots of it. Duncan laughed as he told Nellie, "By God, if I'm going to be a farmer, I'm going to do it first class!"

Nellie came back with an off-the-cuff request. "Sweetie, since you know I really want to have our friends here with us, what do you think about me designing the town center that you mentioned to me, as well as our new home?"

Duncan responded, "That's a great idea, honey! You're now officially in charge of that. It sure will take a load off of me. Of course, I'd like to have some input as well."

"Like what, Mr. Farmer?" laughed Nellie.

"Well, for instance, in our home here, I want a closet the same size as yours, and I want to see the ocean from my backyard and the hills and mountains from my front yard."

"Done," said Nellie. She had already decided that but wanted to let Duncan think he'd gotten his way. She continued, "I've already decided our new home will be at that beautiful point where we had our picnic."

Duncan added, "I knew that at the picnic; you were already in la-la land, smiling like a teenager as you looked around. I know it will be a beautiful home." Then he said, "I want the town to have some guy things—sports bars, sports complexes, a giant auditorium. I also want the streets to be well lit and a lot like the main street in Disney World—brick-curbed streets with plenty of benches, lots of fountains, lakes, and parks. Cars won't be allowed on Kent Avenue. Everything should be within walking distance. Parking garages should be close and sufficient but well hidden or camouflaged, like the parking garages in Vegas. A lot of the parking will be for golf carts."

"No problem. I like all of that. Done, done, and done," replied Nellie.

Both Duncan and Nellie knew that this was not going to be an ordinary farm by any measure. In fact, they knew it would be a combination of a fully self-contained town that would include farms, industrial facilities, power, and shipping. During their return from Tapora, they had agreed to call it "The Farm," at least for the time being, until they came up with a better name.

Nellie continued. "What about our home in Destin? Should we sell it and move everything here?"

"I think it's just a bit early, honey. Maybe we'll sell in a few years. This plan is going to take at least three years, and I'll need to be in Destin a lot of the time to get the infrastructure planned and the needed resources for our plan to work.

"Also, you do realize that it's time to sell Grainteck? Blocked Canyon's asshole president, Jay Cameron, has been bugging me for eight years now to sell it to him. Perhaps I can get him to pay the price now!"

Chapter 5
STAYING LONGER

Duncan rang the front desk and asked to be transferred to the hotel manager. He wanted to book his suite for the next three months. The manager was more than happy to accommodate him at a special rate of $1,000 per night and offered to have the restaurant send up a complimentary dinner to his room. Duncan accepted and was transferred to the hotel restaurant to place their room service order. His next call was to the hotel bar. He ordered three bottles of New Zealand Chardonnay and a full bottle of Jack Daniels Old No. 7 and a dozen cokes.

The rest of the weekend was spent researching architectural firms, engineering firms, and construction companies on the Internet. They needed the best help possible. By the end of the weekend, Duncan had narrowed his search to three companies, with Crown Engineering being number one. Nellie had found ten architectural firms in Auckland and decided to call and see if any one of them had the capacity to build an entire town.

Monday, Duncan contacted the business-development for the City of Auckland, William Bowen, and set up a meeting for that evening at 6:00 over dinner.

Duncan arrived at the restaurant at 5:30 and was eager to get started. He secured a private room for undisturbed conversation. It was a critical meeting that would determine if Duncan and Nellie could move forward with their new ideas. William arrived right on time.

After a cordial greeting, they each ordered a glass of New Zealand red wine that William recommended. They talked in general about each of their backgrounds before the waitress took their orders.

Once the food order was completed, Duncan began, "William, I've just contracted for a very large tract of farm and ranch lands near Tapora. My initial plan was to have a small genetic research laboratory here and a part-time farm and ranch for my wife and my twilight years. However, we're considering a much larger possibility. Our secondary interest is to bring in a massive construction project and substantial industry. It would be a long-term project that would use large quantities of materials from Auckland businesses. For a general idea, I'm talking about spending more than $10 billion US on the front end and likely much more."

"Tell me more," smiled William.

Duncan continued, "We're just in the conceptual stage and if, I repeat *if*, I go forward with this, it will include a marina, a power plant, food-processing facilities, schools, hospitals, homes, condos, and multiple factories; a whole town built from scratch. It will be a total Research Project, and everything would eventually be totally private, much like a private island except for contracted products that would ship into the project from New Zealand and other places. Our research and operations would all be strictly confidential and very restricted from outside access and intervention. We would be doing research on the people as well as the capability of the town to be isolated from the outside. Of course, all New Zealand laws would be followed. We would have our own security, but we would work in concert with the local and national law enforcement operations. I'll need to bring in several thousand new residents to run the operations on a permanent basis. Is this something you can help us accomplish, or do I need to look elsewhere?"

William quickly answered, "You bet I'll help. It's not often that someone comes in with such a large investment. But, I would like to have an idea of what the objective of the research is."

"Fair enough," Duncan answered. "The objective will be to establish the physical and mental baseline and changes over time of a population that is isolated in a community that has full employment and is not subject to the stresses and perils of their current life situations."

"That sounds very interesting. Thanks for sharing that information with me, Duncan," responded William.

Duncan gave William a concerned look and said, "To move forward, I'll need some fast assistance with a few things:

"All of the people involved will need to have New Zealand citizenship.

"We'll also need a local and national business tax special exemption for at least ten years for all operations inside our gates. I'm willing to offer a $20 million upfront startup and approval fee to be divided as desired by the local and national governments and an annual alternative flat tax payment of $10 million US.

"We'll also need a New Zealand government liaison to handle interface issues with local and state officials, and a business liaison to coordinate business activities with New Zealand contractors. We'll pay a nice salary for the right people in these roles.

"And, last but not least, I need the New Zealand government to establish a special research privacy zone that provides the restrictions and privacy necessary for the research to function properly without outside intervention."

Duncan finished talking just as their meal arrived. The conversation on the project continued throughout dinner. As it turned out, William was well connected with the local and national governments and as such felt confident that a deal was workable. He had seen other deals done that were a lot less economically attractive than Duncan's proposed research operations.

As they finished an after-dinner cocktail, Duncan said, "William, I've enjoyed the discussion tonight, and I'm encouraged by your confidence to meet my needs for moving forward. When do you think you can get an offer from the local and national governments back to me for review and approval?"

William responded, "I'm going to make this my top priority, and I may be able to get an offer to you within two weeks. Will that work?"

"I think that will work just fine. Here's my card. Call me every couple of days to update me on your progress. I'm going to start tomorrow on the assumption that you'll come through for me," smiled Duncan.

On Tuesday, Duncan called Crown Engineering's president, Rick Sweeny, and set up an urgent lunch meeting. He left the hotel at 11:30 and took a cab to Alexandria's Restaurant. At the restaurant, he arranged for a private dining room. The room was on the second floor overlooking the bay. Rick showed up right on time. They introduced themselves and ordered lunch.

Duncan began the business discussion before the food arrived. "Rick, I've just purchased 40,000 acres of farmland in Tapora. The purchase will close in two weeks. Your firm has a great reputation, and I want to hire you. It'll be a lot of work and will need to be fast tracked.

"I want most everything completed in three years. I want you to design and construct a completely self-sustained two thousand-acre manufacturing and support complex that will do everything and even more than any port city would do. The complex would include a seaport, a power plant, electrical transmission, water, sewer, disposal, recycling, communications, natural gas pipelines, fuel distribution—all of the resources to support up to twenty thousand families, with ten thousand as an initial population for our 5,000 families.

"It will include a medium-sized town that would emulate a Disney World look. I need you to work with my wife and help her select an architectural firm to build the town itself. We'll be building offices, stores, a bank, condos, homes, parks, lakes, roads, and even a golf course.

"Although small in volume, the base manufacturing plants that I want to build will include the manufacture of concrete, lumber, steel, glass, paper, and other needed raw materials. We'll build a special genetic seed plant, which I already have some designs completed for. We'll need finished products made here, such as clothing, medicines, automobiles, boats, golf carts, farming equipment, electronics, furniture, jewelry, you name it . . . everything possible! The intent is that this place would be off the grid, completely isolated from the world at some future time. I know I'm asking a lot in a short time, but money isn't an issue. I'll be putting an initial deposit in a New Zealand bank of $4 billion US, but I know it'll cost more for everything I want to accomplish.

"I would propose that we keep the cost simple and do an all-in cost plus 10 percent contract paid monthly, with me doing all of the operational funding, with an initial $10 million line of credit to get you started.

"If, at the end, you have met the targeted startup date, you'll receive an additional 2 percent of the project cost as a bonus. Oh, yes, and lastly, we'll need to make this a very low-key and quiet project. What do you think?"

Lunch arrived right when Duncan finished his proposal. Duncan had ordered salmon and a salad, and Rick got lamb with soup. As they began to eat, Rick answered, "Duncan,

I like your offer. You've done your homework. You know what I need to make things move fast. I believe we can do this, but it will be expensive. I believe my board of directors will approve it. I'll call them tomorrow, set up a meeting, and get a confirmation. We have a lot of people to hire quickly for the design phase."

"Okay, then. We have a deal," replied Duncan.

They shook hands and continued to discuss ideas and generalities of the project and ate their lunch. Rick invited Duncan to ride back with him to their main office to see their operation. Duncan accepted, saying, "I'll need to have some offices set up in your building for myself and some of my people."

"We can do that, but due to the size of this project, we'll likely need to rent a large building or operate from rental spaces in several buildings," said Rick.

"Good. I would like a large office for me near your office starting two weeks from today. Get me a desk and a good secretary. Let me know the bank you want to use for me to deposit your first draw. I know I'm hitting you with a lot in one meeting, but I would guess that you'll be earning some serious bonuses with this deal, right?"

"I think so, Duncan, and I look forward to making it happen. Are you ready to head over to the office?" replied Rick.

"Yeah, let's go," said Duncan.

Nellie made phone calls on Tuesday to several architectural firms around Auckland. Most were not prepared to take on such a large project. Late in the day, she found one, Edwards Architectural, who showed interest and had a long history of successful large projects in New Zealand. She set up an appointment with Robert Neal, the company president, for the following day, and, after a couple of hours into the meeting, both Nellie and Robert realized that Edwards Architectural was not capable of handling the project alone. They were very knowledgeable in New Zealand design and construction, including the need for protection from earthquakes that were still quite common in the area. She learned that the Pacific plate's movement toward the west had actually formed New Zealand. The plate was still moving, and New Zealand was still growing. Nellie threw out an idea that Robert really liked. Nellie would have Robert contract with one of the architectural firms in the United States that had designed one of the large theme parks in Florida to provide the base design work, with oversight by Edwards Architectural. It was a good plan. Robert would get things moving tomorrow. He would have a general layout done within the week for her to review prior to the actual architectural work. The cost was no bid, just time and materials, and would include construction oversight.

Days flew by with Duncan and Nellie busy planning meetings. Duncan received his regular calls from William Bowen on his progress on government approvals. Two weeks after their first meeting, Duncan was presented with a proposal from the New Zealand government's Economic Development Council that met all of Duncan's conditions. The project was now ready to move forward at full speed.

Duncan made four phone calls Tuesday night around midnight New Zealand time to catch his Board members around noon on Monday. He contacted John Earnest, Tom Clark, Bob Erickson, and Bruce Bills. Each one was told the same thing, "I want you on our corporate jet tomorrow headed to Auckland. I'll have Debbie Tullos, my new secretary, get your rooms at the Hotel Sofitel, where we're staying, and reserve a board room here for the week so we can use it anytime we need it."

Chapter 6
DISCLOSURE TO
THE BOARD

The corporate jet landed, and the Board members were shuttled to the hotel, where their rooms were waiting. It had been a long flight, and speculation as to the urgency of the meeting had kept them awake most of the trip. Fortunately, their arrival time was late in the evening in New Zealand, so a good night's sleep would be welcome. Duncan had asked them to meet him in his penthouse suite at 9:00 the next morning after breakfast.

The Board arrived right on time at the penthouse suite, where Duncan and Nellie were waiting. They visited for a moment and then settled into the living room to hear the reason for this meeting that was urgent enough for a trip halfway around the world.

At noon, they took a lunch break. Duncan had all of their heads spinning with disbelief. That led to hundreds of questions, many of which Duncan and Nellie couldn't answer yet. The questions continued through lunch and back at the penthouse. Finally, at 6, the Board had concluded that The Farm and other projects that the Kents had described made sense, but would need a lot of effort to pull together in a timely manner. Duncan asked each director to join him in this adventure, and everyone agreed. They were his family, his trusted partners, the leaders he could rely on to make these projects a reality.

Duncan decided to offer positions that would support his plan. He asked John to continue to run Grainteck until the company was sold, hopefully to Blocked Canyon. Bob was asked to take on all construction activities and would move here within thirty days. Bruce would continue as CFO of Grainteck and in addition would take on the CFO position at The Farm. Tom would be in charge of recruitment for town members and also handle negotiations with Blocked Canyon.

On Wednesday, Duncan took his team to The Farm to see firsthand the location of the project. The day was filled with more questions, suggestions, and ideas. The base concepts began to firm up with the new ideas and suggestions from the Board members.

Thursday, Friday, and Saturday were spent with the engineering, construction, and architectural firms to continue with planning and budget development. On Sunday, everyone but Bob flew home to San Diego. Bob had decided to spend the following week finding a furnished rental apartment near the Crown Engineering office and get his office set up in Crown headquarters.

Chapter 7
CONSTRUCTION PLANS

Robert Neal contacted Nellie and was asked to review the preliminary plot map for the city and residences. The meeting lasted four hours, with several suggested changes by Nellie. One of the things she added was a golf course with lakes. The golf course included more than one thousand home lots. The main road passed the clubhouse and continued to the westernmost point of the property. It ended at the point where Nellie drew out the location for their new home.

Nellie selected names for the town and streets. The Kents' new home would be located at No. 1 Secret Street. Secret Street would contain massive estate-home sites for the Board members. They would build a total of seven homes on the street, but the street would have another twenty lots that would be left vacant. She had made the decision that the town itself would be named Kent City. After all, the Kents had funded everything. Other street names included Genetic Drive, Kent Avenue, Gold Circle, Solution Street, Chance Street, Escape

Road, and Colony Lane. Colony Lane would be the main road leading into the town from the main entrance gate. Escape Road would lead from town to the industrial and dock area. Chance Street would run by all of the condos. Kent Avenue would be the main street through town. Gold Circle would cover a small circle downtown that included the local financial operations and executive offices. Solution Street and Chance Street would be the primary streets in the golf course homes community Genetic Drive would be the road from town to the genetic research facility.

Nellie spent hours working on her new home design with one of the senior architects assigned by Robert. His name was Travis Cole. Travis was fifty-two years old and had designed many large executive homes in New Zealand. After talking with Nellie, Travis knew this house would be beyond anything he'd ever done before. Nellie gave Travis a list of the things she wanted in order to make an incredible two-story, twenty thousand-square-foot house that would be world class. Her list included:

1. Both floors would have twelve-foot ceilings.
2. A stone driveway.
3. A *porte-cochère* driveway entry.
4. Tall columns on the front. Shorter columns in the back.
5. Large, stained wooden entry doors with special glass inserts.
6. A two-story foyer with wide double-arched stairs on each side wall and a large hidden elevator.
7. A huge entry chandelier.

8. Polished marble floors.

9. A large gourmet kitchen with a large island cabinet and adjacent bar.

10. The den would be close to the front entrance, behind the stairways, and would be the narrowest part of the house.

11. All main living areas would have massive windows with views to the back and Tasman Sea.

12. The windows in the den overlooking the patio would be at least ten feet in clear width and would fully retract up into the second floor, opening the den to the back patio.

13. The master bedroom would be one thousand six-hundred square feet minimum, plus two master bathroom and closet areas, one for her and one for Duncan.

14. The back patio would be partially covered and recessed three feet to keep the sea views clear.

15. All patio areas would have stone flooring, with a large firepit and rock or stone sitting areas that would work with patio furniture.

16. A covered patio kitchen matching the indoor kitchen would be off to the side and against the house.

17. An indoor spa with massage tables, workout room, outdoor hot tub, and heated pool with waterfalls.

18. A party room that could accommodate up to one hundred and twenty guests would be located near the main kitchen.

19. A TV room with stadium seating to accommodate thirty people.

20. Extensive landscaping with natural rock ledges.
21. Outside lighting would be extensive and illuminate the entire home with hidden lights. All trees would have substantial LED light coverings.
22. The roof would be colorful slate.

The list had been reviewed with Duncan, and they could hardly wait to see what Travis would come up with for the design. Travis told Nellie that the home design would be ready for review in three months.

The design of the town itself would require many meetings over the coming months with the American architects and perhaps a trip or two back to New Zealand during the next six-months. Massive construction work would begin quickly after the drawings were all approved.

In the six weeks since they had purchased The Farm, it was time to get back to Destin for a little rest and relaxation before the hard work really got started.

Chapter 8
BACK IN DESTIN

Nellie's birthday breakfast on the patio in Destin had set the tone for the day. It would be a good one. Duncan and Nellie's meeting with Joe Hawkins was at the attorney's office at ten o'clock.

The drive toward Mid-Bay Bridge that connected Destin and Niceville usually caused Duncan to grumble about the road name approaching the bridge. It was named after some football player who had won the Heisman trophy. Duncan would always get worked up and say, "Whoopty-doo . . . . Why on earth would those dumb-ass elected idiots name a road after a ball player and not someone who had actually done something really big and productive for mankind, someone who actually helped people? I don't have a road named after me, and I've saved millions from starvation. That just shows what our government and society has degraded to." His voice grew louder as he became more irritated. Nellie would just smile and say, "I know, dear; you're right."

They arrived at their lawyer's office a few minutes early. Joe's secretary offered them coffee and donuts, but they declined. Joe came in at five minutes before ten and was somewhat surprised that they were already there.

Joe was overweight and medium height. He always looked disheveled, with his gray hair unkept. He even had one side of his shirttails out. His shoes were dusty and unpolished. His socks actually matched each other today.

He wasn't your typical lawyer. Joe was a widower. His wife of forty years had passed away as the result of a car accident five years earlier.

Joe greeted Duncan and Nellie with firm handshakes and a smile. "Welcome, folks. It's good to see you again. What brings you here today?"

"How long have we known each other, Joe?" asked Duncan.

"Well, I guess that would be about forty-five years now, Duncan," Joe responded.

"You know we first met in that foxhole in Vietnam with bullets flying everywhere. You didn't know me from squat, but you carried me more than four hundred yards to safety when I was wounded," said Duncan.

"Yeah, well, I guess, with everyone else gone on a patrol, I was a little lonely, so, I had to keep you around for company!" Joe replied with a big grin and laugh.

Then Duncan said, "Have I thanked you lately for saving my life that day?"

Joe quickly responded, "You sent me a case of 2010 Daniel Gehrs Fireside Port for Christmas, and it's really good."

"I'm glad you liked it," said Duncan, "but, thanks again for saving me from those Gooks.

"How's your workload?" asked Duncan

"Duncan, I'm in the twilight of my lackluster career. I've been cutting back over the last two years, and you're just about my last real client. I do appreciate being a consultant for your Grainteck Board for the last six years, as well as the personal legal work you have given me over the last year," said Joe.

"Joe," said Duncan, "I need to have a conversation with you that can be life changing for you. I want you to join me on a grand adventure. And I need only one good lawyer for this. I'm going to share with you right now the full depth of my plan. As my lawyer, you are obligated to keep it confidential whether you choose to participate or not. Do I have your word?"

Joe suddenly sat upright and gave a positive nod. Duncan had never been so serious with him before.

Chapter 9
THE GRAINTECK EXIT PLAN

For the next four hours, they talked. Duncan and Nellie explained in detail what they had planned and why. Duncan stated, "It's time to work on an exit plan for Grainteck. I'm ready now to fully retire. A buyer has approached me, and I'll be negotiation with them over the next several months. I'll get you involved soon in that part. Second, we'll need to deal with the proceeds of the sale and update our will to support our retirement plan and activities after retirement. Third, we have a very elaborate plan outlined for what we want to do with all of our money. Here is a packet of sketches and drawings as well as a timetable for implementation of this dream of ours."

Together they reviewed the plan and the sketches. It took almost two hours, there were a lot of plans. Joe had many questions. When finished, they asked Joe if he wanted the job that would be based here in Destin. It would be full-time for at least three years. After some discussions on the scope of the job, when Duncan offered him a shocking rate of $1,000 per hour, Joe accepted immediately. That would be at least $6 million. The money would be an awesome addition to Joe's retirement. Duncan and Nellie were happy to have Joe, as they knew they could trust him.

Once Joe had agreed, Duncan surprised him with one more proposal. "Joe, Nellie and I would like to make an additional offer to you. Would you be willing to join us for the ESCAPE Research Project at our international location? If you would, the compensation we just agreed upon would be the same, but we would offer you a bonus of $10 million in gold. Additionally, I would want you to be on the Board for The Farm."

Joe was shocked again. While he had done well with the legal profession, raising three children and losing his wife had taken a toll on his retirement savings. He owned his house and would certainly have plenty after he received the three years of pay from Duncan. Joe said, "Wow, I appreciate the offer. And based on everything you've told me, I'll accept if you would allow me to bring my three grown children, their spouses, and my grandchildren if they should want to come. As you know, all of my kids and their spouses have college degrees and could fit into the project as valuable team members."

Duncan and Nellie agreed and told Joe that each of his three children's families would be offered jobs and receive the same compensation as the other team families. However, it would be his children's decisions if they wanted to accept the jobs and go or not. Duncan owed Joe his life, and he would do anything for him.

"How many people know about this?" Joe asked.

"Right now, besides Nellie and me, just you, Bruce Bills, Bob Erickson, John Earnest and Tom Clark—essentially just the Grainteck Board of Directors," Duncan replied. "I want all of you on my new project Board, too. No families have signed up so far. The families who do sign up won't know the full picture until I know the plan for the project is working. They'll only know of it as a Research Project within a somewhat contained community that's designed to measure physical and mental properties of an isolated society.

"I want to get around ten thousand families into the project. We need to keep the project very quiet with minimal publicity for it to work. We plan to withhold the complete details of the plan from the families for at least three years after we have all of the families relocated and fully ready to begin.

"Our start date is very optimistic, but I'm already throwing money at it to get it moving now and moving rapidly. Time is of the essence. I need for you to close this office now and move into our Destin office until we all head out to the ESCAPE Research Project.

"Get with Tom tomorrow; he's in charge, and he'll get things moving for you. We want you to help screen applicants, do background checks, send interview letters, and prepare commitment letters, confidentiality agreements, and contracts. You'll also need to prepare contracts with suppliers and shippers. We have at least two thousand three hundred families to get on board before October and another two thousand and seven hundred or so no later than fourteen months later. This is a hard date, and money isn't an issue. And, remember, we need to change our wills to coincide with our plan, and I want that done within a week."

After another hour working on details of the will and discussing many issues, the Kents were finally ready to leave. They shook hands, Joe and Nellie hugged, and Duncan told Joe, "If you have any questions just call me, Nellie, or Tom anytime."

"I will," replied Joe.

Chapter 10
THE DRIVE BACK FROM JOE'S OFFICE

As Duncan and Nellie drove home from Joe's office, his mind relived an event from ten years earlier. He had thought about it many times and what truth had been expressed that evening.

Nellie had been hosting a party for her friends in San Diego, and that gave Duncan a chance to leave town and invite a few of his best friends to stay with him for some golf and recreation. The Kents had just bought a beautiful, five thousand-square-foot temporary, transitional getaway home in Destin's Kelly Plantation subdivision as a break from his work in San Diego. That getaway time would be spent focusing on the planning process for his retirement which was coming up within a few short years. Duncan had invited Tom Clark, John Earnest, and Bob Erickson for a four-night, three-day weekend at the new home.

The three friends were also directors of Grainteck. Tom was the VP of sales. John was the VP of operations. Bob was the VP of security. Golf was planned for all three days. The first round was scheduled on Friday at Kelly Plantation Golf Club, followed by a round on Saturday at Regatta Bay, with a return to Kelly Plantation on Sunday for the final round. On Saturday, after a good dinner at the Marina Restaurant, they returned to Duncan's home and sat out under the stars around the pool and firepit for some guy talk.

Duncan loved the new pool that he had just finished. He'd been very involved in its design and wanted it to be a place of relaxation and enjoyment. A ten-foot tall wall of synthetic concrete sandstone boulders surrounded the pool. There were sitting ledges and stainless climb-out ladders in various places, but some of the rocks went below the pool's water line. The rocks were a brownish-red color sculpted to look like the sandstones of mountain rock near Red Rock Canyon just west of Las Vegas. The rock was hand stained by a specialist flown in from Las Vegas. The specialist had done hundreds of rock stainings, and it looked like real sandstone with cracks and color variations. At one end of the pool was an eight-foot cascading waterfall, and at the other end of the forty-foot pool was a hot tub that also cascaded water into the pool as an overflow. The pool was relatively narrow to give the appearance of a flowing river. It was about fifteen feet wide, except where the waterfall flowed into a deep-end pool area where it spread out to about twenty-five feet wide. The rocks were graced with imbedded flower planters on some of the tops and green plants draping down to almost touch the water in places. Duncan started the gas firepit and brought out a cart loaded with liquor and wine. It was going to be a very good night!

The crew began to come downstairs from their individual rooms to the pool at about 9:00, as planned. After three rounds of drinks, the conversation became much more lively. They no longer felt the soreness from two days of golf. The conversation was typical guy talk—sports, past funny events and situations, and women. Another round of drinks, and the volume got really fired up, especially when Tom started talking about the downfall of the world. That was a pretty broad topic, so everyone chimed in to contribute—and did they contribute!

"High taxes, that's the problem," said Duncan.

John exclaimed, "Right on! Taxes have to be high to pay the dickheads that run the government and give all of the working people's money to the ones who don't work."

Then Duncan chimed in. "Well, tips are just as hosed up. You never know what your bill is going to be from a menu. Damn it, they ought to just put the price on the menu and include tips and taxes. It's just a stupid process, and I feel that I get ripped off every time I have to tip."

Bob added, "No, tax and tips is just the little stuff; it's all caused by drugs and crime."

Then Tom chirped in, "You guys have it all wrong; it is all these so-called religions. They all hate each other, and everyone thinks that if you believe in a different religion, then you're going to hell."

"Yeah, and some of those bastards like to blow themselves up just to kill someone who doesn't believe like themselves," said Duncan.

"Is it ignorance or stupidity that would cause people to do that? Or is it both?" exclaimed Tom.

Bob argued, "Religion is just one symptom of the problem. I think there is just one big problem; I think it's just too damn many people."

Duncan raised his voice, "Hell, Bob, you are right, too; we have limited food, energy, and fresh water, and yet all the dumb asses in the world are breeding like crazy. The world's living organisms evolved for millions of years as survival of the fittest—but no, not now for humans. We do everything possible to keep everybody alive with any means necessary.

"I hate it when I hear about saving a life when it's not saving it at all, when it's just simply prolonging it along with its ultimate certain suffering down the road either from the affliction or the unnatural 'survival of the unfit' that further strains the limited resources of earth.

"It also means that genetic specimens that would not normally survive in nature are breeding and creating a continuation of genetically deficient humans."

Duncan was in his element talking genetics and was letting it all hang out. "You know, guys, I was thinking about our little black Pomeranian dog, Bailey. We loved that little dog. But to help prevent dog overpopulation, we did the right thing and had her spayed when she was young. Then, twelve years later, when she was suffering badly from congestive heart failure, we shortened her continually worsening pain and suffering with euthanasia.

"And, you know, that made me start to think; if we humans are considered kind to do this for animals, then why the hell don't we do both of these acts of kindness for people?" stated Duncan.

"Religion and politics, religion and politics, it's always the same thing over and over again, Duncan. And, that causes opinions that will never change or converge for the benefit of mankind," answered Tom.

"Yep, you're right, Tom," said Bob.

"Ya'll are right, guys, and nobody can fix religion and politics, so I'm going to fix me another drink," chuckled John.

Duncan yelled, "Another round, boys. Tomorrow our gene pool will drown us all." They all laughed. They were beginning to laugh at everything, funny or not!

After another round, Tom exclaimed, "This world-problem crap reminds me of the problem with the old country boy whose roof leaked and who was told that if he didn't fix it, the roof would soon be leaking even more. His answer was, 'In that case, I'll get a bigger bucket!' Fixing it was just too hard and too much work."

With that, John said, "That makes sense; our politicians and world leaders don't want to do the hard work and fix anything. They just want to make all the money they can while in power and move on to finish what's left of their short, little pathetic lives. Screw the world, screw the people, screw the planet . . . that's their philosophy!"

"The bastards, the sons-of-bitches, the assholes. I wish there was something we could do to stop all that crap," responded Bob.

Tom added, "Yeah, that would be great; we have a good case of buzzards' luck with those bastards."

"What the hell is 'buzzards' luck'?" asked Duncan.

Tom responded, "That's when nothing is dying and you can't kill! It means those bastards who are supposed to solve problems aren't going to die and we can't legally kill them. And that leaves the world starving to death and getting worse every year. It's just a matter of time before the food, water, and air get so bad there has to be a world event that is likely to destroy mankind. Most likely nuclear, I would bet."

Everyone was getting louder now. Duncan's speech was beginning to slur a bit, as was everyone else's. With a loud voice, Duncan shouted, "What if there was something we could do?"

"Bullshit, Duncan—there is nothing we can do," replied John.

"Play 'What if?' with me a minute, guys. What if we could? What would we do?

"What if we were gods!" stated Duncan.

"Or at least one of them; there must be at least thirty or more of them," laughed John.

"I wanna be Buddha and drink more beer!" said Bob, laughing loudly.

"Well, I . . . I think everyone in the world but me should stop having sex—that would roll the population back to something that the earth could actually support," stuttered Bob.

"Hell, Bob, there would only be about ten people left in the world after that, 'cause you would peter out after just a few kids!" chuckled Duncan. Tom and John both laughed.

Bob retorted quickly. "Oh, you jealous bastards, remember: I am God, and I would let those ten who were left live longer and healthier; that way, the productive years, from twenty-five to sixty-five wouldn't be so short. Hell, we spend half of our lives too young or too old; that leaves us with only about forty years of some kind of good life, and then we spend 30 percent of that asleep."

"Or drunk," replied Duncan with a smile while waving his bourbon glass above his head. They were on a roll now, and all began laughing again. Everything was funny now. They were in their "creative mode," as Duncan called it. You could say anything without any repercussions.

John slurred, "I would get rid of all religions. You can't tell a good one from a bad one, anyway. I thought the Catholics were pretty good, until we find out they were a bunch of child molesters in sheep's clothing!"

"I would get rid of all of the lawyers, because most all of them are leeches on society! They become the politicians who make the laws so they'll make more money when they go back into law or lobbying. They don't produce one goddamn thing that you can eat, drink, or wear, but they bill you like there's no tomorrow!" yelled Duncan.

"And the military. If you don't have wars, you would not need to waste any resources on blowing up people and stuff, and you wouldn't need good, decent young people getting killed to do it. Most of the time all we really get out of it is a bunch of mangled or dead good men and women who shouldn't have fought those political and religious wars anyway," shouted Tom.

Bob responded, "And let's make insurance illegal! That's such a joke anyway. You're spending money betting you have problems while those money-hungry bastards selling the insurance are betting you don't have any problems and that you won't collect any of the money you gave them! And just try to collect on a claim. The insurance companies will pay you off with a pathetic value calculated by some paid-off appraiser. But, oh no, they're not shy about wanting your money every month. As a matter of fact, they charge me the same every month for collision insurance even though the replacement value of my car goes down every month. Now that pisses me off! Go figure!"

Duncan chimed in again, "And while we're at it, no taxes. Oh, didn't I say that already? Shit, I think I'm getting drunk. I don't want to pay those crooked politicians anything. I think our government should be run by volunteers with *zero* pay and *zero* benefits, one term only. That means no reelections wasting our money. One country. One leader. And a lot less of these sons-of-bitches in the House and Senate—who, by the way, don't represent us anyway but only their damn political party! They think their *party* voted them into office! No parties, if I was God, just real representation of the people . . . and, again, no pay and just one term!"

"And prisons," replied Tom, "I wouldn't have any. None. Such a waste anyway. Crime, if any, would be punished by civil service labor assignments. If the crime was bad, and I would have to think about what 'bad' actually was, the criminal should be sent away to live in solitude for the rest of their life. I don't want to spend $40,000 a year taking care of a damn criminal in prison. We try to rehabilitate the bastards and release them back into society to do more bad stuff.

"Hell, their life in prison is better than many honest, hard-working people. They get free food, clothes, shelter, utilities, TV, Internet, exercise, medical care, dental care, and legal services.

"I saw on TV last week that an eighty-five years old criminal who had escaped twenty-five years ago had decided to turn himself in, in order to get medical care. The bastard was paralyzed from the waist down and had spent all of his stolen money. By turning himself in, he would be well taken care of!

"And, they don't have to pay taxes on the cost of all the free support we provide from our tax money! They don't even have to worry about being able to pay their bills because we pay for all of it. Good, honest, hard-working people having to pay to support criminals. I think the punishment is actually on the good guys!"

"I can't see," Bob yelled suddenly.

"Open your goddamn eyes, Bob," Duncan yelled back.

"Oh, that worked! I must be drunk," said Bob.

"We all are," said Tom, "but we solved all of the world's problems, didn't we?"

Yeah, right," said John. "I'm going to bed."

"Me, too," said Tom.

"I'll cut the lights off. See ya'll in the morning," said Duncan.

Chapter 11
ILENE WALLACE
(nine months later) Shreveport, Louisiana

Ilene Wallace, shift RN at the Schumpert Medical Center, in Shreveport, Louisiana, was depressed. The new Affordable Care Act had been having a devastating effect on all of the hospital financials. The other hospitals in the area had already laid off employees or reduced their work hours to part-time with reduced benefits. It just didn't make sense because they were always shorthanded. The hospitals needed people to work double shifts whenever any scheduled nurse happened to call in sick or just not show up. Ilene had volunteered whenever possible just to help with the family income. She hadn't had a pay raise in two years, but the cost of living continued to rise.

Layoffs had been in the rumor mill for months, but now, every employee had been individually scheduled for a meeting with the human resources manager. Ilene's meeting was scheduled for 2 o'clock on Friday. She feared the worst, as most layoffs usually occur on Friday. She didn't want to tell Ken.

He was already stressed out about their growing budget deficit eating into what little savings they had. Any income reduction would be devastating. She had decided to wait until after the meeting and would only then tell Ken if she'd been laid off.

Today, she'd been required to stay over to handle an emergency situation with a patient having a heart attack and not expected to live. She didn't get to leave with the normal shift change crowd at 2:30. That was okay though, because the overtime for this month had been less than usual.

Immediately after graduating four years earlier from Louisiana State University in Shreveport, Ilene started working at this hospital. It was a profession she thought would benefit people. She was a giver. But, the horrible rudeness of the patients and cost cutting in the nursing field had led to a growing dissatisfaction. They needed the money, and that drove her to try to hang in a little longer.

Ilene's husband, Ken, at thirty-four years old, had spent four years in the Marines, serving in Afghanistan fighting the Taliban. While Ken was a gentle and kind person, he was an aggressive fighter. In battle, he had fought to win and knew he'd killed several enemy combatants, two of them in hand-to-hand with a knife. He didn't talk about it much; it was just his job to fight and protect his fellow Marines.

Post-traumatic stress syndrome was non-existent with Ken. Perhaps it was his upbringing in the north Louisiana rolling hills, where hunting and killing game animals was a normal part of the culture. After completing his military service, he decided to attend college. Using the GI Bill, he earned a degree in electrical engineering from Louisiana Tech University. He had worked for nine years in power generation for the local power company.

Both Ken and Ilene had always been told, "to get a good job, get a good education." They'd gotten that "good education" but now felt they were getting nowhere for all of their hard work.

She and Ken had been married for nine years and had two children, a seven-year-old son, David, and a four-year-old daughter, Jan. Once Ilene knew about the overtime, she had called ahead from work and had the daycare center prepared for a late pickup for Jan. David would ride the bus and get into the house on his own using the key hidden in the front porch flower pot. She didn't like doing that to David, but she had little choice. Ken wouldn't normally get off until 5 and often had to work overtime with no extra pay. It was very depressing to Ken. He'd spent years going into debt to get his degree. Had he not gone to college and made money as simply an hourly worker at the plant, he would have been much better off financially. Additionally, those same hourly workers got overtime pay and he did not. That meant the hourly workers were actually making more money on their W-2s than Ken. It was just not fair, and Ken was always complaining about the inequity.

Ilene Wallace finally left from the day shift at 4 and walked to the employee parking lot.

As Ilene walked through the parking lot to her eight-year-old tan Honda Accord, she saw that, with the normal hospital shift change over, the lot was empty of all hospital workers. It appeared no one else was around. There were no parking lot guards. It was daylight, though, so she felt safe enough. As she was about to unlock her car door, two men in black masks jumped from behind adjacent cars and trapped her. Her heart raced. She screamed! Then everything went black.

Chapter 12
ILENE WAKES UP

Ilene awoke two hours later in the hospital emergency room. Her head was hurting, and her vision was blurry. She was disoriented. She thought, *Where am I?* Then she heard a familiar voice.

"Honey, you're going to be okay." It was Ken. He was by her side. Ken was holding her hand as her vision began to clear. She focused on his caring face.

"What happened?" Ken asked. She didn't remember anything past leaving the hospital.

Ilene answered faintly, "I . . . I don't know. How did I get here?"

Ken replied, "A relief employee found you by your car bleeding and unconscious. Apparently you were beaten and robbed. Your purse was nowhere to be found. The doctors said you have a concussion. They put ten stitches in your head just over your right ear."

Just then, the emergency room doctor, Kerry Giles, walked in. Ilene had worked with Dr. Giles many times in the past, but never as a patient. "Well, Ilene, it's good to see you awake. How do you feel?"

"My head hurts," she replied.

Dr. Giles replied, "You're going to be okay. You just need to rest, and we need to watch you closely for a day or two. You'll need to stay here overnight at least and possibly a day or two to be sure the concussion isn't going to cause any internal bleeding."

"I want to go home," she replied.

Dr. Giles responded, "We'll have your room ready in about an hour, and we'll discuss your leaving again tomorrow morning. Until then, no further discussion, okay?"

"Okay," she said in a sad tone. Then she asked her husband, "Where are the kids? I was supposed to pick Jan up at 4:30 from daycare."

Ken answered, "They're at Billy and Joan's house; I called them, and they picked up Jan from daycare and David from home. They said they'd keep them until you're home and better." Billy and Joan were their best friends, and they lived on the same block. Their kids were the same age, and they attended the same school and daycare. Since neither couple had any relatives nearby, they always helped each other during scheduling conflicts or illnesses.

As Dr. Giles left the room, a Shreveport police officer walked into the room. "Mrs. Wallace, I'm Officer Jones." Officer Jones had on a gray uniform with blue trim. Her vision still somewhat blurry, Ilene couldn't make out his name on his badge. "Can you tell me anything about what happened today in the parking lot?"

Ilene thought hard. "I . . . I can't . . . I don't remember. Wait, I remember clocking out, but I can't remember anything after that," she said.

Officer Jones replied, "Well, maybe you'll remember more tomorrow when you're feeling better. I'll come back tomorrow. Here's my card. If you do remember anything before then, please give me a call."

"I will," replied Ilene.

Chapter 13
KEN WALLACE

Ken stayed the night at the hospital with Ilene but got very little sleep. He'd seen the crime rate grow steadily in the area. It had gotten to the point that he feared for his family's safety, and this event could have been so much worse. He'd considered other towns and cities to move to, but it seemed that everywhere was in decline, what with gangs, drugs, and crime on the increase.

He and Ilene had often discussed moving but couldn't come up with a good solution. If only they were rich and could afford to live in a nice gated community somewhere in an upscale neighborhood and send the kids to private schools. With living costs so high, it just didn't seem possible, even with both of them working. Having both grown up in rural Louisiana near Farmerville, they knew how to keep their costs down by hunting, fishing, and farming. But, living in a city with both of them working, there was little time to do those things anymore, especially with kids.

Saving for the kids' education was out of the question, as they still owed more than $80,000 for their own college costs. Both of their cars were approaching the ten-year mark, and the maintenance costs had been steadily increasing. They were paid for though, and the idea of two new car payments was scary.

To make matters worse, they'd bought a house, but with market conditions falling, they were still upside down on their equity and after six years their home value still hadn't recovered to their purchase price of $175,000. They had seriously considered just walking away and letting the bank have the house, but walking away from an obligation was just not who they were, and if they walked away, where would they live? Their friends told them that it was just business and was the smart thing to do.

Maybe it was, and maybe they should. Their two children were a true blessing and the bright points in their otherwise workaday lives. If only Ilene could stay home with them and not have to put them in a daycare center to be animals in a herd. They had wanted a third child, and though her clock was ticking, they just couldn't afford one more right now.

Ken didn't have any solutions, and the financial stress was beginning to affect their relationship. They were arguing more and were starting to yell at the kids. Something had to change.

Most of the time Ken stayed at Ilene's bedside, but to keep himself awake, he walked the inside and outside of the hospital a couple of times. He also took full advantage of the coffee at the nurse's station.

Just before sunrise while Ilene was still asleep, Ken slipped down to the first floor of the hospital for some breakfast. He realized he hadn't eaten any dinner the evening before. On his way to the cafeteria, he decided to get the *Shreveport Times* paper. Selecting a tray, he chose bacon, scrambled eggs, toast, and coffee from the buffet and paid the casher $2.75. Hospital cafeteria food was still a good value as they kept the prices low for the employees and the patients' families. The same meal a block away would have cost $6 or more. The warm coffee felt good as he sipped it first. He realized he was tired and he needed a hot shower and a shave.

With their financial issues always on his mind, Ken usually opened the jobs section of the newspaper first. But, the front page caught his attention, with large bold headlines stating:

Federal taxes are going up, along with Social Security taxes, and retirement age increases

Crap, more costs. He felt helpless! There was absolutely nothing he could do about all of the bad news that was always dominating the headlines nowadays. He hated the sports section, as the athletes were being paid millions of dollars to throw balls through a hole, and many could barely speak intelligently. So much for getting a good education.

There were only a few jobs for electrical engineers, and they were the typical crappy jobs that weren't real career opportunities, such as sawmills, electrical supply houses, or entry-level positions, often with long hours. Suddenly, at the end of the professional jobs list, his eyes caught an unusually large job advertisement that read:

Wanted:

A unique social Research Project known as the ESCAPE Project is looking for professional family teams with children. Only a few highly qualified families will be accepted, but the benefits will be phenomenal.

The job involves moving to a safe, private, international location. Substantial pay and benefits. Requires a high IQ or college degree, five-year minimum skills, and work experience in a wide range of disciplines, English speaking, and a willingness to commit for a ten-year minimum contract.

Excellent family health and medical history, home provided. If interested, e-mail your and your spouse's resumes along with family information, including religious beliefs and three generations of longevity background as well as approval for background checks to The ESCAPE Project attention: jhawkins@ social-research.org

The job advertisement generated a lot of curiosity, and Ken wondered what kind of company and job this might be. Surely it was something in the Middle East, and he definitely didn't want to go there. Rarely would a job advertisement care about longevity, and he'd never seen a company wanting a family team. In fact, most companies would be considered to be breaking US discrimination laws if they were selecting employees based on marital, religious, and/or medical status.

However, with the assault and robbery of Ilene yesterday, his curiosity was high. He cut out the advertisement and put it in his billfold. He thought that Ilene would begin to awake soon, so he dumped the paper along with his breakfast trash and headed back to her room.

Two days later, Ilene was released by Dr. Giles and sent home. She wouldn't be able to go back to work until after a one-week checkup. When she got home, the personnel manager called and advised her that she was being laid off. It had not been a good week.

Chapter 14
RESEARCH PROJECT INTERVIEW OFFER

Ilene picked up the mail and saw a letter with the return address of:

> ESCAPE Research Project
>
> 981 Hwy 98 East
>
> Destin, Florida 32541

The letter came back exactly two months after their resumes and personal information had been submitted. She was afraid to open it without Ken. Ken would be home within a couple of hours. They were anxious to hear back since Ilene's job termination was effective three weeks after her parking lot attack. A three-month severance package was pretty much used up already, and they were getting desperate.

Ken arrived home at 5:15, and Ilene served a dinner of Hamburger Helper , English peas and milk. It was economical and everyone liked it. After dinner, the kids played until their normal 8:30 bedtime.

Ken had grown tired of asking if anything had come back from the Research Project and was shocked when Ilene pitched the manila envelope onto his lap. She said, "Ken, I just couldn't open it. I'm afraid of rejection!"

Ken replied, "Honey, we'll never know unless we open it," and then he ripped the envelope open and read the cover sheet.

Dear Mr. and Mrs. Wallace,

Your resume and information has been received and reviewed. You are approved to move to the next step in our hiring process and learn more about the ESCAPE Research Project.

Please secure time for your entire family to have a five-day trip to Destin, Florida, beginning October 1. Your family will be picked up at the Shreveport Regional Airport and flown by private jet to the Destin Airport and return upon completion of your stay. We have secured a three-bedroom condo for you during your stay, and childcare services have been arranged for the periods of your interview. The remainder of the time you will be on your own to enjoy the beach and other Destin-area attractions, as you may desire. A full-sized SUV has been rented for you and will be available for pickup at the airport. Details of your schedule and reservations are attached in this package. Included in your packet is a check for $2,000 to use for incidentals, meals, and entertainment as you see fit on your trip.

Please call and confirm your acceptance of this formal interview package, and we will release the check for cashing.

Regards,

Donna Bacon,
Personnel Manager
Research Project
Destin, Florida
Phone # 1-800-2ESCAPE ext. 302

Both Ken and Ilene were in shock. This wasn't a normal interview! What were they dealing with here? This invitation even included fun, a vacation. They hadn't been able to afford a real vacation since their honeymoon. They decided to forgo school for David for Wednesday through Friday so the entire family could be a part of this experience. They could hardly wait until morning to confirm the trip.

Chapter 15
THE INTERVIEW TRIP

The private jet was ready to board at 6:30 Saturday morning when the Wallace family arrived at the airport. They were welcomed onto the plane by the pilots, Jim Beard and Larry Stuart. The plane was a beautiful twin-jet Citation with an all-leather cabin with seating for twelve. A refrigerator held drinks and snacks. Ken asked Jim if this was his only flight today, and Jim replied, "Oh, hell no! We do a minimum of four flights every day. Our next pick-up will be in Kansas City at 9:15." Ken and Ilene got their family seated and buckled up. The flight from Shreveport to Destin was a fast fifty minutes.

Their schedule was to begin meetings just before lunch and go through dinner on the first day. Ken received the keys for a GMC Denali at the Research Project concierge desk set up inside the airport. He drove the Denali to a rented condo at the Silver Shells condos, located adjacent to Henderson State Park. The views from the condo overlooked the Gulf of Mexico and almost two miles of state-park beaches. Ken and Ilene unpacked and checked the time. It was 7:30. They decided to head over to the Donut Hole restaurant. It was close by, and they had read good reviews about the breakfast.

David and Jan were so excited to get to eat away from home. Ken and Ilene had never been anywhere outside of the ArkLaTex area around Shreveport, and everything they saw and did was a new experience to them. After breakfast they drove around town for a while and found the office where they were to meet at 10; then they drove back to the condo for a little rest before the meeting.

As prearranged in their interview packet, a young woman named Salina McDonald, with the Project childcare department, was picking up David and Jan at 11 and taking them to Big Kahuna's Water Park. Salina knocked on the door of the condo right on time. She appeared to be about thirty years old and was quite trim. She was introduced to David and Jan and began to share with them her plans for them during the day. After about fifteen minutes of cell-phone-number swaps and discussions, Ken and Ilene were on their way to the scheduled interview.

The weather was the typical warm and humid for October. Some thunder could be heard to the north across Choctawhatchee Bay. Ken wore a suit, which seemed a bit out of place; everyone else they saw that day was in shorts and T-shirts. This was a resort town, and the streets were packed with tourists. Ilene wore a light yellow sundress and was obviously a lot more comfortable than Ken.

Chapter 16
THE INTERVIEW

Tom Clark met Ken and Ilene in the lobby of the Cornerstone office complex on Commons Drive. Tom appeared to be in his mid-fifties with a trim look and salt-and-pepper hair. His firm handshake and a bold southern, "Glad to have you here, folks," welcomed them. Ken and Ilene both thanked him for the wonderful hospitality and the opportunity to interview with them.

Tom offered refreshments and the location of the restrooms if needed. They took an elevator to the third floor and followed Tom into his plush corner office. The large plate glass windows overlooked Kelly Plantation Golf Club, and a glimpse of the bay could be seen above the pine trees. They were asked to sit in maroon leather chairs that were placed around a walnut office table across the room from Tom's desk.

Tom began by explaining his position with The Research Project. "I'm the company senior vice president, and I've been put in charge of the complete team selection for the entire project. You are potentially one family of five thousand families who will be selected. If, at any time during this interview and selection process, you want to stop and not go any further, please let me know, and you'll be free to go and enjoy the rest of your time here in Destin—all on our dime, of course. We're quite far into the selection process, but I want to take as much time as necessary to make you comfortable with joining us and to be a part of something big.

"Our company is called The Research Project for several reasons:

"What we're going to do has never been done before. We'll be establishing a working colony of sorts in a country outside of the United States. The location will be shared with you only if you accept an offer. This colony will consist of the five thousand families who will build the colony from the ground up. It will be made up of hardworking individuals who have the skills needed for a successful team effort. Travel will not be allowed away from or into the colony once the project's start date. There will be schools, hospitals, farms, homes, power plants, water- and waste-treatment plants, security, communications, and everything necessary for a fully self-sufficient community. It will be a massive undertaking, requiring a wide range of skills.

"As part of the normal forty-hour workweek or schooling, each resident age fourteen and up will be required to work eight hours as needed and assigned on functions that would normally be provided by a government or for fill-in work.

"The 'research' will consist of tracking and monitoring general aspects of the people, families, functions, interactions, work, and operations of a colony. The goal is the determination of the ability of the colony to exist completely independent, as much as possible, of all external involvement.

"The details, including the purpose of the project, will be top secret. Additional details will be shared with the family teams along the way. The ten-year commitment is necessary to assure a time period that can validate the research goal success."

Any questions so far?"

At the same time, Ken and Ilene both replied, "Not yet."

Tom continued, "This project is scheduled to officially start on January 1, which is just about four months away. We have more than four thousand families already signed up. Most have already arrived at the site.

"Our selection process involves a large cross section of various life backgrounds, skills, and perspectives. We particularly liked your rural, small town, history. The wide array of backgrounds we're recruiting is necessary to add the different perspectives to the project results that we need. We need both of your skills, Ken as an electrical engineer and Ilene as an RN. There will be others with similar skills and backgrounds. Both of you were straight-A students through college, so we know your IQ is high. You have no criminal past and no medical issues. Each of your jobs will involve work of about thirty-two hours per week in your area of expertise as assigned, and additionally you will be required to perform a variety of necessary community service functions and training in other skills as needed and as assigned for an additional eight hours per week.

"A large condo complex has already been completed on the site, and it's substantial enough to house everyone. However, because of the duration of the project, one additional aspect will be the construction of individual homes by the team. Schools, roads, hospitals, and infrastructures are being constructed right now by outside contractors and supervised by some on-site project team members. Massive amounts of construction materials are being delivered to warehouses there now."

Tom suggested a short ten-minute break so he could prepare for his next interview and suggested that Ken and Ilene talk about what they'd heard.

Once Tom left, Ilene said to Ken, "It sounds exciting." Then she asked, "I wonder if they'll make us an offer?"

Chapter 17
THE OFFER

After ten minutes, Tom returned to the office and immediately stated, "Folks, we'd like you to join us at the Research Project. So, let's talk money. Funding for the project is being done by a fully funded gold reserve in a private bank. Everyone making the commitment will receive a personal coordinator and transfer agent who will pay off any existing debts and purchase your home for the market price or for the payoff, whichever is greater.

"Since all of the families will work as a team, compensation will not be necessary while the project is ongoing. One hundred percent of all expenses will be covered with your own personal electronic payment card at the expense of the project. You will not need any monthly compensation at all. By not having a monthly compensation structure, you will not pay any taxes. Each family account will receive a deposit each month of real gold into a private safe deposit box that will be fully viewable by you within the Colony Bank at the project. But, the gold will not be vested at all until you complete three years. After three years, you vest at 50 percent. Deposits will continue for at least ten years. Any potential tax liability that might exist will be covered by the project.

"I'm sure you're wondering what that contribution would be, right?"

Ken and Ilene were in some level of shock. This was a lot to absorb, as this wasn't anything normal. How can all this work? This was really different. *But,* they thought, *it sounded pretty good so far.* Ken finally responded to Tom as Ilene nodded. "Please tell us, Tom—you have our full attention!"

Tom replied, "All two-person working families will receive a standard monthly gold deposit of thirty ounces of gold per month effective the day they arrive at the site. At current rates of $1,350 per ounce, that would be in the range of more than $40,000 per month, which comes to $480,000 per year. Additionally, once you commit, you will begin immediately earning a weekly temporary allowance of $5,000 US per week until you board the aircraft to the colony, at which time you will be given your colony expense cards. Do I have your interest now?"

Ken and Ilene were speechless. Both of their faces flushed. Together they currently grossed about $115,000 per year, and that necessitated considerable overtime. After federal and state taxes and insurance, their take-home pay was around $5,000 per month.

"Tom, I'll take a glass of water now, if I may," stammered Ken.

"I would like one, too," said Ilene with a higher pitched voice than normal.

Tom got them both a glass of water and then said, "I have given you a lot of information, so I will leave you two together for a few more minutes to gather your thoughts and questions. I'll be back in about fifteen minutes, and you can ask any questions that you may have." Tom left the room and closed the door.

Neither Ken nor Ilene could speak for a full two minutes. Their thoughts were everywhere but couldn't seem to form words and sentences. Their level of excitement was now through the roof! Finally, with a sheepish grin, Ken asked Ilene, "Can this be for real?"

Chapter 18
LUNCH, RELIGION, AND DINNER

Once Tom returned, Ken and Ilene began firing question after question. Concerns over children, moving, and communication with relatives were all answered satisfactorily to their pleasant surprise.

One particular question concerning religion was answered by Tom saying, "Your personal data supplied with your application indicated that you were not affiliated with any religion. That's a critical part of our project. Year after year, wars and conflict over religious differences have been generating distrust, hate, and contempt. We don't want any religious differences or beliefs to cause conflict or discord between team members. By excluding religious individuals, we feel we'll be removing that controversial issue completely out of the population, leading to a more harmonious working community. This will allow the research to be free of that distraction and bias.

"Ken and Ilene, do we have a problem in that area?"

"Not at all," they both replied.

"Good, otherwise we'd need to terminate our offer," replied Tom. After a few more minutes, when all of the questions were answered, Tom paged for Debbie to come to his office. He told Debbie to take care of Ken and Ilene for lunch and he would take care of them for dinner.

The afternoon was spent with Tom's new assistant, Debbie Tullos. Debbie explained that she had previously been the president's secretary but had been promoted temporarily to Tom's assistant for the recruiting process. There was a planned lunch meeting in the cafeteria room at 1:30 for about thirty new research team employees who were already working and were engaged in the planning here at the US headquarters. About twenty prospective employee couples were also planning to attend.

Lunch was barbecued pork ribs and chicken catered from Sonny's BBQ in Fort Walton Beach, along with various sides and thick, buttered garlic toast. Sweet and unsweetened southern tea was served from two large stainless tea containers. The food was served in a buffet fashion on the coffee bar in the room. Debbie had bought ten key lime pies from the Publix grocery store down the street. It was everyone's favorite, and Debbie said it was the best key lime pie in town. About eight tables were set up, and Ken and Ilene picked an empty table. The table quickly filled with other people.

Lunch was followed by a planning session discussion that was outlined on a white wallboard.

The discussion was about hospital construction. During lunch, they'd met doctors, dentists, engineers, nurses, builders, carpenters, teachers, computer technicians, plumbers, and electricians. Each team member had shared their initial assignments and encouraged them to sign on. Every team member they met was anxious to get to the new worksite. When Ken and Ilene asked, none would divulge the project location.

They returned to the condo at 4.

Salina left once Ken and Ilene arrived but would return at 6:30. David and Jan were to remain at the condo for the evening, and Salina had ordered pizza. Ken and Ilene were scheduled to meet Tom at 7 at Ruth's Chris Steak House next to their condo at Silver Shells.

Tom greeted Ken and Ilene at the restaurant entrance, and they were seated immediately. Tom suggested cocktails to start, along with some appetizers. Ken ordered Jack Daniels and Coke, and Ilene had a glass of the house Chardonnay. Tom had a glass of the J. Lohr Cabernet. The conversation that night consisted of sharing life backgrounds and a few questions and answers about the day's discussions. Asking about Tom's background, they found out that Tom had worked as a senior research pharmacist and was a board member of a company called Grainteck. Having hired many professional people in his career, he was assigned the initial role of recruitment and selection. There was no other consultation involved in the decision process to hire a family. He explained that one of his future assignments would be to assure that proper and sufficient medicines were available for the doctors and team members. He would be running all aspects of the medicine and medical equipment operations.

Tom asked, "Ilene, perhaps your interest and contributions as a nurse could be as part of my group? Or you could select to work with the doctors and hospital operations group. There are still a few openings in both groups right now. Ken, I selected you for a shift manager role in electrical power generation. Is that okay with you?"

Ken replied, "I really enjoy that type of work, but is there a way to have the job be a bit more challenging?"

Tom responded, "What if you were also in charge of power distribution lines and transformers in the whole area? Consider that, and we can discuss it again tomorrow."

They ordered another round of drinks to go with filet mignon steaks. Ilene and Ken smiled at each other. They had rarely eaten out, and, when they did, it was at the Western Sizzlin'. They would always get the sirloin. The sirloin was good, although a bit tough, but was priced within their small budget for eating out. It was definitely not a filet mignon.

The steaks were sizzling on their individual hot plates. A large cloth napkin was given to each of them to protect their clothing from splatter. The steaks had a wonderful, buttery smell. Their mouths watered. The steak was so good! How could they ever go back to the Western Sizzlin'?

They left the restaurant at 9:30, agreeing to meet at three o'clock the next day at the office. Tom had other interviews until then. At the condo, Salina had the kids in bed already. Ilene asked Salina how she was affiliated with the Research Project, expecting to hear that she was a temporary worker from some daycare center. Instead, Salina replied: "I have a master's degree in social science and have special training in child development.

I love children! I will be the manager in charge of all childcare at the Project when parents are at work as well as education of children ages three through six. We expect to have perhaps one thousand children who will fit in that category and will have the capacity to expand more if needed."

"Wow," replied Ilene, "I had no idea."

Salina continued, "It's going to be fun. My husband is a surgeon, and he'll be on the project, too. He left about three weeks ago to set up the hospital and exam rooms."

"That's great, Salina. We appreciate you taking care of David and Jan for us," said Ilene as she escorted Salina to the door.

Chapter 19
THE ACCEPTANCE

The rest of the week was mixed between fun and meetings. Fun consisted of beach time at the condo and included a four-hour pontoon boat rental from Luther's Rentals in Destin Harbor for an excursion to Crab Island. Crab Island was a surprise in that it wasn't actually an island. Instead, it was a large shallow sand bar just north of the Destin Harbor bridge.

The water was clear and only two feet deep at its most shallow places. Dozens of boats of all types were anchored in close proximity. People of all ages were wading in the shallow water and enjoying the unique water attraction. Vending boats were scattered throughout the area renting jet skis, paddleboards, and kayaks. Food concessions consisted of burgers, boiled peanuts, and even ice cream. They talked about the events of the week and reflected upon such a life-changing time. They could hardly believe that the five days were almost over.

The following day turned out to be overcast, with light rain expected throughout the day. They were meeting Tom for breakfast at 8:00 at the Palms condo. The kids were invited. After they were seated and had ordered coffee, and milk for the kids, Tom asked the first question.

"Well, folks, how do you feel about what you've learned this week?"

Ken responded, "We're really impressed! We had no idea what to expect, and this appears to be the answer to our hopes and our dreams. We're ready to sign on for the adventure." Ilene nodded in agreement and smiled.

"That's just wonderful! Welcome aboard," replied Tom as he reached over the table to shake their hands. "Are you ready to learn where your new home is?"

"I can't wait any longer!" said Ilene. "Where are we going?"

Tom handed her an envelope. "This contains the name of the country, the GPS location, and general details about the colony construction and schedule. Please sign this sheet of commitment and confidentiality, and then you may open it." The document committed to ten years with options for leaving after three years with half of the gold bonus. A statement, the "Breach of Certain Clearly Defined Issues," was critical, and a violation would be severe and would result in a full forfeiture of the gold bonus and other potential benefits of being at the colony. They both read and signed the document and read the location of the colony and the Research Project. Ken and Ilene both smiled! Slowly opening the packet, they saw for the first time where they would soon be living. They were ecstatic.

Tom turned the conversation to their start date. He explained that their move team could have them ready to go in two weeks. They finally agreed on one month to be sure to give their parents in Farmerville some time to spend with their grandkids. They would have to explain to their parents that they would not be coming back for at least ten years. They knew that would be a tough conversation, but a necessary one. They would spend a couple of weeks with them before the move. Both knew that there would be lots of tears and sadness.

Tom added that their personal coordinator and relocation specialists would call them the next day and begin the process. They talked through breakfast about what to expect before and after the move. Once their breakfast was finished, they thanked Tom for the courtesies shown to them and for the wonderful times they all had in the area. A few minutes later, back at the condo, they loaded their luggage and headed to the airport.

The Citation flew out of Destin at 11:30, and they were back at their home in the early afternoon. They read their packet several times and talked until 3 the next morning. The excitement was continuing to build. They felt happy but somewhat scared. They felt so many emotions at the same time. Life felt good for the first time in a long while.

Ken decided that he would resign with two weeks' notice first thing the next day, which would allow them to head to Farmerville in twelve days. Since Ilene had already been laid off, she would begin to pack things they would store in the States and things they would need to take to the colony. The brochure was very complete, with moving lists already prepared for them to use.

Chapter 20

BLOCKED CANYON— THE SALE

The meeting was scheduled for 8 o'clock on Wednesday morning, November 12, in the San Diego boardroom offices of Grainteck. Duncan arrived around 7:30. He parked his Denali in his reserved parking spot next to the entrance. He strolled into the office and went directly to the boardroom. The table had been set up by his office assistant, and water glasses with pitchers of water were supplied. A side table had plates and fruit bowls and pastries. Coffee had been brewed and was ready for anyone who needed a boost. Soft drinks and bottles of orange juice were stacked in a large bowl and surrounded with ice cubes. Having not had breakfast, Duncan poured himself a cup of coffee and grabbed an apple strudel. He then sat down at the head of the table and contemplated his long career and the changes that were very likely to occur. If a deal is actually struck today, then Grainteck, his baby, would be gone forever. It would be a sad, yet happy day.

Whether Grainteck sold or not, it would surely be emotional for him. It was time to show firmness and strength for the negotiations. He couldn't get emotional now. Duncan had invited four of his key people to attend the meeting with Blocked Canyon and help with the negotiations. He had prepared them for what he wanted in a deal and how any agreement would need to be structured.

Bruce Bills, Grainteck's CFO, was critical for the meeting. Bruce was the financial brain of the company and was critical for structuring the sale of Grainteck if that were to occur. Bruce was fifty-eight years old and married with no children. After graduating from college with a Master's in accounting, he had worked for several years at a major Wall Street firm and had gained experience in portfolio management, mergers and acquisitions, and banking. Duncan had recruited Bruce twenty-five years earlier, when his then-CFO suffered a major heart attack and had to retire. Bruce had made a huge impact on the growth of Grainteck, and now there was one more challenge for him.

Tom Clark had been the VP of sales for Grainteck for thirty years. Duncan had hired Tom because Grainteck's growing young business had just gotten too big, and Duncan could no longer juggle sales and product development. He'd met Tom at a Cadillac dealership, where Tom, at twenty-five, did a real sales job on the Kents, selling every bell, whistle, warranty, and service package that existed. Duncan liked Tom and, after buying the car, made Tom an offer to join Grainteck. Before retiring at age fifty-five, Tom managed a global sales team of five hundred and twenty two employees.

Duncan had talked Tom into coming out of retirement at age sixty to help in the negotiations with Blocked Canyon and also to work on his new project.

John Earnest, the current president of Grainteck, had been with the company for twenty years and was intimately familiar with all of the operations of the company. John was approaching sixty and was considering an early retirement so that he and his wife, Carole, could enjoy some travel and more golf. He pretty much ran everything, with the exception of R&D. R&D was Duncan's baby, and he wouldn't let go of the details of genetic research and design.

Joe Hawkins, as Duncan's personal attorney, currently on retainer for Grainteck, needed to be there to cover any legal issues that might come up for this particular meeting.

Six members of the strategic acquisitions team of the Blocked Canyon Investment Company walked in at exactly 8 a.m. After introductions and some small talk, their CEO, Jay Cameron, began his pitch.

"Gentlemen, Blocked Canyon is very interested in acquiring Grainteck. Duncan, we know you and your wife own 100 percent of all of the outstanding shares, and we would like to make an offer of $65 billion for all of your company shares. We have secured all necessary financing and can close in sixty days after satisfactory completion of all due diligence issues. Would that be acceptable to you, Duncan?"

Duncan had known the CEO of Blocked Canyon for thirty years and hated the fifty-two-year-old smart-ass who thought he knew everything. Jay was a privileged youngster with very rich parents. He had chosen to attend college and major in genetics. Working for Duncan for five years right out of college until age twenty-seven, Jay's attitude was always self-serving and egotistical. Jay was an only child. He always wanted to have his way and did not work well as a team member or as anyone's subordinate. He would literally throw tantrums that grew worse over time when he didn't get his way.

Duncan had suspected some serious mental flaws with Jay, but with Duncan's heavy workload, he hadn't dealt with the growing situation. During his fifth year at Grainteck, Jay's wealthy parents died when their private plane crashed into the Caribbean Sea. The plane was never recovered, and the cause of the crash had never been determined.

Jay was suppose to fly with his parents that day, but had decided to take a cruise back to Florida from Barbados. With his parents' death, he had inherited more than $10 billion. Immediately after he received his inheritance, Jay resigned from Grainteck, to the delight of everyone at the office.

Then, a few days later, it was discovered that Jay had started his own company. Duncan quickly discovered that Jay had stolen Duncan's DNA designs and some of Grainteck's customers. With Jay having way more money for legal fees than Duncan, it would be useless to file suit for damages. Over the next ten years, Jay had leveraged that money through some risky investments that by some luck had quadrupled his money. Jay then started an investment company and solicited investors for his new hedge fund. His fund now boasted more than $250 billion in assets and had been buying up any companies that he wanted.

Now was the perfect time to do some serious negotiations with Jay.

Duncan said, "Jay, you know we have a business that's a true cash-flow machine. It's essentially a monopoly for genetically modified seeds in corn, rice, and wheat. Additionally, we have a potentially new generation of seeds that haven't yet been tested and evaluated for effects on humans by our laboratory. These untested genetically modified seeds designs will go with the sale, but I caution you to not release them, until they have been fully tested and are suitable for human consumption.

"Our sales net income is more than $10 billion per year and growing at a 10 percent clip. If you give me an 8× multiplier on the current net income, that would be $80 billion. You know you could take that public in a couple of years if you wanted to and probably double your money, so I think the $80 billion should work for both of us."

Jay responded. "Duncan, we are only $15 billion apart; let's meet in the middle."

Then Duncan replied, "I think I will turn this over to Tom Clark and let him handle the negotiations from here!"

Duncan had already briefed Tom and the Grainteck attendees, and they knew exactly what he needed to end up with. Duncan despised Jay and knew that, if he were to stay in the room with him for any length of time during this negotiation, he would get pissed off and walk out of any deal that might be possible. Both parties had put a stake in the ground, and Duncan knew the negotiations should be workable with

Jay open to a $65 billion payment and Duncan asking for an $80 billion sale price. Duncan left the room and returned to his office.

At 4:21 the Grainteck team came into Duncan's executive office to review the tentative offer and acceptance. The Blocked Canyon team was waiting in the boardroom for Duncan to return to accept. The current agreement would be for $76 billion. Full transfer of all of the shares of stock in Grainteck would occur at midnight on December 31, along with a 100 percent payment by wire transfer to the account of Duncan and Nellie Kent.

Blocked Canyon would take over 100 percent of all assets and liabilities, including the ownership of all of the untested genetically modified seeds currently in development and pending production for possible sale in the next three years.

All of the seeds currently in development and in pending production must be evaluated by Blocked Canyon geneticists for any side effects prior to any potential commercial sales for human or animal consumption. No genetically modified seed production has yet been started beyond three years.

Duncan Kent must sign a non-compete clause for the total world area with one exception: he would be allowed to own and retain one small plant currently under construction in New Zealand for research & development (R&D) and testing purposes, and the plant would not sell any product outside of New Zealand. That plant and any associated production farms would not carry the Grainteck name or trademarks and would not be associated with Grainteck and Blocked Canyon in any way. The plant would be totally owned by a New Zealand LLC that would be owned and managed by Duncan Kent and his board of directors.

Additionally, Bruce and John would stay with Grainteck through the closing date and would retire at that time. Any severance package for Bruce and John would be at the discretion of Duncan as well as any consulting fees and bonuses for Tom and Joe.

At 5, the Grainteck negotiating team returned to the boardroom, where the Blocked Canyon team was anxiously waiting. Duncan stood at the head of the table, looked around the room, perhaps just realizing that this moment would be his last time at the head of the table and as the president of Grainteck.

After at least a full minute, he began.

"Gentlemen, I want to thank all of you for your hard work on this. I had my doubts that it could be done today, if even at all. But, my friends, we have a deal. Congratulations! Joe and Bruce, you can take it from here."

He shook hands with everyone on the Blocked Canyon team and then left the room.

On his drive home, he couldn't help but smile, because unknown to anyone except Nellie, he had really . . . really . . . really made a good deal today and not just for the money—hell, he would've taken the $65 billion offer!

Chapter 21
LEAVING

The jet was a chartered 747 from Dallas. It had been modified from the normal seating structure of mostly coach seats to entirely first class. The plane was now on its fifth charter in two weeks. There had already been one each from New York, Seattle, London, and Toronto. Most charters would have at least one stop along the way. Five or six more charters were scheduled over the next few weeks.

Ken, Ilene, David, and Jan boarded at 11 a.m. They were pleasantly surprised about the seats being all first class. Now that was the way to travel! They settled into their seats and just watched the expressions on every passenger's face as they, too, realized that there was only first-class seating. There appeared to be about one hundred people on board. The drinks were flowing, and the food service that the flight attendant announced was going to be first class, just like the seats. A few tired kids would whine and cry occasionally, but, Bose headsets had been provided to minimize any noise problems. The flight was scheduled for stops in Phoenix for an hour to pick up more people and for two hours in Honolulu for more people and refueling.

Across the aisle from Ken's seat was a couple with their 3 daughters. Ken introduced himself and then his family. The couple was Stacy and Audria Baltzegar. Their children were seventeen-year-old Shelby, thirteen-year-old Alexis and eleven-year-old Britney. They were from Houston, Texas.

Stacy was a forty-four-year-old mechanical engineer with extensive experience in automated controls and reliability in industrial plants. He was scheduled to be the maintenance and reliability manager of two of the plants recently constructed at the colony. One plant was a small oil refinery and gas processing plant, and the other was the same one hundred-megawatt power plant that Ken would be working at. Both plants were up and running already.

His wife, Audria, was forty-three and would be working at the corporate office in the logistics department for various import and export of goods for the colony. They seemed to have a lot in common, and Ken explained that he would be working at the generating plant. Ken and Stacy talked "engineering shop talk" for several hours while leaving their wives to care for their restless and bored children.

Menus were passed around for everyone to order their meals well in advance. Lunch was a selection of a warm sandwich, soup, and a fruit bowl. Dinner was a choice of filet mignon, baked potato, and carrots or baked halibut with cream sauce, mashed potatoes, and asparagus. Ken ordered steak, and Ilene ordered fish. David and Jan got the steak.

After dinner, everyone's full stomachs made sleep come easily. First, the kids crashed, and then Ken leaned his head against the plane's interior wall and began to snore lightly. Once the rest of the family was asleep, Ilene could relax, and she slowly drifted off to sleep.

Chapter 22

ARRIVAL

After a restless six hours of sleep, the passengers began to raise their window covers. The light grew brighter as more covers were raised. Looking out of the windows, there was nothing to see but water below.

Seventeen hours after takeoff, they landed at the Auckland International Airport at 3:00 in the afternoon. After getting through customs, everyone was whisked away in a string of chartered busses to the colony. Bags had been tagged and were being delivered directly to their personal condos.

Their packet had completely explained the transfer and the details of the Colony Property. After a three-hour drive through Auckland to the northwest, they crossed a gated land bridge onto an area that was almost an island surrounded by a large bay off of the Tasman Sea. The island was more like a peninsula jutting out from the main north island. Guards were at the gates that controlled the access across the single road that led to the island.

The entire island consisted of one hundred and fifty square miles of hills, woodlands, farmland, lakes, and three small rivers. The island's geography was made up of two groups of large hills with a wide, fertile valley on the west end. A large part of the island had been purchased two years earlier for the Research Project for $57 million from four ranchers who were ready to sell out and move into town with their children. Their farm and ranch hands had all been given a substantial severance pay to work for two more years and then move on to other farms and ranches. The four ranch houses were in close proximity in the valley area and had been used for the last two years as construction and operations headquarters.

The entire condo complex consisted of 6 major individual complexes, with three stories in each complex. There were palm trees everywhere with various surrounding small lakes, with waterfalls and rock streams connecting the lakes. Swimming pools were everywhere. From the outside, they could see large covered balconies that appeared to be about four hundred square feet.

The condo check-in was easy as all units were pre-assigned. The Wallace family was escorted to their condo by a part-time New Zealand college student earning money for college. They had been assigned a three-bedroom unit. As they entered the condo, they were amazed to find eleven-foot ceilings with full eight-foot doors. There were beautiful dark wooden floors and warm tan walls. The kitchen was large and complete with granite countertops with at least twenty-five feet of cabinets. The units were completely furnished. Large windows overlooked one of the many rock streams. David and Jan ran into their rooms and shouted with excitement.

The kitchen was furnished with dishes and pans. When Ilene opened the refrigerator, she found the refrigerator stocked with bacon, eggs, hamburger meat, chicken, milk and butter. The pantry had cooking oil, bread, flour, corn meal, sugar, and coffee. The table was centered with a large bowl of fruits, including bananas, apples, oranges, plums, avocados, and, of course, kiwis.

A beige envelope was located next to the fruit. Ken opened the envelope and read it. It was an invitation for the next day's events.

They were tired from the long trip that day. They quickly unpacked their travel bags, ate a sandwich from the ingredients in the refrigerator, and then talked for another hour. Sleep came quickly for their first night.

Chapter 23
THE FIRST EVENT

The kick-off meeting was scheduled for the morning of the tenth of November. The invitation stated that the orientation meeting was mandatory for all new arrivals, with children welcome. It was to start promptly at 10 in the auditorium. Immediately following the meeting, there would be a picnic lunch in the adjacent park. Dress was casual.

The Wallace family made their way down the wide red brick pathway that connected all of the condos and ran along a stream through the park to the town center. The pathway was full of families all walking in the same direction and stopping occasionally to enjoy the beauty of the park. According to the map and information in their packet, the auditorium was the largest building in town and could hold twenty thousand people at its maximum capacity. It was the first building on the right as they left the park.

Across the street from the auditorium, Ilene noticed the Personal Care Center. The sign on the front showed that it contained the complete services of a spa, salon, barbershop, massages, manicures, and pedicures. Ken noticed a bank, a grocery store, and a café before the street disappeared to the left. All of the buildings were of the Colonial Williamsburg Virginia style. Wood or red brick and white columns were the standard. The roads were all brick, as were the raised sidewalks. It reminded them somewhat of Disney World, which had been their one and only vacation one year after they had married.

The street was crowded with families visiting before the meeting. They saw the Baltzegars and visited with them for about five minutes. Audria mentioned that they had gotten a four-bedroom condo. Apparently all children would get their own room here. They were located in the second condo complex from the park and on the bottom floor, overlooking the lake. Their girls had already found the pool and game room. Their youngest, Britney, was a high-energy child and would run around harassing her sisters and anyone else she could get to with her antics. Ilene was sure that the whole family was delighted to have Britney in her own room as often as possible.

Audria was laughing and exclaimed, "Well, I am so disappointed with this place."

Everyone looked shocked. "Why, Audria? Everything is so nice and new!" said Ilene.

Audria quickly answered, knowing full well that she had their undivided attention. "Stacy and I have searched and looked everywhere in this town, and can you believe, there is not one Walmart, Sam's, or Costco in this whole place!"

They all laughed, because they knew that cost didn't matter since all living costs were being paid for through the colony allowances.

The auditorium was huge; it doubled as a theater and a training classroom. This necessitated the use of giant LED video screens so that everyone could see the stage participants. The sound was great, and many sports teams would have been proud to have such a stadium. All the seating was stadium style with large, soft seats. Giant dark brown curtains draped the walls to enhance the quality of the sound.

There was a balcony, but that section was closed and roped off. Ken and Ilene wanted to sit near the front, but the auditorium was already three-quarters of the way full. They chose four seats on the right side. As they looked around, they saw a couple of families who were on the 747 with them when they had flown in. The room filled with the buzz of conversations. The stage was set with a single podium and microphone. Tom Clark walked to the podium at precisely 10 a.m.

"Good morning, everyone," Tom shouted to kick things off. "Welcome to New Zealand and the Colony Research Project. I trust that everyone likes their condos?"

There was wild applause.

Tom continued. "Today I want to share with you what the Research Project is about and what we will be attempting to do here:

First, we've have developed this place as you see it here today with the help of outside engineering, architectural, and construction firms during the last year and a half. It was a farm. Now it's *a working town* with most of the amenities that you're familiar with from your former homes. It hasn't been easy to do this in such short order, and it's not finished yet. We'll need your help to continue with its progress.

We currently have a base structure for a government, a research department, a bank, schools, a college, a hospital, an airport that's under construction, a farm, a genetic seed plant, an electric power plant, a small oil refinery, a water and waste system complete with a recycling center, a communications center and phone department, and a manufacturing and industrial complex, a grocery store, café and restaurants, a department store, a hardware store, a gas station, a construction company, a transportation complex and center, a marina and harbor, shipping and receiving, a home furnishings store, this auditorium, a parks and recreation complex—with gym, pools, and sports center—a spa and salon, and a childcare center. There's a city services department and a security staff. Duncan and Nellie Kent have spent a total so far of $8 billion US to build this colony. We've had, at times, more than twenty thousand workers to construct this place.

We'll be adding to functions here as we move toward our objectives.

Secondly, our **goals and objectives** here are to try to attain a totally self-sufficient colony. We'll attempt to wean ourselves from all outside products and services, without giving up too much of what we're all accustomed to. Our goal is to be 90 percent complete within three years. We realize that we cannot be 100 percent self-sufficient, as there are many raw materials and manufactured items we need that just don't exist here and will never exist here. To be as self-sufficient as possible, we've built and will continue to build a warehouse complex second to none in the world. We've ordered more than $800 million worth of tractors, autos, trucks, lumber, lighting, and many other construction items not manufactured here currently. We're building small plants everywhere in our industrial complex. Our intent is to manufacture as much right here as possible. We would like to get to 100 percent someday.

Obviously, since we will need to import some materials and products, it will be necessary to export some products to essentially make it a revenue-neutral process. Our initial exports are targeted for one year from now and are planned to be meat, vegetables, fruits, and wine. Our agriculture department is in full swing with massive farming efforts. We have more than twelve thousand acres currently in some level of production.

Third, the research work will consist of **measuring** the progress of our self sufficiency from where we currently are, which is about 50 percent toward that goal of 90 percent in three years. Beyond three years, we will be measuring the progress from 90 percent to perhaps 95 to 98 percent in ten years.

The research will not only measure our progress as a colony, but will also measure your individual and family capacity to function, contribute, and to develop a society within the colony. We call this a colony because we're effectively not unlike the Pilgrims who established a colony at

Plymouth Rock, Massachusetts, in 1620. Those individuals had to be self-sufficient and learn to work together for the benefit of their society.

You'll receive questionnaires on a regular basis and will be required to complete them. We want your honest answers, as that will be critical for good data collection for our research.

Next, regarding **communications.** We have local phones in your homes and in all business, as well as cell phones for everyone. You may have in-bound and out-bound international phone calls and write and receive letters. Internet service is also available and may even be necessary to fully function in your job. You may not send or receive any package of products or food. Any of those items that are absolutely necessary must go through the shipping department, as well as security, for approval. There will be a limited amount of television, radio, and movies, but due to research purposes, those will be highly managed for content. Perhaps you as a colony will want to develop your own entertainment systems. We would encourage that.

The fifth item on our list, **travel** to and from the colony won't be allowed for you or anyone from outside. You all knew this and agreed to it prior to joining the Project. There will be shipments that come in and go out by ship, by air, and by truck, but that will be done in the highly restricted shipping and receiving complex. You probably saw that complex as you came across the gated entrance on the way in. The truck complex is just inside the gate, and the dock is about eight miles from the town center on the bay. An airport, currently under construction, is along the waterfront beside the dock area.

Next, you'll have a week to learn and enjoy your new hometown before you report to **work** on the November 7. Please get familiar with your living area as well as get acquainted with the many new friends that you will make here. Information on where to go for your first day of work will be in your mailbox located at the front of your condo complex. If your work is more than one mile from your condo, busses or shuttles will be running to transport you to and from work. Since most of you will work within a mile, walking or biking will be your likely mode of travel. Bikes will be supplied to all of you and your children this week. You may keep them in the bike garage located in each condo complex.

Social interaction is important for a successful Research Project, and we've scheduled small social events every day this week. Nellie Kent is in charge of these events, and we encourage you to attend. Schedules will be in your mailbox this afternoon.

Government for the colony hasn't been necessary until now. We'll eventually be running the government as a thirty-one-person structure that includes seven lifetime Board members with authority for all aspects of the local government. The seven colony Board members are Duncan and Nellie Kent, Bruce Bills, John Earnest, Bob Erickson, Joe Hawkins and me, Tom Clark. The Board will select members of this government instead of an election and political process. Our plan has yet to be completely formulated but we'll get there. Ultimately, we'll have methods for appointments to a representative type of government, and these representatives will make recommendations to the Board for approval and implementation. We plan to start that evolution within two or three years.

Finally, I want to talk about **pay and bonuses.** The Colony Bank has safe deposit boxes for each family. Even though you cannot touch the gold in your accounts, these safe deposit boxes are designed with a bulletproof Plexiglas window so that you may unlock your box and then view your personal gold pay and bonus cache at any time. Gold will be added monthly from the treasury into your box. Bruce Bills will be heading up the bank. Bruce's wife, Lorraine, will be in charge of the colony spending accounts and your Colony Cards. Please visit Bruce and get to know him and Lorraine.

"While all of you have already received your Colony Card for expenditures, you will also note that it contains a photo of you on the front. That is to assure that no one other than you can use your card. It will be necessary to establish a form of credits for work and services as well as debits for expenditures. This will allow everyone to choose and manage their purchases and make appropriate decisions for their family. Essentially, this is your family spending allowance on a debit card. We've determined that two thousand colony units will be deposited each week into each family's card account for each forty hours of work and/or community service. Two members working will receive four thousand colony units. Additionally, each family with a dependent child under eighteen years of age will receive an additional one thousand colony units per child. However, all of you will start off with a balance of ten thousand units. These are not in any type of country currency, such as US or New Zealand dollars. We have priced all goods and services in colony units. The colony units are not convertible into any type of cash.

"And now, I want to thank you all for being here today. I hope that you will join us for our first of many colony picnics here in our wonderful park. We've planned many activities this afternoon for the children as well as adults. Please introduce yourself to all of our Board members at the picnic, and welcome to the colony!"

With that, Tom left the podium, and everyone got up to leave the auditorium and head out to the park.

Chapter 24
THE PICNIC

The picnic lunch was somewhat unusual. As everyone left the auditorium and went into the park, several forty-foot-long tables were set up with a large transfer truck behind each table. Complete wooden picnic baskets about twenty-four inches by eighteen inches were being handed out to each family from the table. The baskets were labeled as 1, 2, 3, and 4 to match up with the number of people in each family. Families with more than four members had two baskets that added up to the number of family members.

Ilene was handed a basket marked with a 4. As she walked away, she peeked inside. She saw a blanket, four sack meals, a small ice container, four sodas, a bottle of Chardonnay, and four cups. They strolled along with the crowd. People were spreading their blankets on picnic tables, and some were putting them on the ground. Ken selected a table within a group of six tables near the edge of the lake. Three of the tables were already filled and the remaining two were quickly taken.

David and Jan began talking to the other kids playing on the adjacent swings. Within minutes, one would think they had been playmates for years.

The closest table had a couple who appeared to be in their mid-thirties. Since the tables were only fifteen feet apart, they began talking and introduced themselves as Newton and Stormy Baker from Glendora, California. Their one daughter, Brooke, age seven, was busy playing with the iPad that Newton had brought to keep her occupied.

Ken asked Newton, "What will you guys be doing for work here?"

Newton replied, "Both Stormy and I will be working in the school system; I'll teach math, and Stormy will teach biology. We completed our PhDs five years ago and have been teaching at UCLA. We were so happy to get out of California with all of the smog and gangs and drugs. We just didn't want our children to grow up in that deteriorating culture with high taxes. We jumped at this opportunity to get away and have a great adventure. So far . . . so good!"

Ilene said, "Us, too. We're so excited to be here."

The conversation went on for about an hour as they ate their lunch and drank the bottle of Chardonnay. It was a beautiful day in New Zealand, and the temperature was a nice seventy-five degrees. They found out that Newton and Stormy were also in Condo Complex #1, where they were located. They decided they would get together later in the week for dinner. Ken would barbeque some pork ribs and beans on the outdoor grill, and Newton would bring the corn-on-the-cob and some dessert.

Ken, Ilene, David, and Jan got back to the condo at a little after 2. They were still tired from their travels the previous day, so they decided to take a nap. When they woke, it was almost 6 p.m. Ilene said, "Let's cook dinner in our new home tonight. I saw some chicken in the refrigerator, and I'm just dying to have some good southern fried chicken and rolls with mashed potatoes and gravy."

"That would be great," replied Ken.

David and Jan were busy with their iPads, playing games in their new rooms. The living room was equipped with a fifty-five-inch flat screen smart television, a Blue Ray DVD player and surround sound. Ken turned on the TV with the remote. The channel guide came on first, and he saw that the stations were the same as he was accustomed to in Shreveport on cable.

Turning to Fox News, he wanted to catch up on the recent events in the States. Ken was a news junky and watched it every day. The news was always the same, just bad things happening everywhere. He always tried to guess the day's bad events before the news started. It was usually a Middle East bombing, a racial issue over some thug whose rights to steal had been violated, a Democrat versus Republican argument, a financial crisis in some country, a weather catastrophe, a viral epidemic, or starving children in some desert. That night it was forest fires on the west coast and more bombings in the Middle East.

After a few minutes, the smell of the frying chicken filled the room. Once the chicken was fried, Ken's job was to make the gravy to go with the mashed potatoes that Ilene was finishing. This was a simple process handed down from his grandma. He would simply dump all of the hot oil down the sink drain except for a cup. Keeping that remaining cup of oil hot in the skillet and turning the heat to high he would add enough flour to absorb the oil, and stir until it was light brown. It browned quickly, usually within thirty to forty seconds. Then lastly, with the burner still on high, add a full large glass of cold tap water. This caused the flour to swell and thicken. The whole process took only two minutes. The rolls came out of the oven right on time. Dinner was ready at 7:30. It was their first home-cooked dinner, and it was great.

Chapter 25
TOWN VISIT

The Wallace family woke up on Tuesday just after sunrise. They still had not adjusted to the time zone changes and jet lag. David and Jan were sleepy and still worn out from travel. After a breakfast of pancakes, maple syrup, strawberries, milk, and coffee for the adults, the kids were beginning to come alive.

Over breakfast, Ilene said, "I want to see our deposit box at the bank first thing this morning. It'll make me feel good that this is really happening." They headed out through the park to town. There were already many people out in the park. It was a beautiful day, with only a few morning clouds that had drifted in from the sea. The temperature was a mild sixty-five degrees, and the high was to be seventy-nine. Some of the young boys had already found friends and were playing soccer. David wanted to play, but Ken told him that he would need to wait until later, after their town visit.

Their first stop after their stroll through the park area was the Colony Bank. They entered the bank just as it opened at 9. The bank had a colonial look on the outside, and the inside was clean and smelled fresh. It was not elaborate and plush but more of a simple, homelike look. They were met by a friendly receptionist.

"Hi, my name is Kate Matthews," she said with a warm smile. She extended her hand to Ilene first and then to Ken. "How may I help you today?"

Ilene replied, "Hi, Kate, I'm Ilene Wallace, and this is my husband Ken and our two children, David and Jan. We want to see our safe deposit box today and just check it out, if that is all right?"

"That's great, Ilene. We just deposited everybody's first gold on Monday. Let's leave David and Jan in our play area for a few minutes, because children aren't allowed inside of the vault."

David and Jan were excited about that because there were at least twenty children in the play area.

"Follow me to the vault," Kate said. They walked to the back of the bank, where a large wall of shelves contained the alphabetical sign-in books. She found their personalized leather book, drew it from the bookshelf, and placed it on a glass waist-high table. She opened the new book, and Ken and Ilene noticed that their names were embossed in gold letters on the top of the first page.

"For any visit, you'll need to show your Colony Card, and we'll also do a retinal ID scan today to assure that only you or Ken can view your box going forward."

After the scan was done, Kate escorted them into the massive vault. Kate mentioned that the vault had steel walls, roofs, and floors that were sandwiched around four feet of concrete. Their box was located midway down one of at least thirty corridors that were twenty feet long. All of the boxes were large, measuring eighteen inches tall and fourteen inches wide. Each column of four boxes started six inches above the floor all the way up to more than six feet high. Their box was second from the bottom, about midway on the right side. Their box number was 2020. Kate showed them the electronic lock, where they could key in their own personal bank code. She explained that the code would not work unless they first swiped their Colony Card across the reader located next to the keypad. Kate left the room, and they were alone. Ilene swiped her Colony Card and keyed in their personal bank code. The code was 1112. They had selected that code number because November 12 was the date that they left to start their new lives. But, they wondered if a lot of the other families had done the same thing.

Once the code was entered, they swiped their Colony Card again on the keypad, and the cover door swung open. The inside of the box appeared to be about twenty inches deep. Behind a thick Plexiglas window and on the first of three shelves were thirty one-ounce gold coins all stacked in a single column just under three inches tall. They were all new and quite shiny. A chill came over both of them as they both smiled. It was real. It was really happening, just like they were promised. They closed the door, and it locked automatically.

They stopped by Kate's desk on the way out, and she reminded them that they also had safe deposit boxes available for personal items if they wanted one. Ilene said, "Come to think of it, we do have some documents, jewelry, and cash we'd like to keep away from the house in a safe place. So yes, please put us down for one."

Kate wrote their names down in her book and said, "I'll assign you a box when you come in to drop off the items."

Ilene responded, "Thanks so much for your help, Kate; we'll see you later this week."

Their next stop was at the fitness center next to the bank. They walked in and met a young man named Billy Jenkins. Billy introduced himself and told them about his background and credentials. He had a Master's degree in physical therapy from Baylor. He had also participated in the last Olympics in the decathlon. His job at the colony was to enhance the physical well-being of everyone.

Billy explained, "Part of the research being monitored here at the colony is the total fitness level of each person, and we'll measure that data no less than once a month." He needed everyone to commit to a minimum of two one-hour visits per week at the gym. The fitness center included spa services, a gym, swimming pool, lockers, showers, sauna, and steam room. All costs would go on the Colony Card and would consume only a one-unit debit per visit per person. After some thought and discussion, Ken signed up for Monday and Thursday from 4 to 5 p.m., and Ilene signed up for Tuesday and Friday from 7 to 8 a.m. Ilene also signed up for the spa services every Thursday beginning at 6 p.m. This schedule made sense for them since Ken would be working 5 a.m. to 3:30 p.m., and Ilene would be working from 9 a.m. to 5:30 p.m.

Billy then took them on a tour. The gym had it all. It included a six thousand square-foot weight room, an indoor Olympic-size pool, men's and women's hot tubs, and a large room for yoga, aerobics, and dance. It even had a boxing ring and its associated areas. The spa included four massage rooms complete with a by-appointment chiropractor service five days a week. Steam rooms and saunas were next to a relaxation room that played continuous soft music.

Next door to the Fitness Center were the hair salon and barbershop. A large library was also nearby, and like the smaller shops, they had the name of the operator on the front of the store. The hair salon had Samantha Crowder as its operator, and the library had Carole Earnest as its operator.

Ilene felt she'd get to know those people since she loved to get her hair done and the kids really enjoyed reading books when they weren't on their computer games.

The kids were beginning to get restless so Ken promised them ice cream after they had finished touring the salon and barber shop. They walked into the shop and found a receptionist area with a smiling receptionist behind a small desk. To the left, they saw a row of eight barbers at work with a receptionist at the entrance. All chairs were occupied, and there were about a dozen people waiting in a large reception area. To the right, they noticed a room for the ladies' hair that was twice as large as the barber shop. It, too, was fully utilized. The vent fans that made a continuous purring sound minimized the smell of chemicals used for hair color. The reception area had coffee, soft drinks, water, and snacks. Magazines and newspapers filled racks on the wall. There were multiple conversations going on in the waiting room. It was a lively place. Ken made a recurring appointment with the receptionist for a haircut every two weeks on Monday at 5:15 p.m., and Ilene scheduled her hair appointments for every two weeks on Tuesdays at 5:45 p.m.

Their schedule was beginning to fill up already, but they wanted some level of structure in their lives after having such a horrific work structure in Shreveport. Certainly this wouldn't be bad since their commutes were all less than fifteen minutes walking time away.

The ice cream and bakery shop was next to the auditorium, located across the street and adjacent to the park. The glass front revealed two people scooping ice cream for about ten customers. They walked in and took their place in line. David ordered a double scoop chocolate cone, and Jan ordered a single vanilla cone. Ken and Ilene each got a double pralines and cream cone. They walked out and strolled into the park, where chairs and tables were available. As they sat down, David's double chocolate scoops fell off of the cone, and the look on his face was almost funny. You could see the tears beginning to well up in his eyes. Ken quickly solved the problems with a quick run into the ice cream shop for a new cone for David.

Their map showed the library, the department store, and the ESCAPE Research offices on the next block. Since the kids were getting a bit tired, they decided to head back to the condo.

The colony grocery store was directly across the street from the ice cream shop. They quickly walked through just to get a feel for what was there. The sign on the front named it as CGS, which everyone knew simply meant Colony Grocery Store. It seemed well stocked. It also had a pharmacy near the front. Most stores back in the States put the pharmacy in the back so people would buy spontaneously as they were forced to travel the aisles to get to what they really wanted. But here, additional sales were not important because there was no markup on the cost of the products or services. That meant the pharmacy could be up front to allow for a more efficient pharmacy-only experience.

"The pharmacy at the front really makes sense to me," said Ilene.

As they walked back to their condo, they saw that behind the CGS was a large building that was marked with a large sign on the side of the building that read: "The Colony Medical Center." This would be where Ilene would work.

"Wow, I can get here fast and pick up groceries on the way home. Even the workout will be only a few steps from work and home," said Ilene.

As they reached the condo and went inside, Ilene exclaimed, "I want to go to the school tomorrow."

Ken replied, "I really would like to go to the marina." As they made ham sandwiches for lunch, Ken suggested that they do both items separately.

"That sounds good to me," said Ilene. "I'll take the kids to daycare services and head out to the school. After that, I want to get my hair done. I have 747-jet hair, and it won't do anything. I may even get a massage first. You go to the marina and check it out. Maybe you can find a boat that takes people out fishing or a fishing pier that we could all enjoy for an outing day. We've been under each other's butts for four weeks now, and this would give us some time for ourselves." Ken agreed, and the next day's plan was set.

Chapter 26
SCHOOL AND TOWN VISIT

After dropping off the kids at the daycare center, located between condo buildings #3 and #4, Ilene checked out a bike at Condo #3 and biked to the school at the center of town.

The town was so cute and compact. The whole town was currently only four blocks, but some construction was still going on at the end of Kent Avenue, five blocks from the park, to add additional buildings.

Although the school was not open for students, parents could visit and learn about the schedules and curriculums. The introduction brochure on the school system said that the school would be manned this week by two of the teachers who had arrived a month before and were prepared for a busy week. Each teacher had a table and sat patiently behind it with stacks of booklets and forms to hand out to each newly arriving parent. A sign on the left table read "K through 6." Ilene walked up to the lady on the left and introduced herself.

"Oh, hello, Mrs. Wallace. My name is Paula French. I'll be the principal for K through 6, and I believe that I saw where you have a student who will be starting next week in grade 3 and another that will be starting next year in kindergarten. Is that right?"

"Yes," replied a surprised Ilene.

Paula continued, "Here is the school packet for your son, David. Let me review the items that will be different from your previous experience with schools:

"First: There will be no homework. We believe that parents work hard both at work and at home, and they don't need to be further pressured to be doing the work that is the teacher's responsibility. We want you to spend time with your children doing fun things and building lasting family experiences as well as good family exercise and activities. We want you to teach them to be good citizens with good morals. We want your children to like you! Play baseball, volleyball, bowling, badminton, biking, fishing, make cookies—you decide—but make sure you develop relationships and memories that will last a lifetime."

Ilene couldn't even speak. She'd hated having to come home from a long working day and force David to sit at a table and work on some assignment that a teacher had assigned just so she could complete all of the government forms before the end of the week. All of the homework had been to force teaching work onto the parents so that the schools could get a "good" rating that was sufficient to get the most federal dollars possible. David had felt like he was always being punished, because his little sister didn't do homework and could just play.

Paula continued, "Second, we'll be doing IQ testing beginning in every grade on every child. Children will be placed in grades that are relative to IQ and not age. We don't want to hold back children from learning to their potential just because of the number of times the sun has orbited the earth since their birth.

"Third, school will begin at 9 and end at 5:30 each day. Young children can come fifteen minutes early and leave fifteen minutes late, but longer in family or work emergencies. We will not work the kids that long on school work, though. We'll have recess and supervised play for three hours each day. Lunch will be at noon for thirty minutes, and healthy snacks, such as fruits, will be provided in the morning at 10:30 and in the afternoon at 2 and at 4. Hopefully, they won't come home starving, as most children typically do from previous school systems.

"Ilene, you'll need to bring David to this entrance on Monday and take him to Room 7. Are there any other issues that we need to cover?"

Ilene answered, "I can't think of any right now. Thank you very much, Paula,"

"You're welcome, and thanks for coming by today," said Paula.

Chapter 27
THE SPA

Ilene left the school and biked back toward the spa. The morning sun had already warmed the air to seventy degrees. It was summer in New Zealand, and the day's high was expected to be seventy-eight degrees. The town center was busy with folks going in every direction. She stopped next to the spa and parked her bike in the bike slots along the street and walked into the coffee shop. She ordered a cup of latte and a donut and sat down at a table next to the window to enjoy her treat. She took her time, as she needed her time alone. Through the window she watched the people. They all seemed young and happy, not unlike her and Ken. There were no homeless people, no people walking around with their pants half off, their underwear all exposed, and their hats on backward.

She noticed there were no older people here and assumed that was simply because this community was indeed a workplace town and retired older people would not be working anymore. The second thing she took note of was there were absolutely no advertisements on the buildings or store windows, and that made the whole town just gorgeous. Signs and advertisements were not needed in this place. The roads were all brick, so there would be no blacktop tracks on her condo carpets.

She finished her treat and walked to the spa and barbershop. For some strange reason, they were joined with a common entrance and reception area. Perhaps it was because the colony owned everything, and there were no individuals competing in this town.

Her massage was scheduled for 9:15 with Penny Lyons. She had booked a one-hour deep-tissue massage. Over the past three weeks, she had been packing, lugging, dragging, lifting, walking, and otherwise cramped to the point where her muscles just plain ached.

Penny introduced herself and said, "Good morning Ilene. I'm going to give you a great massage today, so get undressed and cover up on the table, face down. I'll be back momentarily." She left Ilene to disrobe and climb onto the massage table. Penny returned, dimmed the lights, and turned on some soft and soothing music.

Penny rubbed oils onto the back of her left leg and started the massage. Penny really knew how to use her elbows to get that deep tissue softened and unknotted. Penny said, "Ilene, as part of the research program, I'll be measuring your fat density during the massage and inputting it into the computer. I guess it's so they can track whether you're getting healthier or not. As I understand it, and I do hear a lot in this job, effective next January 15, no food except proteins such as fish and meat will be allowed to come into the colony. We'll have to produce it all here, and that includes any grains. I see that the farms outside of the city are really active with the preparations and harvesting.

Finally getting a word in, Ilene asked, "Penny, why did you come here?"

Penny replied, "I got a PhD in physical therapy from the University of Kansas when I was twenty; then I worked at a local hospital for three years. I liked helping people, but with Medicare, Medicaid, and then Obamacare, they were cutting my hours and lowering my pay. The paperwork was overwhelming, and the customer care was deteriorating like hell. The hospital was going to make their profit and to hell with the needs of the workers or patients.

We were giving half of the normal and necessary service time for every procedure. And then we were charging the customer or government for the full standard time. That was pure fraud. I didn't want to be involved in fraud.

"At the colony, I can work at the spa and the hospital and get paid well. I get to do the work right, no pressure. I think it's just great."

"How did you get a PhD at age twenty?" asked Ilene.

"Well, books were always easy for me. I pretty much retain everything that I read. I finished high school at sixteen and got a Bachelor's degree in math at eighteen, but I thought the math was boring, so I wanted a more social profession. Basically, I found that I like people more than numbers."

"And your husband?" asked Ilene.

Penny responded, "My husband is working on the farm here. He's an agricultural engineer. You just can't take the farm out of those Kansas boys, you know! He just loves it. We came here more than nine months ago because they needed the farm up and running faster than the rest of the stuff. Since the colony was consolidating four farms to start with when it was purchased, it was critical to keep the farm operating.

"We have one kid, and he's only two years old. We want to have about four more now that our lives are more settled and financially secure."

Ilene shared her background and why they'd left Louisiana for the colony. The conversation lasted only a few minutes, and the massage was feeling really good, so Ilene stopped talking and let her body go totally limp. Penny knew exactly how to make the muscles relax and soften. The smell of the aromatic lotion made Ilene feel that she was in a flower garden. When the massage was over, Penny let her lie still for another thirty minutes before getting up. Penny came in at 10:45 let her know it was time to leave.

Ilene sat up startled. "Oh, sorry, Penny. I felt so good that I dozed off. Wow, I feel like a new woman. How much do I owe you?"

She handed Penny her card.

"Six units," said Penny. "Oh, and by the way, you were lucky to get in today. Had it not been for a cancellation, you would've had to wait at least a week. You need to book regular appointments well in advance," Penny added.

Ilene responded, "Sure, Penny, I will. Give me a few days to figure out my schedule, and I'll come by and get on your schedule.

"What about a tip?" asked Ilene.

Penny replied, "There is *no tipping* anywhere in the colony. Everyone gets paid very well. Anyone accepting a tip has to go before Tom Clark for a private meeting! Didn't you read that in your booklet?"

Ilene responded. "I was lax in reading it all. I guess I'd better read all of it!"

Chapter 28
THE HAIRDRESSER

Ilene walked from the spa to the salon just in time for the 11 o'clock appointment she'd scheduled earlier that morning. Her hairdresser was Samantha Crowder.

Samantha had been at the colony for two weeks. She took one look at Ilene and said, "Girl, you have been in that spa massage too long this morning; you have a red ring around your face. That Penny can do a number on a person, can't she?" She was laughing loudly. Her black skin made her white teeth look even brighter.

As she started to wash Ilene's hair (still laughing), she stated, "Now, I know you're going to ask me how I ended up here, so save your breath. Everyone here wants to know about everybody, so I'll start, but you'll have to tell me your story next. I'm thirty-two and single and was formerly working as a college professor in chemistry. I got so tired of the politics and mess associated with the students that were disrespectful and obscene, as well as the low pay and cutbacks, that I just stepped back and started doing hair. It paid about the same.

"I saw an ad in the paper for college chemistry teachers and responded. They offered me the opportunity to do both hair and teach college chemistry with good pay, so what the hell—I took it. I don't think they needed a full-time college chemistry teacher anyway."

"I thought there were only families here," replied Ilene.

"Oh, no," replied Samantha. "They decided to take singles, too. They told me there were four hundred singles here and that half were men. That cinched it for me. I figured that if there were exactly two hundred men and two hundred women, and it got down to the end and I was the last woman, then the last guy would have to take me. So, honey, I am already planning my wedding! They're having a singles' reception Saturday night, and I can hardly wait. Keep your eye out for a hot single black stud for me, not that I don't like the white boys too, if he's really hot." She smiled with those pretty white teeth again and winked.

Ilene could tell that Samantha enjoyed the banter. She decided to have some fun with Samantha and exclaimed, "You know, I saw a young man this morning with some large blue jean pants, extra large tee shirt, red underwear, and a hat that was going in the wrong direction on his head!"

Samantha responded, "Girl, you are full of shit! This is a high-class place. There ain't any of those dumb-ass idiots here. There's class here. You can't get in this place without a high IQ, and those rapper assholes don't even have IQs."

Samantha started laughing again and said, with a big laugh, "I am going to get you for that, girl. I think I'll just give you half a haircut today—and make you come back tomorrow for the other half."

"Okay, okay, I give up. I'll be nice. Please cut my hair right," begged Ilene.

As she finished washing Ilene's hair, she added, "Now, I need to make you aware that, as part of the Research program here, I'll be inputting data into the system on you. I'll have to measure your hair-follicle density per square inch and the hair growth rate."

"I'm going to have to measure a lot of stuff in the college classes, too," Ilene replied.

"That's fine with me. I figured that a Research Project with 'colony' in the name would have lots of issues that needed to be measured to ensure a successful and worthwhile experience."

Ilene looked at her finished hair in the mirror. She had naturally brown hair, but she liked to have some highlights in it. Her hair was done perfectly. She smiled and handed Samantha her card. "I really like it. How much is it?" asked Ilene.

"It's five units," replied Samantha.

"Thank you, Samantha. See you again soon," said Ilene as she left the salon.

Chapter 29
KEN'S RIDE

Ken took the bike right after breakfast and pedaled through town toward the marina. He saw joggers, cyclers, walkers, and even people doing yoga. The air was cool, and that let him pedal a little harder. Some light fog was in the lowest areas around the lake and valley floors. As he left the town center and ventured beyond the construction area, the beautiful farmland of New Zealand revealed itself. The colony farm had rolling hills of pastureland, cattle, and orchards. Beautifully shaped deciduous trees were scattered along the rolling hills to provide shade for the cattle. Far away, on the side of a large hillside, he could see one of the large sheep herds that the country was famous for. He passed orchards of apples, peaches, plums, kiwis, cantaloupe, and watermelon.

Through openings in a few large hothouses near the road, he could see tomatoes, peppers, and okra plants growing. The orchards gave way to fields of mature corn, cantaloupe, watermelon and wheat. Near the harbor, a large flat area where a small river approached the Tasman Sea, the pastureland turned to hay fields and, after half a mile, the lower hayfield was being converted to rice fields.

Suddenly, three pheasants flew up from along the ditch next to the road. The beating wings were loud and sudden. The noise almost made Ken lose control of the bike. His heart raced as he recovered control. The pheasants had made Ken's mind flash back to the days in Farmerville, when hunting was a big part of his younger years. He was disappointed that he wasn't able to bring his guns with him to New Zealand. He was a good shot, and it had paid off as a US Marine. Hunting pheasants or deer in New Zealand would be fun, if he could find a gun. He wondered if his brother back in north Louisiana was keeping his guns well oiled for when he returned.

The five miles to the marina took him only twelve minutes, but what a great ride. It was mostly downhill, but that meant the return trip would be mostly uphill.

The marina and port were located in a protected cove. To the right, about a mile away, he could see the power plant where he'd be working and the small refinery. It looked like a typical industrial park area, and he could see that construction was underway. He remembered from the map in his welcome packet that the current construction plans included building a fertilizer plant, a steel foundry, a lumber mill, and many more unidentified shaded layouts on the map for future additions.

There were a lot more trucks moving around than in the town and condo area. Construction work required a lot of people and equipment. Trucks coming in with supplies from Auckland were traveling through the entrance bridge along the beach road to the construction site. A hotel had been constructed at the marina for construction workers, as they too weren't allowed into the farmland and town center. He could see the paved parking lot around the marina, and it was bustling with fishermen and freight-handling equipment. As he approached the parking lot around the last curve, there was a guard gate, and a guard was on duty.

Ken stopped, and the guard asked, "May I see your Colony Card, please?" Ken handed the guard his card, and the guard scanned it through the card reader, handed him the card back, and then raised the gate for him to pass.

"Have a great day," the guard shouted as Ken rode through.

Ken expected to find a small sandwich shop or café in the marina area. He walked into the marina shop at the start of the pier and asked if there was a café. The casher replied, "We have a café, but it's closed today and tomorrow for equipment changes. There's coffee inside the dining area and vending machines that have soft drinks, tea, water, peanuts, sunflower seeds, and fruit and such."

Ken walked into the dining area, scanned his Colony Card, and got a bottle of water and a bag of peanuts. He sat down for a brief rest from his morning ride.

A group of shrimpers were drinking coffee at the table next to him. They were talking about the previous night's shrimp fishing. It had been a decent haul, but the increase in fuel costs was hurting their ability to make a profit. Ken noticed they were using New Zealand money to operate the machines and not a Colony Card. That meant they weren't part of the Research Project and were either contract employees or independent suppliers using the marina as a working base. A few construction workers also were at the far corner of the dining area, eating meals from brown paper bags, and they, too, had bought drinks with New Zealand money.

The dining area had a wall of windows that looked out over the dock. He decided to take a stroll down the dock. The first boat he saw was a beautiful Hattarus 86, and the name on the side read "Colony Fishing Charter One."

Brochures were in a waterproof box next to the boat. Ken took one and read it as he walked. There were four charter boats available. Prices were in colony units and offered bottom fishing and trolling. Whole-day and half-day charters were available with a minimum of three fishermen over age twelve and a maximum of six fishermen. Ken stuffed the brochure into his back pocket and walked on down the dock. Ken noticed that there were about a dozen boats at the dock and about the same number of empty spaces. He wasn't sure if the boats were at sea or just unfilled slots. Seagulls were swarming and landing on the shrimp boat to pick up morsels left by the three shrimpers in the dining room. Toward the end of the dock, yellow tape blocked any further progress. A pile-driving machine was parked at the end and was apparently adding to the size of the dock. Even though it was a weekday, there were no workers present. Ken turned around and headed back to get his bike.

Rather than ride back, Ken decided to go on to the power plant so that he would know how to get into his workplace come Monday. He rode along the beach road to the plant. He noticed that near the power plant entrance, there was a paved jetty going out about one hundred yards into the bay. A two hundred foot-long dock was located near the end of the jetty, with piping in place to unload the incoming fuel oil that would be burned in the power plant boilers. The warm water discharge pipes from the power plant was also visible at the end of the jetty. Ken knew that back in Shreveport, the warm discharge water was clean and when dumped into cooler water would attract baitfish. In turn, the larger fish would come in to eat the baitfish. *This would be a great spot for a family fishing day,* Ken thought. Ken rode his bike to the end of the jetty, turned around, and headed home. The mostly uphill climb home left him sweaty and tired. He took a hot shower and a short nap when he reached the condo, which proved to be just what he needed at the end of a great ride.

Chapter 30
DINNER WITH NEWTON AND STORMY

Newton and Stormy arrived at 4 on Thursday afternoon. They brought twelve ears of corn and a chocolate pie that Stormy had made that day. They also had a six pack of colony beer. Ken knew that it might not be enough so he had bought a case of beer earlier in the day when he bought the baby back ribs, chicken, beans, and barbecue sauce. He liked the KC Masterpiece sauce, and, to Ken's surprise, the colony barbecue sauce tasted about the same.

Jan could hardly wait to show Brooke her iPad. She knew Brooke liked the iPad games from the day they had first met. The girls went into Jan's room and started to play almost immediately. David followed them into the room to aggravate and annoy them.

Ken and Newton ungentlemanly popped open a beer for themselves and then asked Ilene and Stormy if they wanted one.

"Of course, we do, you goofballs," Ilene replied as Stormy nodded. Ilene had gotten out some chips and green onion dip for a snack. The guys dove into them.

Almost immediately, the women started to talk about kid stuff. Stormy said, "I went to the school this week, and I was excited about the kids not having homework. The school times would work in unison with the work times, and that's just awesome. I'll be teaching biology for the older students.

"I was also told that there would be about two hundred and fifty students for each age range. However, the school system wouldn't be set up with just typical grades or children's ages, but instead would be based on IQ testing. This way, the students could advance at a pace that their brains could reasonably handle and not be held back or moved forward based on the number of rotations of the earth around the sun since they were born."

"That's what I was told too. It's a very novel approach. I like it," said Ilene.

Stormy added, "They might even have Newton for some math classes, since he'll be teaching at all math skill levels. Although it's unusual for younger kids to have multiple teachers, I do feel that it would allow the kids to advance faster in specific subjects versus just following the herd of their grade." Ilene agreed with a nod of her head.

It turned out Newton and Ken had a lot in common. Neither one really liked to watch sports on TV. Newton said to Ken, "To me, it's just ridiculous to pay some moron $250 million over five years to throw a ball through a hole ten feet above the ground. It reminds me of the movie *Idiocracy* and the current state of the United States whereby smart, highly educated people were becoming rarer, leaving the idiots in charge." They had a good discussion about whether the folks in government were idiots or just stupid. They agreed you can't cure stupid, so if they were just idiots, there was some hope with a little education. Ken added," It's highly unlikely the United States politicians could be educated. They just don't know they're stupid, so we'll just have to describe them as *ignorantly stupid.* "That would work. Pass me another beer, Ken," said Newton.

Further talk revealed they both liked to fish. Ken told Newton about the bike ride and the nice jetty and the colony charter boat. They decided they'd go to the jetty one day and test out the fishing there.

Ken said, "One thing that really makes me happy about fishing here is that there are no snakes in New Zealand. I hate snakes. Back where I grew up in Farmerville, Louisiana, there was a freshwater lake called Lake D'arbone. The water moccasins were really bad around the edges and feeder creeks, and then if you get out into the woods, the rattlesnakes can be anywhere. Some get up to six feet long, so you always have to be on guard for those bastards."

Newton replied, "Me, too. I have the philosophy that a good poisonous snake is a dead poisonous snake! Those tree huggers who want to save them are such hypocrites. If they want to save things that can kill humans, because they have a right to live, then they ought to consider saving the polio virus, the smallpox virus and the Ebola bacteria. Don't they have a right to live? No, they won't do that. I'll bet those tree huggers are all vaccinated for measles, polio, diphtheria, and all sorts of stuff that would deny those sweet little viruses a little dinner!"

Ken was cracking up laughing. Then he said, "Good point, Newton! I'll drink to those tree-hugging hypocrites starving and killing those poor deadly bugs and protecting those poor deadly snakes!"

Newton and Ken were really hitting it off well, and both were enjoying being cynical. They agreed that it was fun and made them feel good about themselves blasting others who couldn't defend their positions. What a deal!

At 5, they moved out from the condo to the lake picnic area in the back. They picked a nice shady spot, dropped the charcoal onto the grill base, and lit it. They agreed it was time for another beer while the fire heated up.

"Newton, what do you think about all of this research they're doing here?" asked Ken.

Newton answered, "Well, Ken, they're sure measuring a lot of stuff. I kind of think it's trying to measure the changes that can and would take place if people were more self-sufficient again. Seems they're trying to get the government controls and business propaganda out of the structure and measure its effect on people in the group. So far, though, I haven't seen or heard anything that bothers me. How about you?"

Ken pondered a moment and then replied, "This is by far the biggest, most expensive Research Project I've ever heard of, although I haven't been involved in any other ones. If we stick it out until the ten years is over, we'll be filthy rich."

"Yes, but why are they paying us in gold and not letting us use New Zealand money?" asked Newton.

Ken said, "I don't know, but just imagine if the price of gold doubles in the next ten years."

"I know—its crazy," replied Newton.

Ken popped the top on another beer and handed it to Newton, and then he popped one for himself. Ilene and Stormy were off strolling down by the lake with the kids. Ken grabbed the ribs and loaded them onto the grill. He had them soaking for a couple of hours in the barbecue sauce. Ken's secret, though, was to boil the ribs for thirty minutes prior to marinating them in the barbecue sauce. That would make the ribs tender and easy to cook; only about twenty more minutes was needed to cook in the sauce. There was just enough room on the grill to add the corn. Ilene had made the barbecue beans earlier, and they were staying warm in the Crockpot.

Back on the topic, Ken asked Newton if he had any idea what all of this would cost and how the research company was going to make any money from this venture. Newton answered, "If I had to guess, I'd say more than $4 or $5 billion so far for a cost. Those folks spend money like there's no tomorrow! As far as I can tell, there's nothing to sell. I can't imagine who would want to buy this type of research information when it is done. I just can't figure out that one."

The food that evening was just great. They continued to talk until dark and then went back up to the condo for another two hours before calling it a night.

Chapter 31
WORK

Ilene and Ken headed out for work on Monday morning. The morning was beautiful, with a slight sea breeze blowing from the Tasman Sea. It was a bit cool at fifty-five degrees, but was expected to warm up to about sixty-eight degrees for a high. A light breakfast of fresh New Zealand fruit was filling after eating and drinking too much the night before.

Ken biked to work, and Ilene walked to the school with David, after dropping off Jan at daycare. Ilene walked into the office of the director of medical facilities, Dr. Andy Jackson, right at her scheduled time. Dr. Jackson introduced himself and welcomed her to the colony.

"Ilene, we don't have many sick people here, and our population is such that we probably won't have many except for accidents and a few illnesses that pop up. Most of the folks here on the project are younger than fifty, and that's usually a time in life where the typical illnesses of old age have yet to begin. But we have skilled doctors in most every field here. When they don't have work, they'll be teaching each other, nurses, and students in our high school and college. In general, our efforts will be centered on wellness and measurements for the Research Project. Our doctors and dentists all have their offices located in the hospital. I want you to work in both the doctors' offices and the hospital itself on occasion."

Dr. Jackson paused and then continued. "We're unlike most hospitals in that they have to make a profit, and we do not. They buy expensive testing devices and then charge huge prices, when a test is required or desired, to help pay for the equipment. We've bought the finest testing devices available. For example, we'll be running full-body-scans MRIs on everyone at the colony. We'll baseline everyone and look for any problems or potential problems. We'll also monitor body fat and are hopeful that we'll see improvements with exercise and a healthier diet, without fast-food chains or sodium- and sugar-laden snacks. We'll rescan everyone every three months. It's a lot of work, but we'll be able to spot any development of an abnormality early and, as you know, early diagnosis is the key to surviving most diseases.

"What I would really like for you to do is work in the office of Dr. Carolyn Davis, our gynecologist, to be in support for all of our women here at the colony. I want you to work with the radiologists to secure reports on all women's reproductive test scans for diagnostics and recording purposes of the Research Project. We'll need to know results of the scans, as well as personal surveys, during office visits. You may need to attend and assist with some births as well as measure and log in some specific data.

"Ilene, are you okay with those assignments?"

Ilene answered, "Yes, but will these assignments change?"

"They could. It really depends upon our particular needs at any given time," answered Dr. Jackson.

Ilene knew that any new job would require some adjustment and getting used to, so she didn't have any other questions for now. It was obvious, with this place being brand new, it was difficult to plan all medical issues in advance. She thanked Dr. Jackson and proceeded to Dr. Davis's office to report for work and orientation.

Chapter 32
DR. CAROLYN DAVIS

Dr. Carolyn Davis was a forty-five-year-old gynecologist who had graduated summa cum laude from medical school at age twenty-eight. She was the mother of two children, both girls, fifteen and thirteen. Her husband, Larry, was also a doctor who specialized in internal surgery.

Carolyn walked into the lobby and called for Ilene to join her. She showed Ilene around the office and reviewed the work schedule. Carolyn pointed out that the project required some systematic patient measurements, and a questionnaire would be necessary with each patient visit. They included the woman's detailed period dates, frequency of intercourse, breast measurements, exercise frequency and duration, weight, height, blood work, etc.

"Additionally, you'll need to go into the hospital to visit with patients and any newborn babies to continue the work scope," Dr. Davis added.

All women would be required to visit the doctor's office at least quarterly. CAT scans would be run at least annually. Carolyn explained that the uniforms would be standard hospital white and would be supplied by the hospital.

Cleaning was also supplied. Ilene would simply arrive at the office and go to the changing room to locker her home clothes and get into the cleaned nurse uniforms and shoes.

Ilene spent the rest of the day in her own office, setting up her desk and files and getting her uniform information to the hospital supply room.

Ilene was excited for the opportunity to work with Carolyn and was happy that she wouldn't be mugged again like she was in Shreveport.

Chapter 33
KEN REPORTS TO WORK

Although he wanted to bike to work the first day, a light rain helped Ken decide to take the shuttle to the power plant. The shuttle pulled up to his condo block at 7. Ken arrived at the plant about fifteen minutes early and went directly to the manager's office.

The manager was Gene Winfree. Gene was a big man, about six foot three, weighed about two hundred and fifty pounds, and appeared to be about forty years old, with slightly graying hair. Gene welcomed Ken to his new job and showed him to his office. Ken hadn't talked previously with Gene about exactly what his new position would be, so he was a bit nervous. He'd been an operations engineer before.

As he went into his new office, he noticed the title just below his name on the entry door. It read:

Ken Wallace
Electrical Superintendent

Ken suddenly realized that he'd received quite a promotion. He was in charge of all of the power plant's electrical generation systems. While surprised, he knew that, for the amount of money he was being paid, he would surely have more responsibility. That was okay, as he felt he'd been ready for several promotions in the past, but promotions in his old power plant required either a death or a retirement.

Gene took Ken for a grand tour of the facilities. That took almost two hours, as Gene gave a lot of details on each piece of equipment.

Gene then took Ken back to the office, where he introduced him to two of his six new direct reports. There were only two in the office because two were on different shift duties, and the last two were yet to arrive in New Zealand. All of his new reports were electrical engineers with about five years of experience and around twenty-eight years old. Two were women. Most of the day was spent just following Gene around and learning the operations.

After a full day of orientation and learning his new job, Ken returned home on the shuttle to share his day with Ilene.

Chapter 34
THE FIRST FISHING TRIP

After four months and numerous discussions on who was the best fisherman, Ken scheduled a fishing trip with Newton Baker and Stacy Baltzegar. Ken had chartered the colony fishing boat for a full day on Sunday. Splitting the cost among three people on the Colony Card made it very reasonable for everyone. They were hoping for some tuna and grouper. Ken biked to the dock and arrived at 5:15. Newton was already there, and Stacy arrived five minutes later.

The forty-foot ship was named the "Colony Escape," and the name was quite suitable for a good getaway day. The captain was Tim White. Tim had served in the Navy and, using the GI bill, had finished college with a degree in marine biology. Tim was a stout two hundred and twenty pound man about forty years old. He had a full head of light gray hair but still had dark brown eyebrows. He was beginning to get a small beer belly that hung ever so slightly over his belt. He was wearing only a T-shirt, shorts, and deck shoes. He had moved to the colony from Pascagoula, Mississippi, where he had done commercial fishing and later moved on to running his own small charter boat. The "Colony Escape" was anchored at the dock, which was separate from the commercial and worker docks, but were still in close proximity to each other.

"Good morning, everyone," shouted Captain Tim. "You all look half awake. I have coffee in the galley; put your gear onboard, and I'll shove off."

Captain Tim went immediately to work, and the ship was headed out within a minute. Captain Tim passed out a new straw fishing hat with a four-inch brim and a cool logo patch of a sailfish on the front that read:

The Colony
ESCAPE PROJECT
FISHING WITH CAPTAIN TIM

As the ship shoved off from the dock, the warm coffee began to bring the fishermen to life, and they began to talk. Captain Tim began telling fishing tales and said that the trip to the best fishing grounds was about an hour and a half from the harbor. They would be fishing with live shrimp for the grouper and an artificial drag bait for the tuna. Tim had prepared the rods to fish drag baits just in case they might get a tuna strike once they left the harbor.

Easing through the harbor, the sun began to rise. The pink and orange colors created a beautiful outline of the New Zealand North Island Mountains. It was going to be a good sunny day with a light westerly breeze. The air was fresh and cool at about fifty-five degrees. They had all been warned by

Captain Tim to bring a jacket and long pants for the early morning hours.

Beginning to move out, they noticed the commercial docks were coming alive as the sun rose. There was a shrimp boat unloading freshly caught shrimp and an oil tanker unloading at the power plant dock. Ken noticed that the tankers were not large, so there would probably be one arriving about every month or so.

Newton asked, "I was wondering why the colony dock is so separate from the commercial business?"

Stacy replied, "They say it's part of the research to assure that influence from the outside is minimized."

"Well, I don't understand what they're trying to measure, but they sure are measuring everything," Ken added.

Captain Tim chimed in and said, "They measure how long we fish, where we fish, what we catch, what we eat, how much fuel we use, who fishes—you name it. It takes us thirty minutes each time to fill out all of the measurements.

"We once had a motor failure and were towed in by a commercial fisherman, and a security team asked me all kinds of questions. They kept harping on whether I ate or drank anything from his boat. I hadn't, but they kept asking, and they wouldn't say why. I think that I do more paperwork as a charter boat captain than I did as a marine biologist back in Mississippi.

"One of the rules they gave us is that we aren't allowed to eat or drink anything from outside of the colony. It has to go through the food-and-drink department and be labeled with the colony label. The exceptions are seafood, tea, coffee, and bananas. All other meats, fruits, and vegetables are being grown on the farm."

Stacy commented, "Have ya'll noticed all of the guards at the bridge's main gate? They check everything that comes onto the island. It's very restricted, and freight cannot come past the bridge unloading parking area and must be shuttled in by colony workers."

"I saw that," replied Newton.

"Very weird, don't you think?" asked Stacy.

"I sure wish we knew what research they were doing. I know they told us it was to measure how well we could function as an isolated colony, but they also said the full details of the research wouldn't be fully available to us for some time," replied Ken.

"Perhaps if we knew, it would skew the results they're looking for," said Newton. They all agreed as Captain Tim yelled, "Fish on!"

Ken grabbed his trolling rod and gave a big tug. The fight was a blast.

After about twenty minutes, Captain Tim hooked the tuna with his gaff and yelled for help. He hauled it over the side of the boat with the help of Newton and Stacy. It turned out to be a nice ninety-pound blue-fin tuna.

Ken was exhausted and had to take a break. His arms ached from the constant straining and reeling on the rod. Ken bragged and told his friends that he was indeed the best fisherman on the boat. The fish continued to bite, and everyone caught fish.

By the end of the day, they had caught four tuna for a total of two hundred and eighty pounds and two grouper for about forty pounds. They'd consumed several sandwiches and, of course, a cooler full of beer, all of which had been part of the package. It was a great package. All they'd done for the entire trip was to show up on time.

They were all back to the dock by 5. Captain Tim took care of the fish cleaning and said they would split it up three ways and flash freeze it in two-pound packages for a pickup any day after Wednesday. They did, however, bring home five pounds of fresh unfrozen grouper each, if for no other reason than to prove to their families that they were indeed great fishermen. It had been a great, adventurous day, and Ken's relationships with his friends were beginning to grow. They all decided to schedule another fishing trip in a few months, once they'd eaten their new catch. This would very likely be a recurring event since they all enjoyed each other's company.

Captain Tim had been a hoot. His humor kept them laughing the whole trip. The story that was the funniest was about "Little Johnny": Little Johnny's second-grade teacher wanted someone in the class to make a sentence using the word "fascinate." Of course, Little Johnny waved his hands wildly and wanted to do it, but the teacher knew that Little Johnny was so bad that he always said something nasty, so she called on Sue in the front row.

Sue exclaimed, "My family went on a trip to the Rocky Mountains last year, and we were fascinated by all of the tall mountains!"

The teacher remarked, "That was good, Sue, but you used the word 'fascinated,' and I want someone to use the word 'fascinate.' Who can do it?"

Little Johnny again began to wave his arms excitedly, but to no avail. The teacher called on Ted in the second row. Ted began, "Our trip here to New Zealand was the most fascinating experience of my life."

The teacher responded, "Ted, that was good, but you used the word 'fascinating,' and I want someone to use the word 'fascinate.'"

Everyone in the class was now afraid to mess up as Sue and Ted had done—all except for Little Johnny, who continued to wave his hands from the back row. Thinking that Little Johnny couldn't do too badly with the word "fascinate," the teacher reluctantly called on little Johnny. Little Johnny stood up and began.

"Last Christmas, my sixteen-year-old sister got a new sweater, and it had ten buttons on it. But, her tits were so big that she could only fascinate."

Chapter 35
THE DOCK CAFÉ

At the end of August, their first winter was almost over, and spring was coming to New Zealand. Ken had become comfortable in his new job. It was easy. He spent a lot of his time teaching his six direct reports and following the production reports. Other than the occasional mechanical breakdowns, his time was his to use as he saw fit. The colony had allocated plenty of money for spare parts, and any breakdown was easy to fix, so far. The cool spring weather was wonderful, and the Wallace family enjoyed picnics, sports, and other family activities. The weeks were rushing by.

On the last Friday of October, Ken decided to take another bike tour of the dock area and have lunch. He had an urge for an oyster po' boy, and they were on the menu at the Dock Café.

Every time he was in the café, he enjoyed listening and sometimes talking to the contract workers in the commercial area. He reached the contractor café area in only five minutes, pulled his bike into the bike parking slots, and started toward the café entrance. A yellow sign was tacked on the front door of the cafe. Ken approached the door and read the sign:

> All on-site contractor work will end on December 31. The café will be permanently closed. All food entering the docks or leaving will be fully inspected by colony inspectors and security.

Ken walked into the café and ordered the oyster po'boy with fries and tea; then he picked a table near some of the contract workers. There were four steel workers at the table next to him, and he could easily hear their conversation. They weren't quiet at all. Perhaps they were loud because they worked around all of the loud equipment.

The workers were all wearing worn blue jeans and ragged, long sleeve work shirts. The man closest to Ken was telling the others what he knew about their pending job losses.

"I hear the work here is being stopped because they don't want us on the island. There are going to be some new jobs back on the mainland that will pick up in January that will ship items onto the island. It'll make it easier on me if that happens because I don't like traveling here every week and staying in the contractor hotel. I'd rather stay home."

Another worker chimed in, "We're almost finished with all of the structural steel work anyway. But what I hear from one of the guards is that they don't want any outsiders on the island at all by January 1. They've been bringing more people in from the States and have built their own town. You can see it from the high levels of our steel work. It looks real fancy. It looks strange, though. They don't have any New Zealanders there that I know of. Our government should be looking into that."

"I think it's some religious cult from America," piped in a third worker.

The fourth worker added, "Bobby Wilson told me that one of their guards broke one of their rules by accepting some bread as a gift from a truck driver from Auckland. The guard's whole family was exiled from the island and is staying in Auckland. It all sounds like a prison to me."

Ken finished his lunch and left the café. The workers had gotten him thinking. Was this really a prison? What if this was a cult? Could it be that he wouldn't get his money when his contract was completed? What would happen if he broke a colony rule? The only management of the colony he had met was Tom Clark at the interview in Destin. Everyone else he'd met were employees of the ESCAPE Project, all hired just like him. The gold in the safe deposit vault was behind Plexiglas, and he couldn't even touch it. Ken knew he needed to talk to Newton and Stacy. He dared not discuss these new concerns with Ilene. She would surely freak out.

That afternoon, back at work, he phoned Stacy and Newton and set up a meeting with them at the pub closest to their condos for 5:30. He told them that he just wanted to buy them a beer and discuss something of interest.

Chapter 36
BAR MEETING

Ken got to the pub a few minutes early to secure a corner table and ordered a colony beer, as there were no other beers allowed on the island. Wine was plentiful, and the island produced plenty of liquor and beer. It wasn't bad, either.

The pub was just beginning to fill up with the evening crowd. It was a popular gathering place for the town. The town supported a total of three identical pubs spread out so as to be located near the homes and condos. The bar theme was all about sports since New Zealand was a country filled with active sports enthusiasts. There was room for more than three hundred in each bar, and seven televisions were continually showing local and international games from the satellite dishes mounted on the roof.

Newton and Stacy arrived together right at 5:30 and found Ken at the corner table. Ken had already gotten them a "Coney," which was short for the colony beer. He was somewhat uneasy about the meeting. He felt that his life was so much better than it had been in Shreveport, and he was beginning to feel disloyal to the company that had made this all possible. But, on the other hand, the lack of information about what they were truly there for was beginning to make him feel insecure and uncertain. The mystery was almost unbearable for an engineer.

Stacy made the first comment. "What's up, Ken? Your call sounded urgent."

Ken replied, "Well, guys, I'm not sure. I was down at the Docks Café, and I found out that the café is closing on December 31. Then I overheard four of the steelworkers talking about being laid off and how the colony wasn't allowing any contractors on-site any more.

"The colony seems to be closing off the rest of the world! In addition, I know they told us that the real objective of the project was secret, but we don't know if it's legal and don't have a clue what it's all about, and that worries me."

Newton added, "I know what you mean. But as with any job, it's not our role to be in the know on all of the issues."

Stacy chimed in, "You're right, Newton, but it sure would be nice to know a little more. I wish they had a monthly newsletter that communicated issues and progress. The construction work is likely reaching a point where the local colony construction team can pick it up and continue with the development efforts, but we don't know that.

"I think the colony is very close to the 5,000 families that were planned. Audria works with the relocation and housing group in the main office, and she told me there were only about one hundred and fifty more families coming, and they had to be here before January 1."

Ken added, "I wish I knew what was so important about January 1. It's like everything has been geared to assuring the kick-off date is not passed, no matter what." Ken knew the meeting wouldn't solve any of his concerns, but he needed to have his buddies on the same page as he was and needed to see if they had the same concerns.

They finished their beers and ordered another round. The conversations continued for another thirty minutes. Ken suggested they resume their discussions on Sunday at noon with a family picnic at the new park next to the power plant docks. It was a beautiful park with large oak trees, covered tables, barbeque grills, and a playground for the kids. The food would consist of the usual hamburgers, hot dogs, and potato chips.

They left the bar with plenty of time to get home to their families for dinner.

Chapter 37
THE PICNIC

Sunday came quickly. Ken had volunteered to bring the food and spent all of Saturday evening getting everything purchased and ready. It was somewhat of a self-punishment for having brought up the whole drama of an unknown problem.

Ken and Ilene got one of the community extra-long golf carts and loaded the food and kids. Jan was all ready and excited to have their friends to play with. David had been all pouty most of the week about not having any boys to play with, so Ken had surprised him and asked a neighbor if their son, Donny, could come along to the picnic. David was now quite happy and had planned to climb a tree with Donny and scan the grounds for a place to fly the two new kites that Ilene had bought for them to play with.

The day turned out to be perfect for a picnic, with a forecast high of seventy-eight, fair skies and a light wind. The ride was fun, and Ken let David drive once they were out of town. He thought he was all grown up. Jan was upset that she couldn't drive. To keep the peace, Ken stopped about a half mile away and let Jan sit in his lap and drive for a few hundred yards.

Ken liked the location of the park and had walked less than five hundred meters from the power plant to the park for lunch many times. He'd sit at one of the tables and just enjoy the shade and the cool breeze. From the park, he could watch all of the activities at the oil dock, the café, the construction projects, the container ships, and the fishing boats.

Things were much quieter and less active now that the construction was winding down. A small oil tanker was pulling into the power plant dock to unload more fuel oil into the storage tanks. A tanker usually arrived every two months and provided all the fuel to feed the boilers in the plant and the small refinery. He noticed that this tanker flew a flag from Qatar. That was typical because the Middle East was much closer than Canada, and the United States did not allow exporting of oil.

They found two shady picnic tables that were strategically placed between two large oaks. Ilene spread red-and-white plaid picnic tablecloths on each table. Stacy, Audria, Shelby, Alexis, and Britney arrived on their bikes ten minutes later. Newton, Stormy, and Brooke arrived about a minute later.

Stormy had brought a soccer ball, and the kids all ran to play on one of the mowed grass fields about fifty yards away. Even though Jan was a bit young, she would run with the rest and think she was playing, too. Ilene, Stormy, and Audria passed around beers to all the men and fixed lemonade for the kids. Stormy had brought a bottle of Chardonnay and poured a plastic glass for each of the women. Ken prepped the grill with charcoal and started the fire.

Within fifteen minutes, the flaming charcoal began to glow a bright orange and gradually turned gray on the crust from the resulting ash. Once the fire was ready, the hamburger meat was placed in the center of the grill, with the wieners along the sides. The grill was large and held twelve patties and eighteen wieners. Ilene got the buns out of the packages along with all the trimmings and spread them out on one of the tables. She'd decided this would be a true buffet picnic and everyone could make his or her own plate. Audria had made a cherry cobbler for dessert. The men could continue drinking beer and talking about guy issues.

The men had been sitting at the eating table and started out talking with almost a whisper, but as the second beer went down, the volume got considerably louder. They were talking about the colony and the secrecy of the Project.

"Newton, you're getting too loud," said Stormy.

"You are, too," said both Ilene and Audria almost in unison to their respective husbands. They all just laughed, as they toned it down, but everyone knew that the volume would be back soon. They needed to eat food to dilute the alcohol.

Ken got up and walked to the grill to turn the meat. After another ten minutes, the meat was done and placed on the table. "Come and get it," Audria yelled to all of the kids, who were still playing soccer.

Ilene had noticed that all of the Baltzegars yelled a lot. Apparently, they had lived in a very large house with multiple stories and no intercom, so the only means of family communication was by yelling. The kids all came running and were the first to fix their plates. They took the table that the men had been at. The preparation table would be for the adults.

The discussion over lunch continued to be about the Project. Audria hadn't participated in the conversation but, having heard all of the issues, suddenly blurted out, "Why don't you men go meet with Tom Clark? He just moved here last week. He told me he'd finished up with all the recruiting and would be here from now on. Maybe he can explain who is doing all of this and why. His office is the corner office in my building."

"Audria, that's a great idea," said Ken. Newton and Stacy agreed. It was settled—they had a plan.

"Let's suggest some better communication, too. Perhaps sending out a monthly newsletter to everyone," suggested Stacy.

"Audria, can you get us a meeting with him Tuesday after work?" asked Ken.

Audria answered, "I will, and I'll call . . ."

Suddenly a bright orange flash and a loud explosion at the dock stopped the conversation mid-sentence and drew everyone's attention toward the sound. The children screamed. Within seconds, metal fragments began to fly by and fall from the sky.

"Get down!" yelled Newton. Everyone fell to the ground except Jan. Ken saw her, jumped up, ran to her, and threw her down to the ground as she screamed.

Ken raised his head enough to see a giant ball of flames and smoke shooting skyward from the ship at the dock. His mind raced. The fuel ship had blown up! It was really close.

He could feel the heat from the blast and fire. The heat was getting more intense. Metal flew through the trees and fell from the sky. The metal pieces seemed to fall for several minutes, but it was actually only a few seconds. The oil in the ship was spreading out, and the flames were getting closer. One large piece of metal fell within a yard of Ken's head. It buried into the ground and gave a hissing sound as its heat contacted the damp ground.

Ken yelled for everyone to run. They all jumped up and ran through the trees toward the grass field in the direction of town. Large twisted metal pieces of the ship more than five feet in length were strewn over the landscape. They had been lucky that one of those hadn't fallen on them.

As they ran, Audria noticed that Stacy had blood on his left arm. His long-sleeved white shirt was torn just below his shoulder and had blood spreading in a downward pattern.

Audria yelled, "Stacy, Stacy, you're bleeding. Look at your arm." He apparently had been hit with a piece of flying metal. Stacy glanced at his arm but kept running. They ran about two hundred more yards and were out of breath. Stacy slowed and was turning pale. He was wobbling and about stumbling. Suddenly he fell to the ground. Shelby yelled, "Daddy, Daddy . . . somebody help Daddy." Everyone stopped and looked toward Stacy.

Ken and Newton were staying in the rear of the pack to make sure everyone was getting away. They saw Stacy fall and ran to his aid. They rolled Stacy over in the thick grass onto his back. Ilene moved in close and began to examine his arm.

Her skills as a nurse were coming in handy. She said little and went to work ripping Stacy's shirtsleeve open around the wound. She told Ken to remove his shirt and then used it to wrap Stacy's wound to apply pressure and stop the bleeding. It looked like his shoulder muscle had been cut on the outside of the arm, and the metal was still imbedded in the tissue.

Ilene yelled, "I'm leaving the metal alone because it's helping to stop the bleeding. We need to get him to the hospital now."

Ken quickly decided that they needed transportation and needed it now. He looked back at the picnic site and, in a full-out run, headed back in the direction of the flaming ship and the picnic site to get the golf cart for Stacy. Ken knew that the golf cart would be the fastest way to get Stacy to the hospital. His heart pounded as he ran. He jumped over patches of hot metal and smoldering grass. Broken and downed tree limbs were everywhere in the park. He reached the golf cart and jumped behind the wheel, stomping the accelerator pedal to the floor. He dodged the debris as best he could and was back to the group in less than a minute. They helped Stacy into the middle of the front passenger seat, and Ilene jumped in beside him.

Audria jumped in the back seat. Ken told Newton to drive the golf cart to the hospital as fast as the cart would go. Newton floored the pedal and headed to the right toward Harbor Road. There was only about three hundred more bumpy yards and he would be off of the grass and headed into town. Newton knew that the five miles into town would take about fifteen minutes at best, since they were going uphill most of the way.

Stormy needed to stay behind and manage the kids, and Ken needed to try to get to the plant. There would likely be injured there, and he had some of his direct reports on duty. The electrical grid might even be down.

Stormy began to walk with the kids in the direction that the golf cart had gone across the field. Sirens and flashing lights were beginning to go off as security and emergency fire vehicles and ambulances arrived on the scene.

As Ken moved closer to the smoke and flames, he could feel the heat becoming more intense. He decided to circle to his right and approach the plant from the backside, away from the flaming ship. There was a back gate in the fencing, but since there was essentially no crime on the island, the gate was never locked. He could feel the heat from the burning ship across his left side as he came closer to the plant.

Ken circled around behind a new food processing plant that had just been completed next to the power plant to avoid the heat and keep some cover between him and the tanker, in case there was another explosion. He ran to the power plant back gate and slipped inside the gate.

Just inside the gate, lying on the concreted yard, he saw two injured employees on their backs and one on his side. The plant safety nurse and a security officer were attending to them. The injured employees appeared to not be in a life-threatening situation, but one appeared to have some nasty burns on his back. Ken ran past them and to the control room, where he found the plant still in operation.

Gene Winfree was there, with a fearful look on his face. His wrinkled forehead expressed his fears as they were unfolding. He was on his two-way radio barking orders to different operation workers. His shift foreman was watching all of the gauges and charts. Ken knew it was time to support Gene and stay focused on his role to keep the electricity on. He needed to help in any way he could. Without speaking, he grabbed his own two-way radio from the charging station and took charge of the electrical operations.

After an hour, Ken was anxious to hear from Ilene. He phoned her and asked how Stacy was doing.

Ilene spoke with a steady voice. "He had the metal removed and has been cleaned up. We put fifteen stitches in his shoulder muscles and another twenty-two in the skin to close up the wound. He didn't need any blood, but he'll have some pain for a couple of days. Pain medicine and antibiotics have been prescribed, and he can go home as soon as Audria gets the prescriptions filled at the hospital pharmacy. He's going to be okay.

"Stormy got a ride when she reached the main road, and she and Newton made it back safely to the condo with all the children. The kids are all shook up. I checked with Stormy a moment ago, and the kids are asking all kinds of questions. When will you be here? I need you back here. Do you know what happened? I'm really scared!"

Ken answered, "Honey, I don't know what happened, other than the oil supply tanker simply blew up. It's still burning and likely will for at least another day. There were four of our power plant people preparing the ship for unloading the oil when it blew. None of the ship personnel have been found. They're all missing and likely didn't make it. Some of the operations people inside the plant were hurt, maybe six or eight total. They're all at or headed to the hospital. There were some contractor employees and fishermen hurt and will be headed to our hospital—I just don't know how many. The New Zealand sheriff, maritime police, and fire departments are all on the scene now. Security had to let them in, but they will be leading the investigation. Our teams will assist in any way we can. It looks like I need to be here the rest of the day until perhaps 10:00 tonight or later. Can you handle that?"

"I'll do my best. I may have to work late, too. They need lots of help here at the hospital. Call me in a couple of hours, okay? I have to run now. I'll call Stormy to see if David and Jan can stay there until late tonight. I know they'll do whatever we need. I love you, Ken. Be safe!" said Ilene.

"Okay—I love you, too," said Ken.

Chapter 38
THE IMPACT ON
THE COLONY

Duncan heard and felt the explosion while sitting by his pool. He knew something bad had happened as he watched the black smoke rise in the south by the power plant. He ran inside, passing Nellie in a rush to his bedroom to change clothes. She followed him, asking, "Duncan, what's happening?"

Duncan answered as he hurriedly grabbed for his cell phone. "Nellie, I don't know, but it's probably not good, not good at all." He immediately phoned Tom, Joe, Bob, John, and Bruce and said to meet him at the boardroom in fifteen minutes.

Nellie looked worried as Duncan hurriedly threw on black pants, a white shirt, and a pair of shoes. He grabbed his briefcase and almost ran to his white Yukon Denali. Starting the car, he thought that perhaps this was something that he had caused. Did he not spend enough money on safety? Were there any injuries? Would this impact the project? There were so many unknown issues, and he needed to know.

He sped down the long paved driveway to the main road. On the way, he called Eddy and asked, "What happened, Eddy?" Eddy didn't know but was headed to the power plant. "Eddy, I want you to get on your pager and let all of security know to let any and every New Zealand official government and safety individual into the colony who wants to come in. Open the gates on the bridge until I instruct you otherwise. This is their country, and we are their guests. We need their help right now."

Officer Tony Brantley of the New Zealand sheriff's office was on the scene of the explosion within twenty minutes. It was indeed a rural area, and the nearest town outside of the island was about fifteen miles away. Officer Brantley had been to the colony many times. His past visits had been to meet with Eddy Jackson, head of security for the Research Project. They had a good working relationship, and Eddy had taken Tony on several tours. The colony had donated a monthly check for $50,000 to help with the sheriff's cost of operations. The sheriff appreciated the extra financial support and had been told the monthly payment would continue as long as the colony was there.

Since the Tapora region was part of Tony's region of the district, Tony was responsible for any illegal or criminal issues that occurred. Tony had made everything easier for the colony by getting New Zealand authorization for Eddy's security team to provide security and to carry weapons. The relationship between Tony and Eddy had been going on for two years with no crime.

Officer Brantley reached the main gate. It was open, and he was motioned by the guard to go through. He sped toward the smoke billowing from the dock area with lights flashing and siren blaring. About three hundred yards from the flames, he saw Eddy's flashing lights. Eddy was already on site. Tony pulled up next to Eddy's SUV and saw Eddy about ten yards in front of the SUV, talking on his cell phone. The colony fire team was much closer to the fire. They were spraying water from the dock high-pressure hoses to try to keep the fire contained to the dock area. A New Zealand fire truck pulled onto the scene moments later to add support.

Both Tony and Eddy knew it was highly unusual for an oil tanker to explode and catch fire. "Let's see if the power plant has any tapes of the dock. I know they have cameras all over the place," said Eddy.

In the control room, they had the shift foreman remove the tape from the recorder and replace them with new ones. Playing the tapes, they found one that showed the tanker as it pulled into the dock and hooked up to the unloading pipes. As they watched, they saw the three power plant dockworkers assisting and getting the appropriate unloading documents from the ship captain. Then, they saw the workers and the captain look up to the boat deck that was about twenty feet above the dock. There on the deck was a man dressed in black and waving his arms. He was holding something in his right hand, but they couldn't make out what it was. Suddenly, the ship erupted in flames. Smoke and shockwaves blinded and blurred the picture, and then the tape went black.

Tony commented, "This looks like one or more terrorists did something to blow up that tanker."

"Yes, it does," replied Eddy.

Tony took the tape and headed back outside. The medical and fire teams with all of the associated flashing lights were everywhere now. The medical teams were loading injured people into the ambulances. Firefighters were surrounding the blaze, but oil spreading over the water in the bay was burning, giving the appearance that the water was burning. Black smoke was getting worse.

"This is a disaster," said Tony. "Let's see if we can help get some of the less severely injured to the hospital, because it looks like there aren't enough ambulances here."

Duncan arrived at the main office and hurried into the boardroom. Everyone was there. John spoke first. "The oil tanker from Qatar had a massive explosion right after docking and hooking up. It appears there were no survivors from the tanker, and we have three power plant workers missing and several others injured. New Zealand fire and rescue are on the way. Tony Brantley is already inside the gate with Eddy. All medical resources from the hospital have been called in."

"What about the power plant?" asked Duncan.

"The electricity has not gone off, so I think the power plant is still okay, at least for now. The flames and smoke are terrible down there right now. The power grid is synchronized with New Zealand power, so if we do have to shut down the plant, we can still have electricity," said John.

Duncan immediately took control and began giving directions. "Okay, I want Tom to go to the hospital and manage the situation there and make sure we support the emotional and stressful issues that the families are surely going through.

"Bruce, I want you to contact our insurance company and get them in here. Bob, I want you to find out what our situation is with fuel supplies and what we need to be doing to keep the fuel supplies to the plant going. We may need to stop future oil shipments if the dock is severely damaged and we cannot unload. Joe, I need you to be our spokesman and handle any communications with the news media. Contact the tanker company, and have them get a representative here now.

"I'll work with security, law enforcement, safety, and the fire department to see if I can find out the cause of this situation. Now, let's get busy and meet back here at 6:00."

Everyone jumped from their seats and headed out to their respective assignments.

Chapter 39
MAKING THE NEWS

Within an hour, five news crews were at the colony gates, wanting to gain entry for the news story. The guards had kept them from entering, but they were filming the distant black smoke plume and recording the on-the-scene reporter from just outside of the entrance gates.

From his office, Duncan watched the evening news, which showed the flow of fire trucks and police vehicles entering the colony, and reporters were speculating about the operations within the gates. No one from the colony itself was there to speak to the reporters.

Duncan thought, *This could be a disaster for the continuation of the project if we don't get control of it and fast.* Then he gave Joe a call. "Joe, as we discussed, I want you to take responsibility for being the spokesman for the project and interface with the press. I want you and you alone to do that and not have anyone else giving out information. Can you meet with them as soon as you get a statement ready?"

"Will do," replied Joe. "I'll run it by you once I draft it up."

The draft took almost thirty minutes to prepare and review with Duncan. Joe called the fire and police leaders on site and advised that they would be holding a press conference at the main entrance at 10 and asked if they would like to join. Both had declined due to the urgency of the situation on the ground but agreed to support any future needs.

Joe hurriedly drove to the main gate and gathered the press around for a briefing.

"Folks, please gather around. I would like to support your news efforts by making a statement on behalf of the Research Project here." Joe spoke loudly to ensure that his words were heard clearly.

"My name is Joe Hawkins, and I will be the spokesperson for the Research Project located beyond this main gate. Currently, what we know is that an oil tanker pulling into our unloading docks from Qatar exploded. The oil being delivered to us was intended to supply our power plant fuel needs for the generation of electricity here at our town and businesses, as well as a small refinery to produce local gasoline and diesel. All onboard the tanker and some of our dockworkers were killed in the explosion. Others on the site and nearby were also injured.

"It appears from witnesses that the explosion was the work of terrorists, but a full investigation is in progress with the New Zealand police and fire departments.

"More information will be shared as it becomes available. Right now, we're focused on the medical issues of those who were injured and working with the New Zealand officials, as they deem appropriate. Going forward, I'll be here at the gate every afternoon at 4 and update everyone on the situation as we move through this investigation. I've talked to the appropriate investigators on this, and they will also be here at these daily meetings to update the press on any of their findings."

The press asked several questions afterward, but Joe explained in each case that the situation was so new that he would not be able to answer any more questions tonight. After ten minutes of repeating the same response, Joe thanked them for their patience, left the main gate area, and returned to the corporate office to advise Duncan of the event with the press.

Duncan's only comment was, "I sure hope we can keep our project out of the news as much as possible. I don't want the press or anyone else questioning what we're doing here and snooping around into our operations."

Chapter 40
RECOVERY

A level of calm began to return after two weeks. The fire and smoke were gone. Stacy's arm was healing. The doctor made him take four weeks off before going back to work. The wounded plant workers were home and healing. The Board had provided counseling for the families of the three workers who'd been killed. They were offered the choice of staying on at the project or returning to the States with a full ten-year compensation package.

Ken returned to work at the power plant near the dock. The power plant system was okay, but the loss of some friends and coworkers had everyone in an unusually quiet mood. Crews were cleaning up the park, but the oil unloading dock was in bad shape.

There was a feeling among the residents that they were not as safe as they had assumed. They were concerned about possible future attacks and what should be done to protect them. They needed some reassurance.

Chapter 41
TERRORISTS

John Earnest called for a Board meeting exactly one month from the day of the explosion. The purpose was to review the status of all of the assignments that Duncan had handed out. Duncan called the meeting to order at 8. Everyone had poured coffee and was preparing for their part. "All right, let's get started. I'll kick it off with the results of the New Zealand government's involvement and results.

"The environmental department has sent in cleaning crews and has about two weeks more to finish the work. We were lucky that the fire burned off most of the oil over ten days, leaving a ship base with ballasts that kept the ship afloat. The remains of the tanker have been towed to a ship salvage yard about twenty-five miles to the south.

"Investigations from the security teams have revealed that it was an Islamic terrorist attack. Two different groups in the Middle East are claiming responsibility. Our power plant video confirms that it was at least one terrorist that detonated the bombs. No extremist group has ever targeted New Zealand.

The logic of the attack was likely because of the appearance of an American-only outpost here. We're not sure how they found out about us, but likely some of the construction workers had a Muslim connection in the Middle East. It was easy for the terrorist group, because of the lax security in this country.

"Based on the New Zealand government's final review report, they have concluded that the attack was one of the radicalized splinter groups from Syria. They don't believe that the colony is under further threat; however, they recommend continued vigilance for the foreseeable future. From a financial standpoint, we're paying all of the New Zealand groups for the cleanup costs and resources that were utilized. They've been great to work with. We don't expect any fines from any organization.

"John, bring us up to speed on the operations."

John began, "With Bob's help, we haven't missed a beat in our operations. The biggest concerns were damage to the dock and oil unloading system. We had adequate oil stocks to run for one month. During construction of the boiler, a natural gas burner system was installed but had never been used. For two weeks, we simply ran an underwater three-inch pipeline across the narrowest part of the bay to a natural gas pipeline run by NZ Gas Company. We have totally switched over to gas and no longer will be bringing in any oil to the docks. We will, however, truck oil in to fill up our tanks and keep them full as a backup fuel.

"Joe, you're up."

Joe stood up. "Guys, I got the tanker owner and his insurance carrier here last week. I made sure they both were here at the same time. Essentially I got them together and told them it wasn't our fault and they needed to stay in the room and figure out who pays for what. I explained that I wanted the tanker company to pay our $5 million deductible. Bruce was in the meeting with them, and he helped stress our position. Bruce and I left them and came back in two hours; they had it settled. They acceded to our demands, and we're paying nothing. Bruce is keeping track of all of our costs to submit to our carrier for reimbursement."

Tom remained seated and began, "I've met with all three families of the deceased team members. They're pretty torn up. Two have decided to stay, and one has decided to return to the United States. The one family left a week ago. The two who are staying have been given two full months off of work and school. They need time to grieve. The community has been very supportive, and several individuals are spending time with them. Our hospital psychologist has met with each family member three times per week and will continue until she is satisfied that everyone is okay.

"The entire population has been traumatized and is quite disturbed. Our psychologist has seen many people and can't get to everyone who wants an appointment. She's recommended that in addition to her own personal help, management needs to provide an update for everyone at the auditorium. They need assurance and need to feel safe again. I recommend we have the meeting this week."

Duncan decided to wrap up the meeting and stood as he began to speak, "Guys, this is good work. I want to thank all of you for your efforts during this trying time. Let's have a general meeting in the auditorium in two days. Tom, please take the lead. You may want to have people from the New Zealand government investigation team at the meeting to discuss their activities and efforts. The meeting will likely be short, unless there are a lot of questions. Let's stay on top of this since it will likely take some time to fully recover.

"As far as our business operations are concerned, Tom, I would like for you to recruit three New Zealand replacement employees for the power plant. We don't have time to get three from the States. We just need to make sure the New Zealanders will not be leaving to visit relatives at all after January 1. Also, I want to tighten up security. Let's make sure that everything coming into the colony has to go through the Main Gate entrance."

"What about the shipping and fishing boats?" asked John.

"Let's put some type of identification on each of our fishing boats and require any freighter ships to fly a certain identifying flag. We can add more guards if needed," replied Tom.

"Okay, that sounds good, but let's also make all of our citizens here aware of a higher level of security, since we don't know for sure if some other terrorist might attack us. During the upcoming general meeting, we can ask everyone to advise security of any issues that seem unusual or out of the norm. Let's conclude this meeting, and I'll have Debbie schedule our next meeting for next month."

Duncan concluded the meeting and headed to his office for other meetings.

Chapter 42
MEETING WITH TOM CLARK

Audria had set up an early morning meeting with Tom Clark. Stacy, Ken, and Newton met at the coffee shop near the colony main office at 7:30. They had one hour to talk before the meeting with Tom Clark would start. They ordered coffee and decided that they would have the barista write a number on a napkin between 1 and 1,000 and they would each write a number in their left hand. The number closest to the barista's number would be the spokesman for the meeting with Tom. It wasn't that no one wanted to do it, but that seemed like a good way to pick.

Ken picked the number 700 and wrote it on his napkin. Newton picked 1000 and wrote it on his napkin. Stacy picked 300 as his number. The barista turned over his secret number and showed 875. Newton had won the draw and was their designated speaker. They finished their coffee and walked to the office to meet with Tom.

They walked into the main office complex and were greeted by the receptionist, Jeanie Sanders. "Good morning, gentlemen." She greeted them with a smile. "Tom is ready for you in his office."

Tom's office was well appointed with pictures of his family and his hobbies. A large striped bass was on one wall, and a large blue marlin was on another. Tom was definitely a fisherman. Jeanie seated Ken, Newton, and Stacy at a round table at one side of the room just below the big marlin. Jeanie asked them if they needed any coffee or water. Everyone decided to have water.

Tom sat down at the table after shaking hands and said, "Guys, it's good to see all of you again. It's been a while now since I hired ya'll back in Destin. I've not even seen ya'll around yet since I just arrived a few weeks ago . . . and then all this terrorist crap! I just haven't had the opportunity to sit down and visit with anyone."

"That is a nice marlin," said Stacy, trying to help ease the tension of his buddies.

"Yes, it was a real thrill to catch him. He weighed three hundred and seventy-eight pounds and was caught off of the southernmost point of the Big Island in Hawaii about four years ago while I was fishing with a dear friend, Andy Ho, there. I'm also looking forward to many great fishing trips here in New Zealand. I've not been on any fishing trips here yet, but I'll surely be doing some very soon. I've been really busy getting everyone hired for this project so that it will be fully ready to go on January 1. I have another meeting in thirty minutes, so what would you gentlemen like to talk about today?"

Newton began. "Tom, we appreciate the opportunity that has been afforded all of us here. The work has been challenging and fun for us, but we were discussing among ourselves and felt like the communication of the objectives of the project is less than optimal. We all know that everything is being measured, and we're gathering some of those measurements, but we just don't know why. Although we know the terms of our contracts are that the purpose of the measurements wouldn't be exposed for some time, we think that at least some communication perhaps could be shared. In other words, are we on target with the objectives? Or are we below? Or are we above? Can anything be shared along the way, or do we have to wait? Perhaps the colony could publish a monthly newsletter to everyone?"

"Well," replied Tom as he sipped from his coffee cup and looked up at his marlin in deep thought, "perhaps ya'll have a good point. I'll need to take this up with the Board of Directors and get their thoughts. I know that the Board has very strict rules on disclosure among themselves, but perhaps some information on the progress could and should be shared. Let me do that for ya'll and get back to you in a few weeks.

"In the meantime, let me go out on a limb here and share with you that we are on target with our objectives, even with the terrorist attack on the oil tanker. I will say that our measurements are providing value and, might I add, positive-trending statistics about the effects of an isolated community free from the negative aspects of politics, threats of war, taxes, religion, special-interest groups, and other issues that have caused problems in the world. The medical services here are first class and are available to everyone. It appears that because of that good medical care and testing, along with less stress, better food habits, and more time for exercise, our population is showing good signs of improved overall health. The average number of high blood pressure, diabetes, and pulmonary issues has been declining steadily.

"Also, other than the oil tanker issue, we've had absolutely no crime here. Our health statistics are now already higher than our baseline averages in the States. Of course, we're measuring a lot more issues, but these are a couple of the big ones. The outside-world community is plagued with military conflicts, religious conflicts, commercial conflicts, discrimination, political discord, thievery, murder, rape, pollution, government entitlement for non-work, exponential debt . . . just too many bad issues and problems to list. We essentially believe that by eliminating a lot of the crap that has evolved in the world, we can prove that a different approach might have value to the world and to the colony members.

"Will that work for your concerns, or is there anything else?"

Newton looked at Stacy and Ken. "I think that will take care of our concerns for now, Tom."

"Okay then, I'll be back with you soon, and thanks for bringing your concerns to my attention," Tom said. He moved his chair back and stood up, indicating that the meeting was over.

Chapter 43
THE NEWSLETTER

A newsletter from the Board of Directors was delivered to each family exactly two months after the meeting with Tom. Ken and Ilene decided to read it together late that evening, when the kids were asleep. Ken had poured two full glasses of Chardonnay, and they sat down next to each other on their bedroom balcony overlooking the park and lake. The moon was full and reflected off of the lake. It was another beautiful night in New Zealand, and they could share some together time. Ilene read the newsletter aloud.

"In an effort to provide more transparency into the management of the Research Project and its associated people, this newsletter is intended to share with each of you how we're currently organized and how we plan to change our management structure in the future.

The Colony and Research Project governing body is, at present, made up of a Board of Directors that consists of:

Duncan Kent	President
Nellie Kent	Executive Vice President
Tom Clark	Vice President of Resources
Bruce Bills	Chief Financial Officer
Joe Hawkins	Vice President of Legal Affairs
John Earnest	Vice President of Operations
Bob Erickson	Vice President, Systems and Services

The Board will be developing a new representative support body for its people. Our new governing process will select one representative per year for each five-year age group on January 1 of each year. The groups' ranges may be amended from time to time, but, to start, they will be as follows:

Group 25 through 29
Group 30 through 34
Group 35 through 39
Group 40 through 44
Group 45 through 49
Group 50 through 54
Group 55 through 59

Each representative serves four years and cannot be re-selected for fifteen years after their last year of service. This means that in the first year, there will be six representatives. The second year will have twelve representatives. The third year will have eighteen representatives, and in the fourth, and afterward, the colony will have twenty-four representatives.

They will be selected for their age group by the highest annual IQ score of a standard testing program currently in place as one of the standard measurements for all individuals. There will be no voting, popularity contests, politics, or lobbying self-interests. Selected individuals serve as volunteers as do all government members and support functions utilizing their mandatory eight hours per week of community service work. Any individual who doesn't want to serve as a representative will be excused and allowed to perform some other assigned community service work for their standard eight hours per week of service.

The representatives will have a single leader who will be selected annually by the full Board to preside over the representative meetings. Joe Hawkins will attend all representative meetings on behalf of the Board and advise the representatives from time to time as needed. All representatives will report to the President of the Board of Directors. They will have no authority to act without the approval of the Board of Directors but will vote on issues that are brought up by themselves or by the Board. All representative votes will be submitted to the Board. The Board and the President will use that information to help determine the will of the people here. Over time, the representatives will likely become more empowered at the direction of the Board.

Beginning in Year Four and each year thereafter, the twenty-four sitting representatives will also select, by drawing, seven of their group to serve as judges for any and all colony violations. Any illegal actions by individuals will be immediately turned over to the local sheriff for any applicable punishment.

A colony rule violation conviction shall be subject to potential dismissal and expulsion from the colony. Any conviction from the local New Zealand government shall also result in expulsion. There will be no incarceration of individuals. The only punishment for any issues would be community service or expulsion from the colony and its associated financial and personal benefits.

The Board of Directors is looking forward to having the counsel and support of the representatives as they manage the colony and its ongoing Research Project. Watch for more newsletters from the Board as we begin this new process.

Regards,

Duncan Kent
Board President

Ken commented to Ilene, "Honey, this sounds really good. I think our meeting with Tom has paid off nicely. Now, the people here on the project will have input and know they'll be heard. It'll also let everyone know who the representatives are and that one can approach them with their thoughts and ideas as needed. Pretty cool, I think."

"I agree. It'll surely put smart people in more control instead of the typical 'politically correct, money hungry, assholes' that run the government in the States," said Ilene.

Ken looked across the lake and gave a sigh. A slight breeze rippled the lake. The smell of the flowers that had been planted in the lush landscaping gave a sweet smell to the breeze. He said, "It's so beautiful here, and being here with you makes it all so wonderful."

Ilene had just finished her glass of wine and so had Ken. Ilene looked at Ken and leaned over and gave him a warm kiss; then she leaned back in her chair and gave him a big smile. "Ken, I do love you! And, I can't help but notice that since we have moved here to New Zealand, I seem to be much more horny than ever before. Maybe it's the lack of stress, but I sure am really wanting you tonight," whispered Ilene.

Ken smiled and held her hand. "I feel the same way, sweetheart. Let's have a good time tonight." Rising from their chairs, they moved from the patio into the bedroom. It was indeed a very passionate night!

Chapter 44
NELLIE GOES TO THE DOCTOR

Nellie couldn't believe they'd been in New Zealand for two and a half years. It was late June and the beginning of winter. The great thing about New Zealand was that the temperature didn't really change much from summer to winter. The sea kept the temperature relatively mild year round. But, there was still a noticeable and welcome change of seasons. There was enough of a temperature change for the leaves to turn to the pretty fall colors on the deciduous trees. The colors were spectacular this year. From her home at the point, Nellie could see globs of small red-and-brown bushes surrounding bright yellow trees, with large evergreen trees in the distant background. It was so pretty and peaceful.

She wasn't hungry at all this morning. She felt weak. She'd stayed in bed all weekend long and was having pain in her abdomen. Her mother had died at age fifty from colon cancer. It had been bad, and Nellie had moved in to help her for six months until she ultimately passed. It was pure horror. Did she now have cancer? Her mind was going crazy considering the possibility that it could be cancer and that her end was near. She thought of Duncan and what would happen to him. Would he go on and remarry, or would he be alone and sad for the rest of his life? Would it kill the project? She could wait no longer; she had to know what was wrong.

Nellie walked in to the hospital at 9:30 on Monday morning. It wasn't necessary to make an appointment.

She headed down the wing with the doctors' offices. The names of the doctors were on the individual doctors' doors. She turned right into the office of Dr. Carolyn Davis. She walked to the receptionist and signed in the registry. The receptionist said, "Dr. Davis will be with you shortly, Mrs. Kent. Please have a seat." All of the chairs in the waiting room were plush cloth with armrests. Some were even recliners. Those amenities were just a few of the ideas Nellie had required of the architect during the town design phase. Nellie found an empty chair near the water dispenser. She filled a glass with the cool water and tried to relax.

At 10 Nurse Ilene Wallace came into the waiting room and called Nellie's name. Nellie walked out of the waiting room following Ilene. They went into one of the exam rooms, and Nellie took a seat in one of the comfortable chairs. The room was large and not cramped as most exam rooms are in the States. The room didn't have the typical wall crap that salesmen leave for doctors to cover their walls with because there were no drug salesmen in the colony. One wall had a long cabinet with sufficient top and lower cabinets to keep all documents, tools, and equipment out of sight and organized.

Ilene knew Nellie from her six quarterly visits that she'd already completed. "Good morning, Mrs. Kent. You just had your regular quarterly scan and checkup four weeks ago. How are you today?" she asked.

"Well, pretty good, but I want to discuss a little problem with Carolyn," replied Nellie.

"Okay," said Ilene, "just fill out this questionnaire sheet and describe your problem while I take your vitals."

Ilene knew of the Kents, as did most everyone in the colony. Rumor was that it was their money that was funding the Research Project. Once she had taken and recorded Nellie's vitals and collected the questionnaire, she left the exam room and hung Nellie's chart on the outside of the door.

Ilene came back into the exam room moments later with Dr. Davis. In a soft voice, Carolyn asked, "Nellie, what is going on with you?"

Nellie, showing some stress said, "Carolyn, I'm afraid I have cancer. I've been having pains in my abdomen now for about three days, and yesterday I noticed some blood. I'm almost seventy years old now, and this doesn't happen unless it's something bad, like cancer."

Carolyn replied, "Now, Nellie, don't be jumping to conclusions. We need to give you an exam and do some testing to find out what's going on."

Ilene assisted Nellie in getting undressed and covered with an exam gown. She then helped her onto the table and into position for the exam.

Once the physical exam was finished, she did a sonogram. Next, she drew blood for testing. She then called for the hospital to do a CT scan specific to the female reproductive system.

Carolyn stated, "Nellie, I want you to go down, get a CT scan, and then come back to the office here; then we'll review the results. Since it will take an hour or so to get the scan results back and read, why don't you go have lunch and come back about 2:00 . . . and stop worrying!"

Nellie left the hospital and walked down the street for a couple of blocks to the restaurant that was simply called "The Italian." She ordered some lasagna with a small Italian salad. A large glass of sweet tea would have to suffice for the coffee she'd skipped earlier. Having skipped breakfast this morning due to her anxiety, she was now quite hungry. The restaurant was beginning to fill up, as it was almost noon. She hadn't told Duncan about her pain issue; she did not want him to be worried. He had enough on his plate right now.

For that matter, she hadn't told anyone. She was so scared. She was afraid to know it was cancer but was also afraid to not know. Would she be able to beat it? Would she have long to live? How would she tell Duncan? Not knowing was awful. She picked at her food and ate only a little. Her stomach cramped, and she felt worse.

Ilene had a few minutes off for lunch and ran down to the hospital cafeteria and ate half of a cheese sandwich and a salad. The cafeteria food was pretty darn good, and, as a hospital employee, Ilene didn't have to use up any Colony Card credits.

It had been a busier morning than usual. There had been six patients this morning, including Nellie Kent. They usually had only ten patients in a typical day. They allotted thirty minutes per patient, and with their personal community service for eight hours per week, the office stayed pretty busy. Fortunately, there were three more gynecologists at the hospital, so that made everything work pretty well for now, but they were talking about cutting back patient time to twenty-five minutes.

Most all of the women in the colony were of child-bearing age, and, with their newly acquired wealth, many were talking about having more children, which in turn was driving the workload up a bit. She'd even thought about another child herself, but was waiting for a good time to talk to Ken. She wondered what he would think. Talking to Stormy, they had already decided to try to have more since they had only 1 daughter. The colony made it easy for parents, so more kids would not be difficult at all.

Ilene finished her lunch and walked back to the office. She saw on her desk the packet from the lab on Nellie's CT scan. She opened the metal clasps on the flap and read the report inside; then she closed the packet and put it with Nellie's appointment papers.

Moments later, Dr. Davis walked in. "We got the report back on Nellie Kent," said Ilene.

"Did you read it?" asked Carolyn.

"Yes, I did. And you need to read it. I don't know what to make of it," Ilene said, with a confused look on her face.

Nellie came in at 2:00 and was immediately taken back by Ilene to an exam room. In an unusual action, Carolyn had told Ilene not to come into the room for the conversation with Nellie.

"Nellie, your report shows that you do not have cancer. So you can rest easy now," stated Carolyn.

Nellie smiled nervously and said, "Oh, that's so good, Carolyn. I'm so relieved. But what is it?"

Carolyn wasn't sure how to tell her, because she had never said this to any patient like Nellie before, but decided to get right to the point.

Carolyn began: "Nellie, our scan and your symptoms show that what you're having is a normal menstrual period. That has never occurred or ever been seen in a woman your age. I know you're very healthy and look more like forty than seventy years old. It's unusual to look so much younger than most women your age. This is one for the books. Your scan shows that you have many eggs in your ovaries and that you can expect this situation to continue monthly for at least a while, but we don't know for how long. Your uterus has a normal thickness and looks typical for a thirty-year-old woman. There are no signs of the cysts that gave you problems in your younger years. Nellie, I think it's entirely possible for you to get pregnant provided there are no problems with Duncan's sperm. I re-emphasize that I've never seen anything like this in my life and we're in some uncharted territory here."

Nellie sat in shock and surprise. A thousand thoughts flashed across her mind. She couldn't speak for a full minute. "Really? Really? Are you sure you're right?" Nellie finally asked.

"That's my professional opinion, Nellie," replied Carolyn.

Regaining her composure, Nellie suddenly knew she needed to do something and had to do it now. "Carolyn, I want you to cancel your appointments or move them to the other doctors right now. I need for you to come home with me and visit with Duncan. Don't mention this to anyone else. I'll wait in the lobby until you're ready to go," exclaimed Nellie.

"But why? You can tell Duncan," replied Carolyn.

"No, I cannot. I'll explain everything when we get there, but we must go and go now," said Nellie.

Nellie wasn't aware that Ilene had read her report.

Chapter 45
ILENE CONFUSED

Ilene left work early when the office shut down at 3. With extra time before picking up David, she walked to the grocery store and did her weekly shopping. The CGS allowed everyone to push the shopping carts home and bring them back on their next trip from the condos to town. She pushed the full cart to the school and then, with David in tow, pushed it to their condo. As she finished unloading the cart, Ken walked in from work. Ilene poured two glasses of New Zealand Chardonnay, made on the colony farm, and asked Ken to sit on the balcony with her.

They sat down on the black wicker patio furniture with light-brown cushions. The wine was a tad sweet, but Ken liked the sweeter wines. He'd been shifting from beer to wine over the past year, except during barbecues, crab and shrimp boils, and fishing trips, where beer was still the drink of choice with his buddies. They talked for a while about Ken's day and the kids, and then the conversation shifted to Ilene's work.

"Well, I had a very interesting day today. I got off a bit early and completed our weekly grocery shopping. It was only one hundred and eighty-five units on our card," said Ilene.

"That's great," replied Ken.

Ilene added, "And, something happened at work that you must promise to keep confidential, or I cannot tell you."

"You know I will—I promise," said Ken.

"Today Nellie Kent came into the office. You know she's almost seventy, and the Kents are about the oldest people here," said Ilene.

"Yep, I know that, but I didn't know she was almost seventy years old. She looks much younger. I would have thought about forty or forty-five," said Ken.

"Well, she thought she had cancer but instead she had started having a period and has started regularly ovulating. Dr. Davis has never seen anything like it before."

"Must be the water and good food here," said Ken smiling.

"Whatever it is, I want to know, and I will be watching this to see if she does get pregnant. It would be a world record, for sure!"

They finished the glass of wine, and Ilene blurted out, "Ken, I want to have another baby. Newton and Stormy are trying, and I'm ready."

Ken stuttered and said, "Wh . . . what? Where did that come from?"

Ilene responded, "I've been thinking about it for a while. We had wanted another child back in Shreveport, but we just couldn't afford it money-wise and time-wise. That's not the case now, and my clock is ticking. So, I just wanted to throw it out there and see what you think, now that we have both time and money."

Ken sat for a moment holding his empty glass and then suddenly held his glass into the air and said, "To more kids. Hell yes, let's do it."

Chapter 46
THE KENT HOUSE

Carolyn left the office with Nellie and got into her Black GMC Denali. Duncan had been disbursing forty of these vehicles per year, and the Board members and their spouses would get a new one each year. The rest of the forty new GMCs would be given to managers needing transportation (security officers, farmers, delivery services, and industrial support services). One of the warehouse clerks had told Carolyn that there were hundreds of these vehicles in storage waiting to be disbursed.

With Carolyn in the passenger seat, Nellie drove past the condo area, and another mile past a new housing development under construction. The houses were being built around a golf course, with winding roads and underground utilities. So far, only about three hundred homes had been completed, and the people getting the houses initially were the directors and managers. Dr. Jackson was getting one built now, but Carolyn was number 431 on the list. The construction group was currently building about ten houses per month, so she was about eighteen months away from moving out of her condo and into a new home. The condo was just fine, but she would not turn down the opportunity to have a single-family home for a more private and slightly less noisy atmosphere.

The road crossed over the golf course on a stone bridge and began winding up a narrow brick paver driveway to the top of a very large hill, perhaps fifteen hundred feet higher than the surrounding hill and valley land. At the top sat a huge two-story beige stucco-and-rock home with large white columns supporting deep porches across the entire front. A *porte-cochère* with matching columns was centered on the front entry. A huge chandelier hung down from the ceiling of the *porte-cochère*. They stopped under the *porte-cochère* and walked through the two giant front doors with glass that depicted a frosted kiwi bird standing on a frosted gold ingot bar on each door. The foyer was a huge round area about twenty-four feet high with two walnut staircases that arched around both sides of the entrance and came together at the center of a second floor balcony. Another gold-colored chandelier that had hundreds of clear crystals and lights hung down from the center of the foyer. The walls were stained walnut wood with amazing carpentry that gave thickness and depth to the walls. The floors were all white and gray marble. On the left wall was a life-sized oil painting of Nellie, and to the right was a matching oil painting of Duncan. They both appeared to be about forty-five years old when the paintings were completed. Carolyn's first impression upon entering the house was one of fabulous wealth and elegance.

Nellie led her beyond the staircases and into the den, where she asked Carolyn to have a seat on one of the four wingback chairs that were placed adjacent to two large peanut-shaped couches. Nellie asked if she would like anything to drink, but Carolyn said "No." Nellie then left the room and said that she might be thirty minutes or so before coming back.

Carolyn turned toward the back of the house, where a wall of windows led to a large, covered patio. She could see that the shady backyard view was looking directly across the Tapora Bay toward the Tasman Sea. It was a breathtaking view. The landscaping was beautiful, with walkways trimmed with monkey grass and flowered areas bordering large beds of English ivy. Everything seemed to be kept low so the fabulous view could be enjoyed from the den.

Nellie walked into Duncan's office and sat in front of his large leather and cherry wood desk. Duncan's large bronze eagle, with spread wings, boldly watched over his desk from a sofa table on Duncan's left. He looked up from his computer screen and saw Nellie staring at him.

Duncan knew something was up and quickly said, "What?" before Nellie had uttered a word.

"Duncan, you know the appointment I had with Dr. Carolyn Davis today," said Nellie.

"Yes," replied Duncan.

Nellie added, "I thought I was having some very serious female problems, but it turns out that I'm having my period. Carolyn ran CT scan tests, and I have lots of eggs in my ovaries. She thinks there's a chance I could get pregnant."

Shock registered on Duncan's face. He couldn't speak. His mouth was open, but no words were coming out. It took a full minute for the news to sink in.

Once it did, Nellie responded, "I brought Carolyn home with me as a necessity but didn't tell her why. I think we need to keep Carolyn from talking about this with anyone."

Duncan said, "My God, Nellie, do you realize what this means? I didn't expect this. I think I'm in shock. This is exciting yet totally unplanned."

Nellie replied, "I know—I am too. I wasn't sure what to do other than bring Carolyn here."

Duncan whispered in deep thought, "Good, Nellie, you were right in doing so. We have to talk to Carolyn now, so let's go have a talk with her."

Carolyn couldn't help but wonder what was going on and why she had to come talk to Duncan in such an urgent rush. She felt uncomfortable and fidgeted as she looked around the room. A wood-and-glass coffee table centered in the room was empty except for a beautiful gold goblet about twelve inches tall filled with light-blue crystals. An apparent unseen battery-powered LED light in the bottom of the bowl gave the crystal a magical glow that forced one to stare at its constant beauty. Carolyn wanted to pick it up and hold it, but fear of damaging it kept her in her chair.

Her pager had been going off for about fifteen minutes, and she finally had a moment to call the office. She dialed the office number, and the receptionist, Katie, answered.

"Dr. Davis, Mrs. Jensen is here and in labor. Ilene is with her in the hospital delivery room. Ilene says she's a four right now, but it won't be long," exclaimed Katie with a sense of urgency.

Carolyn responded, "Tell Ilene that I'll hopefully be back by the time Mrs. Jensen gets to eight; otherwise, she needs to have the ER involved after the patient reaches that point. I'll be back soon; I've got to go now."

She hung up the cell phone as she saw Nellie approaching through the hallway. Duncan was only a few steps behind. Carolyn had never met Duncan but had heard a lot about him from others and from her personal medical sessions with Nellie.

Duncan was tall, at six foot three, and stood straight. His full set of hair showed only touches of gray, giving it a salt-and-pepper look. He was wearing a red turtleneck sweater with khaki slacks. Duncan was very muscular and handsome, and Carolyn's first impression was that there is no way this man could be almost seventy years old—maybe fifty-five at the most. He looked almost as young as her own husband, who had just turned fifty-one.

Duncan and Nellie walked into the den holding hands and sat down on a sofa across from Carolyn. The conversation lasted almost an hour and a half. When it was over, Carolyn had promised to keep everything confidential but looked exhausted and dazed from all that she had heard. Nellie drove Carolyn back to the hospital and then returned home to Duncan.

Chapter 47
THE DISCUSSION

When Nellie came back after taking Carolyn back to the hospital, she walked into Duncan's office and found him leaning back in his office chair in deep thought. He was gazing out the large window onto the well-manicured and landscaped front lawn. She was the first to speak. "You know we've wanted a child for more than forty years. Are you ready to be a father, now?"

Duncan smiled and said, "You bet I am." A wrinkled forehead gave away a worried concern that was yet to be explained.

Nellie asked, "Okay, I see you're worried about something. What is it?"

"Nellie, my concern is that we're in uncharted territory here. This is a side effect that I didn't expect from my efforts to improve our heath here in New Zealand. Are we actually getting younger? Are we reversing the aging process? Is it just you? Never have people our age had children before. We don't know if you could carry a fetus for a full term. Would a baby be healthy? We don't even know if my sperm is potent enough to get you pregnant," stated Duncan.

"You're right, Duncan. Perhaps you need some testing now," said Nellie with a smile.

She knew Duncan hated to go to the doctor, and a sperm fertility test would be something he just wouldn't want to do. Duncan didn't respond for a full minute as he stared at Nellie. Then, as he finally spoke, she could see tears forming in his eyes.

"Nellie, you know I love you with all of my heart and that I would do anything for you. We've always wanted children, and, if there's any chance for us, I want to do it. Would you set me up an appointment with the doctor as soon as possible? We need to get this behind us so we won't be in limbo."

Nellie said, "Okay, my love, I'll set it up for tomorrow. But in the meantime, I'm calling the drug store and getting some feminine products, as these cramps are getting worse. I thought I was over all of that stuff a long time ago! And, by the way, you'd better get ready for a date in about fourteen days." Duncan looked stunned as Nellie smiled, turned, and walked out of the room. As she left the room, she looked back over her shoulder and said with a sheepish smile, "Date night is going to be a wild night, so get ready!"

Chapter 48

INVESTMENTS START TO PAY OFF

It was six months after the project kick-off and 10 in the evening when Bruce Bills unlocked the door to the bank and took the elevator to the top floor. In New York it was a Monday morning, and Bruce had work to do. The bank was the tallest building in town and contained the executive and project main offices on the top three floors. The top three floors provided outstanding views of the farm and ocean. Bruce's office was one of the corner offices just down the hall from Duncan's office and had large windows that looked toward the marina area. It was a plush and comfortable office, with lots of wood and leather. He had two computer screens on his desk. As he walked into his sixth-floor office, he opened the shades to enjoy the full moon and town lights.

This was a special night that Bruce had been planning for five months now. He knew this was the first of at least five nights per week that he'd be working the hours of 10 to midnight for quite some time to come. He'd done his home-work and was ready.

Bruce had been the CFO at Grainteck for twenty-five years. He'd worked for ten years at a major brokerage firm on Wall Street prior to Duncan recruiting him. He was well qualified for this important new task at hand. With a Master's degree in accounting, buying and selling stocks were just a matter of handling the numbers well. Duncan and Nellie had full confidence in his skills and abilities. He loved numbers, and the numbers were continuing to get quite large.

His wife, Lorraine, was also an accountant. She'd decided to use her skills in the Colony Bank so she could see him more often and they could have lunch together. She understood that for a while Bruce needed to work some nights to match the open hours of Wall Street.

Bruce fired up his computers as he brewed himself a large cup of coffee. His coffee cup was special. It was a white cup. At the very top was an inscription in gold that read:

To a NEW Beginning
Duncan & Nellie Kent

On both sides of the cup was an orange and yellow sunrise over a green island amid surrounding blue water. The sunrise was representing the colony island. Although not really an island, it was a peninsula that the fenced and gated entry gave the appearance of an island with water on three sides. Vertically, within the blue water below the island, were the names of the

colony Board members and their title
the CFO, was just below Duncan and

After a few sips of the warm brew, ,
drawer and pulled out a large ledger book. Eve
was quite skilled and would be using his compute.
sell, he wanted to keep a legacy paper document to p.
track his activity. The first page contained a list of fifty sto
that he'd done a lot of research on. He logged onto the colony
brokerage account and checked the balance. It contained
$10 billion in cash. The cash had been established by the Kents
as a specific and separate component of the plan. The cash was
necessary to be able to short stocks in the market. Bruce began
by shorting one hundred thousand shares of the first company
on his list at $77 per share. Shorting stocks would typically be
very risky, but Bruce felt very comfortable that night.

Bruce knew that when stock is "shorted," it's borrowed
from an owner of the stock and sold in the market. But the
stock must be replaced at some indefinite time in the future.
Bruce's plan was to let the stock drop in price by at least 50 percent and then buy it back to close out the short transaction.
By shorting the stock, the colony account would be credited
with all of the money from the sale minus commissions.

With the first short sale of the night, Bruce saw $7,700,000
immediately deposited into the cash account. He'd been given
the authority to select the stocks based on the criteria that
the Board had given him. However, Duncan had specifically requested that Blocked Canyon be shorted, and shorted
heavily, every day. Perhaps Duncan's dislike of Jay Cameron

verriding his good business judgment, but then again, ican was rarely wrong. Blocked Canyon would be his first ort every night.

Bruce continued with the second stock on his list. Again he shorted one hundred thousand shares at $54 per share and watched as another $5,400,000 was added to the cash account.

Bruce continued to short stocks that were on his list for a full hour. When he stopped, the cash account had increased by more than $250 million. This activity would be repeated every night for the next year. He would be selecting various stocks to short. Now, all that would be left for these initial stock bets would be to wait for the downturn on their price. Bruce was certain the upcoming second-quarter financial results report, due in October, would most certainly drive the stocks lower.

His night's work done, he left precisely at midnight to drive his new GMC Denali to his home just down the street from Duncan. Lorraine would likely still be waiting up.

Chapter 49
DUNCAN'S TEST

Duncan left his office and walked to the clinic at the hospital building. He signed in with Dr. Garrett's receptionist and took a seat. He was called back within a couple of minutes and taken to a room. A nurse walked in moments later. She took his temperature and blood pressure; then she asked what problems he was having. Duncan's face was suddenly flushed. This was so embarrassing for him.

"I apologize, but I don't want to discuss this with you! Could you bring in Dr. Garrett, please?" The nurse looked at Duncan and, knowing who he was, lowered her pen and chart, and walked out of the room.

Dr. Garrett walked in and shook Duncan's hand. "How are you doing, Duncan?" he asked.

"Dr. Garrett, I realize this might be a bit strange since I'm almost 70 and my wife is, too, but I need to have my sperm tested."

"Why would you want to do that, Duncan?" asked Dr. Garrett.

Duncan didn't want to tell Dr. Garrett any more than was necessary. He knew that any answer, truth or made up, would present more questions, and he didn't want to answer any questions. "Dr. Garrett, this is an issue that I want to keep in full doctor-patient confidentiality. I don't even want my name on the test report. I don't want any questions—I just want the test and the results," demanded Duncan.

"Okay, Duncan, if that's what you want. We'll do that. Now, do you want to give the sample here or at home and bring it back here?" asked Dr. Garrett.

"I prefer to do it from home. I can get the sample and bring the sample back tomorrow morning," responded Duncan.

"Okay, then. Let me get you a sample cup, and I'll see you in the morning. We can do the test within thirty minutes of receiving the sample, so if you're here at 9, I can have the results for you any time after 9:30. I'll give you a written report and discuss the results with you. Is that going to work for you?" asked Dr. Garrett.

"That works for me, Doc. I'll see you tomorrow morning," responded Duncan. Duncan took his sample bottle, put it into his pocket, and left the clinic. As he left, he thought to himself that this was perhaps the most embarrassing event he'd ever experienced. He wondered how women were able to do so much more invasive testing than this, have it done often, and then make it appear to be just normal.

The following morning, Duncan arrived back at the clinic at exactly 9 o'clock. Refusing to see anyone else, he handed off his sample to Dr. Garrett. He then walked over to the café across the street for some breakfast. He selected a cushioned booth. The waitress knew him by name and brought his usual coffee with Splenda. A container of cream from the colony was brought to the table in lieu of the artificial creamers that Duncan really wanted. His dietary team had chosen to exclude them from the food supplies. He hated not having his Coffemate mixture, but knew that the Project was all about using ingredients grown on the farm whenever possible. He had managed to keep Splenda available since the production of sugar cane was not a viable crop for the area. Duncan was hopeful that his genetic research plant in the colony could develop a strain of sugar cane or sugar beets for the mild climate here. When the waitress returned, Duncan ordered the special that consisted of bacon with two eggs and buttered toast.

Finishing breakfast, Duncan paid with his Colony Card. He knew this was simply about the perception of him participating in the Research Project. In reality, he was personally paying for 100 percent of everything, so tracking his personal expenses wasn't necessary for anything but show. Leaving the café, he walked back to the clinic and into Dr. Garrett's office.

"Duncan, here's your report. I was amazed to find that your sperm test shows that you have very good swimmers and more volume than most young men. You must be doing something right. I went back and checked your last blood test from three months ago, and your testosterone levels were in the eleven hundred range; a normal range for someone your age would be three hundred to five hundred. I think that if you don't want to get some woman pregnant, you'd better wear a condom," said Dr. Garrett.

"Thank you, doctor, for that warning for my safety," smiled Duncan. "Right now, I feel much more potent than I did yesterday. I'm almost afraid of touching any woman now. I think it must be the water here," joked Duncan.

He stood up, thanked Dr. Garrett again, shook his hand, and walked out of the clinic with a smile on his face. He decided to head home and give Nellie the good news. They had work to do!

Chapter 50
NEWS REPORTS

Over his morning coffee, Duncan opened the *Wall Street Journal* newspaper and saw an unusually large headline in bold letters:

World Health Officials Report a Dramatic Drop in Pregnancies

FDA officials express concerns

Duncan anxiously read the article.

"A World Health research firm today announced that the birth rate in the world has slowed to a level never seen before.

"Jeremy Belcher, president of the organization, stated in an interview yesterday that the drop appears to be worldwide. The current birth rate began dropping rapidly over the last eleven months. It appears that the pregnancy rates started changing about twenty months ago and have steadily declined to almost zero at present. Exceptions seem to be remote populations, but their rates are beginning to drop, also.

"This correlation seems to indicate some level of influence from bacteria, virus, or food. Investigations are underway in most countries. Concern of some type of terrorist activity has been thrown out because the population in the Middle East is also being hit.

"The US Department of Health is looking into the situation to determine the cause. Current speculation is that some type of airborne superbug virus affecting fertility has spread rapidly worldwide by air or the world food supply. Superbugs could be carried by any number of animal species, including other humans as well as food supplies, thus providing for rapid transmission of the virus worldwide.

"No virus has been discovered yet, but investigations by medical specialists and collaborative efforts are paramount in all countries. All individuals are being urged to boil their water and fully cook their foods to at least one hundred and eighty degrees in order to protect against the possible virus.

"The possibility of an impact from genetically modified food sources is also being strongly considered. Food sources, including meat, dairy, fruits, vegetables, and grains have been genetically modified for at least thirty years to improve production yields and prevent spoilage during shipment. Testing of these genetically modified foods on humans has been nonexistent and assumed to be safe.

"Several independent health organizations have argued and complained to the FDA for several years about the lack of sufficient testing of genetically modified foods."

The article and news hit Wall Street stocks hard. All of the stock market TV shows were buzzing, as were the news stations. The stock market always fears the unknown, and those headlines reeked of some as yet to be determined problem.

The market was off another 10 percent, with stocks that related to baby food, diapers, baby clothing, car seats, and crib manufacturers being hit even harder. Every stock dealing with infant products and services were being decimated.

Duncan felt sure this was going to happen. He laughed as he wondered how that thieving asshole, Jay Cameron, at Blocked Canyon, was doing. He poured himself a tall glass of Jack and Coke on ice and then whispered to himself, "I'll bet his butt is scrambling right now. The bastard! I knew he wouldn't test the genetically modified grains and would just throw them on the marketplace. His greed has finally caught up with him."

Chapter 51

BLOCKED CANYON URGENT EVENT

Jay Cameron arrived at his corporate office looking disheveled from the lack of sleep. Jay was used to being in command and control, but now he was being treated like a criminal under intense interrogation. He'd spent the entire week with investigators from the FDA. The media was being handled by his PR manager, who had been trying to put a positive spin on the situation by denying everything and pointing out the potential of some new airborne virus. But his board of directors called for a special meeting the following day to assess the situation at hand. Jay had reluctantly agreed and was very fearful for his job.

Jay had already done some analysis and realized the most likely culprit in the world fertility rate was indeed the genetically modified grains that were producing the last two years of food crops. He knew the genetically modified foods and grains grown by his company's seeds were never tested to determine their impact on humans and animals. Duncan had specifically included in the sale agreement that Blocked Canyon was to test the human and animal impact with Jay's geneticists, but Jay had skipped that in order to save money and get product on the market faster. Unlike the extensive testing done by every pharmaceutical company on new medicines, his company could produce a consumable product and sell it simply because it looked like a familiar food that had been consumed for years.

He'd been so anxious to utilize the historically high profit of the Grainteck genetically modified seeds that he'd neglected to check the design or have any tests run by his own geneticists. Those current grain crops were all the end result of what was now purely Blocked Canyon-branded seeds.

Now, with investigations in full swing, there was little doubt that his company was going to be totally destroyed and likewise even his personal fortune would be eroded away with global civil lawsuits. He would likely be sent to prison. Once his wife and children realized that he was responsible for sterilizing their children and grandchildren, he'd be divorced and ostracized from any and all contact.

He could blame Grainteck and Duncan Kent, but he had accepted all liability when he purchased Grainteck. The blame game wouldn't work. He was simply out of options. He knew the only legal maneuver he had left when the lawsuits came was to plead the Fifth. But then, he'd surely end up in prison for the rest of his life. Attempting to run to another country would likely be fruitless since every country in the world would be after him.

It was just not right; Duncan must have done this on purpose! Duncan was still pissed at him for stealing his genetic designs twenty-five years ago when he worked for Grainteck and formed his own company, Blocked Canyon, from the stolen designs. Jay didn't really see it as stealing since Duncan had not patented his seed DNA designs, and they were there for Jay to use. Jay's opinion was that it was just business. While it had worked and been profitable for a couple of years and took some market share from Grainteck, Duncan had quickly modified his DNA codes and began marketing his next-generation, higher-production genetically modified seeds. From then on, Duncan patented everything. But, Duncan never got over it.

Jay knew Duncan had planned this to get even with him. He just knew it. But, then again it was so unlike Duncan to develop a product that would possibly damage mankind. He'd been such a proponent for humanitarian efforts and saving lives. Why would he destroy the entire human species? It didn't make sense! But it had to be Duncan's fault. His anger grew with every thought of Duncan. He hated him. What should he do? Whatever it was, it needed to be done very soon.

Chapter 52
BLOCKED CANYON

The following afternoon, Jay arrived at Blocked Canyon at 1:30. The Board meeting was scheduled for 2 o'clock. As he reached his corner office on the twentieth floor at the top of the BC building, his secretary, Kimberly Maness, handed him a note with two business cards clipped to it and said, "This is from two FBI agents that came by this morning at 10. They stayed for an hour and then left the note. They said they'd be back tomorrow at 10 and wanted to talk to you."

"Okay, Kimberly," replied Jay with no expression on his face.

Jay knew this was inevitable. He felt like a trapped animal. He walked into his office and closed the door behind. Walking over to the wet bar, he poured himself a glass of Wild Turkey on the rocks. That would do for lunch.

Sitting in his red-leather chair, he leaned back and threw his feet onto the very center of his large wooden desk. He'd never done that before, as he'd been so proud and protective

235

of the $30,000 desk with the red chair with the matching leather inserts. Now, he could give a shit!

Looking around the room, he saw pictures of his wife, Tammie, and his two grown daughters, Sheri and Beth. He saw a picture of all of the grandkids, three boys and two girls at their Telluride, Colorado, getaway home. There were golf trophies, a large wall-mounted rainbow trout, a picture of his vintage red 1995 Mercedes SL600 convertible—all trappings of his success. And soon, it will all be trash! Gone!

Finishing his drink and taking a quick glance at his Rolex watch, he stood up and walked out of his office, perhaps for the last time, and toward the boardroom.

Chapter 53
THE WALL STREET ARTICLE

On August 21, a *Wall Street Journal* article announced that the following press release had been issued by a Blocked Canyon spokesperson:

> Jay Cameron, president of Blocked Canyon, has been fired and is being replaced by the executive vice president, Daren Whitehead. Investigations are continuing by both the FDA and the FBI into possible criminal actions against Jay Cameron and Blocked Canyon. Blocked Canyon denies any wrongdoing and said they will cooperate with all investigative units to clear up any issues. Jay Cameron could not be reached for comment.

The news media were all scrambling to get in touch with Jay for an interview. There were no answers to numerous phone calls to his home. The shades were all drawn at his home. No one had found Jay yet. The FBI returned to the office and found Kimberly packing up Jay's office belongings. She had no idea when he would return to pick them up.

Duncan read the article and smiled. He'd gotten the bastard. And, he got him good. And now, he was profiting off of Jay's company falling apart by having shorted thousands of Blocked Canyon's stock. And that profit was in addition to the $76 billion price that Jay had paid for Grainteck. The only hard part had been being nice to Jay before and during the sale negotiations. And now it was over for Jay. Revenge was sweet.

Bruce Bills saw the headlines that night when he came in at 10 and smiled as he checked the cash account. It was up an unusually high amount of $2.15 billion, mostly all from Blocked Canyon shorts. He knew the market would drop even more in the coming weeks and months.

Chapter 54
FLIGHT or FIGHT

At 6 a.m., a taxi pulled up to the front of an independent Fixed Base Operator airport and unloaded one blue medium-sized piece of luggage and a large tan duffle bag. The taxi driver had been paid in advance with $850 cash for the one hundred and ten mile, one-way trip from New York to Philadelphia in the middle of the night. His rider handed him a $100 bill for a tip.

His rider was casually dressed with jogging shoes, jeans, a lightweight black hooded jacket, and a plain black baseball cap. One of the two pilots flying the chartered plane met him in the FBO lobby and offered to carry his luggage to the plane. Jay let him take the duffle bag but kept the rolling luggage. Jay rolled his luggage through the FBO lobby and onto the tarmac and watched as his duffle bag was loaded. He kept his luggage and climbed the stairway onto the Learjet 31A. The second pilot was going through his startup process, but took time to welcome Jay and make sure he was seated, buckled.

Few words were said. One of the pilots offered coffee and donuts. They were accepted without comment.

The chartered Learjet was ready to leave Philadelphia at 7:30. The flight plan showed one-way travel to Vancouver, British Columbia, Canada. Payment was to be in cash at the point of departure.

Five hours later, the jet touched down in a small private airstrip near Vancouver. After getting out of the small airport without the typical security process, Jay Cameron felt some small level of relief. He had decided to run. He was angry, even beyond angry. Duncan Kent had done this to him, and he would pay—somehow, some way, he would pay.

Jay had moved quickly with little rest. Getting out of the country was critical. He knew that if the FBI arrested him, he'd never be able to get out of the country, even if he got out on bail. He had emptied his bank accounts and safe deposit box of all the money that he could and had put $200,000 worth in gold coins in his car three days before in anticipation of the problems to come. His suitcase contained his laptop computer, $2 million in hundreds, three changes of clothes, and toiletries.

Jay made his way by taxi to the Marriott hotel and quickly showered and collapsed into the bed for some needed sleep. Although exhausted from the recent events, he had difficulty sleeping. His mind kept thinking about how he could get that son of a bitch Duncan Kent.

The next day, Jay fired up his laptop. He searched for hours. Finally he found what he was looking for. He'd located Duncan. He'd left the United States and had bought some farm in New Zealand. Jay suspected Duncan was in New

Zealand, since Duncan had reserved his new factory there from the sale during the buyout. Jay would go there, he would find Duncan, and get even with him for destroying his life.

Jay knew that the FBI would be looking for him. He had to keep moving. Staying too long in one place would surely end his plan. So far, his passport was still good. He had to get to New Zealand before it was revoked. On the phone with several jet charter companies, Jay found one that would take him to Hong Kong without stopping in Hawaii or Alaska. He wanted to get far away from the United States. From there he would get yet another charter to New Zealand. The Gulfstream G550 nonstop charter to Hong Kong could leave that night at 10 and, it was already 7. The Canadian leasing company had agreed to accept cash in US dollars for an additional 5 percent. His total cost for the transpacific flight on this large, long-range corporate jet would be $57,000. He quickly packed his bag and checked out of the hotel, paying cash. Taking a cab to the airport, he was on his way to China, the next leg in his New Zealand quest.

After five more days and a third charter, Jay landed in Auckland. He'd studied information and maps on the Internet. He now knew that Duncan's location was near the town of Tapora. He could hardly wait to find him.

Chapter 55
TENTH FISHING TRIP

It was early October, and spring was in full bloom. The wind was calm, and the temperature was a cool sixty-two degrees. Captain Tim had called Ken and told him the fish were really biting in his favorite fishing grounds. That was all the gang of three needed to plan a trip for Saturday. They'd been on nine fishing trips with Captain Tim since coming to New Zealand. They always had loads of fun harassing each other and somehow, even with all the bullshit, still managed to catch plenty of fish.

Ken had told Captain Tim to have plenty of beer for the trip. They left at daylight from the fishing dock. Captain Tim said the best tuna were really hot about a couple of hours boat ride to the northeast. Captain Tim always wore cowboy boots everywhere but would change into deck shoes once he reached the boat.

That day, he had forgotten to change shoes and was still wearing his cowboy boots as they left the harbor and started out to sea. Tim just kept bitching and complaining about his dog that wouldn't get out of the large fenced community dog yard.

"That damn dog! I had to chase him down and get him back into my condo, and that's why I was running a little late this morning."

A few minutes later, he started to make faces and asked, "Do you guys smell anything that stinks?"

"No, I can't smell anything," said Stacy.

"Not me," replied both Ken and Newton.

"Huh, it's strong to me," said Tim. Suddenly, Captain Tim raised his right foot and looked on the sole. Laughing, he said, "Well maybe I stepped in some dog shit when I was in the dog yard in the dark this morning."

"That's possible," said Newton.

Captain Tim said, "Nope—no shit there," as he raised his left foot slowly so that the three fishermen could see the bottom of his boot as he raised it. In front of the raised boot heel in the L-shaped area was a strip of light brown mush that was stuck between the heel and sole. "Oh, my god, there it is, Tim," yelled Stacy as he turned his head to avoid the smell that was sure to emanate from Tim's foot.

"Yep, there it is," added Ken. "There's your smell, Tim. You have dog shit on your boot."

Tim looked shocked. Then with his boot still sticking up where everyone could see the sole, Tim reached down with his left index finger and ran it deep into and along the mushy soft crap and retrieved a spoon-sized glob. He quickly looked at it, sniffed it, then thrust it into his mouth, smacked his lips and said. "You're right—it is dog shit."

The three fishermen yelled in disgust. "Oh, yuck! You sick bastard," said Newton.

"You disgusting pervert," said Ken.

"Anybody who would eat dog shit is just sick and crazy," said Stacy.

As the fishermen were at their highest level of disgust, turning pale, and nearly throwing up from the thought of what Captain Tim had done, Tim began to laugh. He laughed so hard that his face turned red. Then he blurted out, "You dumbasses—it was peanut butter! I put it on this morning when I got out of my car into the crack of my boot, where it wouldn't touch the ground. The joke's on you," laughed Captain Tim.

Everyone looked relieved, but still disgusted, from the mental image of Tim eating what they all thought was dog shit.

"Tim, I'm going to get you for this," said Ken, as Tim continued to laugh at their pale faces. Tim proceeded to remove his cowboy boots and put on his normal deck shoes while still chuckling.

Occasionally, one of the guys would look at Captain Tim and simply say, "Asshole," which would always produce another smile from Tim. He'd gotten them, and gotten them good. This was one prank they'd never forget.

They arrived at the fishing grounds at 9. The fish were really biting well that day. Newton hooked a sixty-pound tuna within a few minutes of starting to fish. Everyone caught fish, and by mid-afternoon, they had more than seven hundred pounds of nice tuna. Captain Tim called a halt and started the return trip from the fishing grounds. It was time for an easy ride home and a few more of Captain Tim's ice-cold beers. The crew seemed to be over Tim's peanut-butter prank.

During the return trip, Captain Tim began complaining about all of the fish he was going to have to clean. They'd caught a lot more than usual, and it would take a while to filet and package the tuna. But, as they came closer to the harbor, Captain Tim's complaining grew worse.

"Since I don't get tips like I did in the States, it ain't fair. You bastards caught too many fish, and now I have to clean all of them by myself. I should've taken you to a bad spot instead of my hot fishing hole."

"Bullshit," said Stacy, "you signed on like all of us, and it's your job to clean all the fish that *we* catch."

"We paid for this trip with our Colony Cards. Maybe you could hire someone with your Colony Card to clean the fish for us," laughed Ken.

Captain Tim fired right back, "Oh, you assholes—you just want to have all of the fun without the real work."

Newton decided to add his two cents to this attack on Captain Tim. "Not true, Captain. You chose this profession because you liked it, and cleaning fish goes with the territory," laughed Newton.

Captain Tim grumbled. "Only because the colony didn't hire any first mates! That should be each one of you sons-o-bitches' standard eight-hour community service jobs: to be my first mate and clean all the fish for me. You'd appreciate me more then."

"All right, Captain, we're now feeling so sorry for poor pitiful you, that we'll degrade ourselves into being your slaves and help you clean the fish," said Ken as they all hung their heads to mock feeling sorry for Captain Tim.

Tim could still see them grinning. "All right then, I guess my plan worked," as he smiled with a big grin. "I'm starting to like you guys again!" laughed Captain Tim.

"Boy, I wonder if he treats all of his customers like this." said Newton.

"Yeah, it's a learned skill that takes years to master," said Captain Tim, still smiling. All of the guys liked Tim, and they all enjoyed picking on each other, but Captain Tim was always a good target for an attack, because he loved to dish it out, too. It was just about as much fun as the fishing itself. They knew there had to be a good trick to pull on Tim the next time they went out and knew Tim would be expecting that. They really didn't mind cleaning the fish anyway. They just had to give Captain Tim a hard time.

After a relatively calm boat ride from the fishing grounds, Captain Tim began to turn his boat to re-enter the protected harbor and dock area. He slowed his boat to under three knots to keep from making a large wake. From his right, Captain Tim noticed something unusual. Another boat was also pulling into the harbor about one hundred yards ahead of them. It wasn't a fishing boat, but a speedy gray sport boat with an orange stripe. The harbor was a no-wake zone, but the speeding boat didn't slow down any. There were no fishing poles showing on the boat. He could see a driver behind the wheel and a single passenger. He knew all the boats that used the dock since he was there every day, and this boat was not one of them.

Captain Tim shouted out loud over the sound of his roaring boat engine. "Hey guys, get a load of this crazy boat up ahead. I can tell you that idiot has never been into this harbor and dock before."

Everyone looked up to see the speedboat barreling toward the dock, creating large waves that were a no-no for the harbor security officers.

Ken yelled over the loud engine. "I thought that passengers coming onto the island had to come through the main gate and get through security."

"That's right," nodded Captain Tim. "They told us to watch for any unauthorized boats coming in, especially after the oil tanker terrorist attack. All non-freighter boats coming in are supposed to have these four-inch blue "C" stickers on both sides like I have on my boat.

As their boat moved closer to the dock, they watched as the passenger jumped onto the dock and was handed a black duffle bag by the boat driver. He quickly headed toward the shore. Without even looking at Captain Tim's oncoming boat, the sports boat captain had pushed off of the dock and was spinning around and headed back out into the bay. As the returning sports boat sped by them, a closer look showed that the boat clearly did not have the colony blue stickers. Captain Tim grabbed his binoculars and quickly wrote down the registration numbers showing on the front of the boat.

They quickly turned their attention and watched as the passenger moved up the dock at a fast walking pace and onto the parking lot with no hesitation whatsoever. They could see that the passenger was wearing sunshades, a black hoodie, and blue jeans.

The dock security officer was responsible for checking all boats coming and going from the dock. Since the terrorist attack, all of the officers were carrying guns. Sitting in his guard shack around one hundred and fifty feet away, he'd seen the sports boat unload its passenger at the dock and leave without signing in or checking in. He walked in the direction of the dock expecting to intercept the passenger, but the passenger began to run when he saw the officer. The officer began to run to catch up to him.

"Something is up with this guy," said Stacy.

"Yeah, look—he's not even going toward town. He's running toward the hill to the brush and trees. That ain't right. Nobody does that," said Captain Tim.

"I know. That's toward the golf course about a half mile away," said Newton.

"He may be another terrorist," said Ken.

"Guys, what should we do?" said Stacy.

Captain Tim replied, "My radio went out yesterday, and I can't call anyone. Did anyone bring a cell phone?" No one had brought one, as there was little need to communicate frequently with anyone.

Captain Tim was just reaching the dock, and he throttled back to slow his boat; Newton threw a tie rope over an anchor stanchion. They continued to watch as the young security officer was gaining on the passenger. Two hundred yards lay between the dock beach and the brush on the hillside. As the officer was about to catch him near the brush, they heard him yelling at the passenger to stop. Suddenly, they saw the stranger spin around with a gun drawn and fire a pistol at the officer. Everyone on board Captain Tim's boat was watching as the guard dropped to the ground and then, a second later, heard the cracking sound of two more gunshots.

"Holy shit, that guy just shot the security officer!" yelled Captain Tim.

Ken jumped from the boat onto the dock and said, "Stacy, come with me. We need to see if there's anything we can do for the officer, but let's keep our distance from this guy and not get shot. Newton, you and Tim get in touch with security somehow and get an ambulance and security here."

"Will do," said Newton.

Stacy jumped from the boat onto the dock and followed Ken as he ran toward the shore. The passenger had entered the brush and was beginning to work his way up the entrance of a shallow gorge. His dark clothes made it difficult to see him. As soon as they were sure the passenger couldn't see them, Ken and Stacy moved quickly toward the fallen security officer.

They approached the guard, who was lying face up. They immediately noticed that a bullet had hit him just below his left eye. He had two more places on his chest that appeared to be wounds from the other two shots. The guard was dead! Ken signaled back at Captain Tim and Newton by shaking his head and pointing thumbs down. Then he motioned for them to go on to get help.

Captain Tim and Newton had quickly thrown another line to another dock anchor to secure the boat. They jumped off the boat and in a dead run, they went from the boat, along the shore, to the security office about one hundred and fifty yards away. Reaching the security office, they found a phone on the desk. Newton grabbed the phone and, not knowing the number, hit the zero button.

"Get security here to the dock fast. The dock security officer has been shot. Bring an ambulance. Hurry please! Come armed; there's a gunman around here somewhere!" yelled Newton.

The operator on the other end said, "Just a second. I'll transfer you to security at the main gate."

The voice on the other end answered: "Security. How may I help you?"

Newton repeated his urgent request and the officer, clearly shaken, held onto the phone but started barking orders to his fellow officers. Then he said, "We're on the way. Stay there. We'll need to talk to you when we get there." The officer hung up.

Captain Tim and Newton knew the main guardhouse was about eight miles away and the road was quite curvy along the coast road that avoided town. That meant it would be at least fifteen minutes before they could get to the dock. The ambulance, however, would be dispatched from town, and that was only five miles away and the roads were fairly straight. They guessed about seven minutes for the ambulance to arrive, but they already knew it was too late for the officer. They looked at each other and wondered what in the hell was going on.

Ken and Stacy moved past the dead officer toward the ridge where the passenger had disappeared. The terrain was getting steeper, and waist-high brush was getting thicker as they reached the side of the ridge. Tall evergreens and eucalyptus trees covered the top of the ridge. Stacy suggested they take the harder path up the side of the ridge instead of following the small ravine taken by the passenger.

Stacy said, "That bastard may be waiting up this draw and we don't want to walk right up on him without any weapons. Let's just slip to the side and see if we can follow him from a distance."

"Sounds good," replied Ken.

The ridge was about fifty feet high and, upon approaching the top, they slowed and moved cautiously by keeping cover with the tree trunks. They reached the top and began scanning the area for the passenger. The ravine was to their right, and it crookedly snaked uphill toward the golf club house but had several branch draws on each side. The passenger could be anywhere in the draw or its tributaries. They watched the field for a good ten minutes and saw nothing. The area just in front of them was a wheat field. Across the field, around four hundred yards away was an old fencerow with a line of eucalyptus trees.

"Should we go for the trees across the field and get a better viewpoint?" asked Stacy.

"Yeah, let's go for it, but stay low," answered Ken.

"Okay, but let's run. It's hard to hit a moving target," added Stacy.

They reached the back of the wheat field in eight minutes. Running bent over was not easy. They were exhausted and dropped down by the first tree they reached. There was

two-foot-high brush under the trees which, when they squat-
ted, gave them good cover. As they caught their breath, they
heard the sound of sirens back at the harbor.

"They must have gotten in touch with security," said Ken.

Suddenly, Ken nudged Stacy. There was the man, about
a quarter of a mile ahead, coming out of the left side of the
ravine and cutting across a field of young peach trees about
four feet high. He quickly disappeared into the orchard but
was headed at a fast pace toward the larger homes on the
even higher ridge at the eastern point of the colony. The
homes were almost a mile and a half away. Ken and Stacy
knew that to follow directly behind the man would be very
risky, so they decided to parallel the man and move to the
east also. They had no idea where the man was headed, but
by keeping an eye on him, perhaps they could later help
security locate him.

The peach orchard had small rolling hills. It was spring,
and the peach trees were in full bloom. Their pink blossoms
were dense, but Ken and Stacy could still see movement over
the tops of the trees from each hill. They topped the first hill
and again saw the man moving over the next hill. He was still
moving toward the East Point. The East Point homes were
only a half mile away from the man, and they were another
three-quarters of a mile away.

Ken said, "Stacy, let's tighten the distance. We need to
be closer so we don't lose him."

They picked up the pace and angled a bit more toward the
man. The next hilltop put them one hundred yards closer than

before. They were gaining. The man was still moving in the same direction, but his bag was definitely slowing him down.

"Stacy, what's he trying to do?" asked Ken.

"I don't know, Ken, but whatever it is, it's not good," answered Stacy as they continued to rush through the peach orchard.

Ken whispered, "If he was another terrorist, why wouldn't he be going toward the more concentrated number of people in town or at the condos? He's headed straight toward the large houses of the leaders and managers of the colony that are located on the seaside of the country club. What we do know is that this guy is a killer, he's headed toward those houses, and is likely intent on killing people there."

About three hundred yards from the homes, the peach orchard ended. The remaining distance was preserved natural land with large scattered oak trees that became denser as the tree preserve approached the large East Point homes. The largest homes were all along the seaside of a dead-end road that extended beyond the other homes scattered within the golf course to the north. Ken had been in the area before on one of his bike rides. He recalled that the biggest house was at the end of Secret Street and that it belonged to the Kents because the name was on the mailbox. It appeared that the man was headed toward that home.

Ken, being a former Marine, quickly knew that he had to go into action. Stacy had no military training.

"Stacy, I want you to go to the right and get about two hundred yards down the road and flag down the first security car that comes. Show them where the man has gone. If you don't see a security car, then get the first resident you can and call security. I'm going to slip in closer to this guy, and I believe I can best do this alone. Go now," said Ken.

Stacy took off in a direction just inside of the peach-orchard fence in a fast pace to the right, parallel to Secret Street.

Ken waited a few seconds; then he ran to the first tree, stopped, and checked to see where the man was. He continued to move from tree to tree, left of the man's path, but carefully picking his way closer.

Chapter 56
THE BREAK-IN

Jay Cameron was beginning to tire as he approached the Kent house. He stopped behind a large oak tree across the street from No. 1 Secret Street. He reached into his bag, pulled out a bottle of water, and quickly drank all of it. His heart still racing; he wondered if Duncan and Nellie were home. It was getting dark, and surely they should be home. He'd chosen Saturday in hopes that they would be there. His speedboat charter got him as close as possible to the Kent home. The agreement with the speedboat owner was that he would return to the dock area at daylight the next day. He hadn't planned on there being an armed guard. He had to shoot him, or the guard would have stopped him from accomplishing his objective.

He took a deep breath, reached into his bag, and pulled out a .38-caliber revolver pistol. He carefully reloaded by replacing the three bullets used to kill the guard at the docks. He put the rest of the box of bullets into his pocket. Jay took off his black hoodie and placed it into his bag. Placing the gun in his belt behind his back, he left his bag behind the tree and walked in a casual, unassuming stroll across the street toward the Kent home. Walking to the front door, Jay wondered if it was locked. *Probably not,* he thought. With a soft click of the handle, he found the door opened easily. He slipped inside. He could hear some noise in the kitchen.

Nellie enjoyed cooking and had promised to make some homemade fried apple pies for dessert. She'd already cooked the apples down and was rolling the dough out and filling the taco-shaped pies with the apple filling. She patiently pinched the edges to seal the dough and keep the apple filling inside. She could fry four at a time in her pan and had planned on making a dozen this evening. It was Duncan's favorite dessert.

Duncan had been unusually busy all day, meeting with the prime contractor and wrapping up some work that was being completed outside of the colony for the dock rebuild. As it got dark, he left his office on Gold Circle and started the fifteen-minute drive home. He'd called Nellie as he left and knew dinner would be ready about the time he reached home. He was anxious to kick back in his leather recliner and have a nice glass of New Zealand wine. He knew that a nice meal of corn soup, salad, and lamb chops awaited him shortly.

Nellie placed the last pie of the second batch of apple pies in the skillet, when suddenly, from the kitchen entrance right behind her, a deep voice suddenly shouted, "Where is Duncan?" Nellie looked up and saw a stranger with a gun in his hand. Her reaction was a loud scream as she jumped backward, dropping the last pie into the hot cooking oil.

"What are you doing in here?" she shouted, still shaking from the sudden shock.

"I want to see Duncan right now—where is he?" said Jay.

"H . . . he's at work," answered Nellie.

Jay pointed his gun at Nellie and demanded, "Get over here in the living room, and sit down."

She moved toward the living room slowly, keeping her eyes on Jay. As she took a seat on the couch, she heard Duncan's SUV pull into the garage.

Stacy was moving along the peach tree edges and was about to head through the trees toward the street when he saw a black SUV headed toward the end of the street. He broke out of the peach trees in a dead run, waving his arms, but the driver of the SUV didn't see him. Stacy continued to the road and onto the sixth house from the end of the street and rang the doorbell. No one answered, so he headed to the next house. He had to find someone—and fast.

From two hundred yards away, Ken saw the man walk up to the front door of the Kents' house and walk inside. He knew that now was the time to move fast. He ran full speed to the side of the house and eased around to the back. He looked in the window and saw no one in the room. Checking the sliding patio door, he quickly slipped into the house. It was the master bedroom. The smell of hot cooking oil caught his attention. He moved quietly through the room and down a long hall toward the smell. He needed a weapon fast, and knew the kitchen offered the opportunity for a good knife. As he moved down the hall toward the cooking oil smell and eased into the kitchen, he heard a man's voice: "Hey, honey—I'm home." It was obviously Duncan Kent.

Jay continued to point his gun at Nellie as Duncan walked into the room. Surprise and shock shook Duncan's whole body.

"What are you doing here, Jay?" Duncan then saw Jay's gun as he turned the gun toward him. "Nellie, are you all right?" Duncan added.

"I'm okay—just a little shook up right now," answered Nellie.

"Get on the couch, Duncan," demanded Jay as he waved his gun at him. Duncan slowly moved to the couch and sat beside Nellie. "Duncan, you ruined my life, and I'm here to kill you and your wife. I want to know why you did this to me. I gave you all that money for your company. Tell me! Why?"

Duncan answered, "Jay, you don't want to do this."

"Oh, yes, I do want to, and I will, but first tell me why!" demanded Jay as he walked over to Nellie and put the gun to her head.

"No, stop, I'll tell you. Just take the gun off of Nellie, please." Jay slowly backed up and pointed the gun at Duncan.

"Okay, talk now, you son of a bitch!" yelled Jay.

Duncan looked at Jay and began to speak, "Jay, you stole my genetic designs. I never liked you after that. I think of you as a crook . . . a thief. But, then you kept calling, trying to buy me out. I'd been considering selling to someone because of my age. It loathed me to sell to you, but you were the only viable offer at the time, and I wanted to sell out and move here, to finish my life and spend my money on good people."

Duncan thought he needed to be really careful here so as not to appear that he'd done anything deliberately.

"Go on!" demanded Jay as he waved his gun.

"But, when you made me an offer, my latest genetic improvements hadn't been checked out as to their effect on humans or animals. The older designs were okay and would be fine for the sale of Grainteck. During the negotiations, and again during due-diligence documents, I told you not to use the new designs until evaluations of the effects on humans and animals were done. But . . . no . . . Jay, you went ahead and put them out onto the market without any testing whatsoever. So now, Jay, you can't blame *me* for that. None of it was my fault."

From his position in the hallway, Ken could hear everything being said in the living room. He knew the man's name was Jay and he was here to kill the Kents. He slowly eased into the kitchen, taking care to avoid being seen from the adjacent living room. He saw a wooden knife block on the island cabinet and took out the two largest knives. One was twelve inches long, and the other was ten inches long. The four apple pies frying in the hot grease were beginning to burn, and the smell and smoke was starting to roll out of the pan. Ken needed a diversion. He increased the burner heat to make it burn faster.

Jay, having been totally focused on getting Duncan, began looking at Nellie and suddenly realized that he could have some fun with Duncan before he killed him. A strange look came over his face that gave the appearance of confusion and anger at the same time.

"Get over here, Nellie. Take your clothes off. You know, you're pretty hot looking for an older woman," said Jay, waving his gun at Nellie's head.

Duncan responded, "Jay, calm down. You don't want to do this. Let Nellie go. She's done nothing to you. Let her go, and deal with me as you want. Come on—let her walk out right now."

The smell of burning cooking oil began to drift into the living room.

"Jay, you've never killed anyone before," said Duncan in an attempt to dissuade Jay from his intended crime.

"Bullshit again, Duncan. You don't know me. I killed both of my parents years ago with a bomb in their plane, and I killed a guard down at the docks about an hour ago. No one is going anywhere. And, I'm going to kill you and Nellie. What is that smell?" asked Jay.

"Oh, no," exclaimed Nellie. "My apple pies are burning. I need to turn the burner off; it's going to catch on fire!"

Jay looked confused, but then he wanted to continue hurting Duncan before he killed him. He wanted him to hurt badly. Shooting him at that moment would spare Duncan of the pain he wanted him to feel. He could kill them both later once he'd had his fun. "Okay, get up, both of you, and go into the kitchen. You first, Nellie. Any funny moves, and I shoot both of you right now."

They slowly walked into the kitchen, with Jay keeping his distance but keeping his gun aimed at Duncan's back. When Nellie reached the stove, she noticed that the frying pan was gone. Someone had moved it. The burner was still on. She moved closer to the stove, confused, wondering where the pan was. Duncan was following closely behind her. Jay had moved close to the island cabinet and was looking beyond Nellie at the stove.

Suddenly, from behind the island cabinet, Ken jumped up, holding the frying pan in his right hand and both knives in his left hand. Stunned, Jay swung to look at him. As Jay turned, Ken slung the pan of hot grease and pies straight at Jay's face. As the hot grease hit Jay's eyes and face, he screamed in instant pain. The empty pan hit Jay in the chest, pushing his gun to the right. Jay began firing at random as he continued screaming. Jay's eyes were burned, and he couldn't see. In the same move of throwing the hot grease, Ken leaped on top of the island. With one knife in each hand and with a single lunge, he dove straight down at Jay. With both hands high above his head, he plunged both knives at the same time into each side of Jay's neck. Ken fell on top of Jay, knocking him to the floor. Ken left both knives in Jay's neck as he reached down and grabbed the gun. Jay had gone limp, and the gun was easily taken away. Ken reached up and handed it to Duncan and said. "Take it, I've been shot, call—." Suddenly, Ken felt dizzy; then he passed out.

Duncan quickly laid the gun onto the cabinet and rolled Ken onto his back. Ken had two blood spots on his lower left stomach and another just below his left shoulder. Duncan held pressure on the wounds as Nellie grabbed towels to help. Nellie heard the front door opening and ran to the entry to find four security officers with their guns drawn and looking for an intruder.

"He's dead!" yelled Nellie. "But the man who saved us is shot. Get an ambulance here! Hurry, please!" One of the officers grabbed his belt radio and called for an ambulance. The other three officers ran into the kitchen and quickly began assisting Duncan with Ken's injuries.

The ambulance arrived and swung into the *porte-cochère*. Two paramedics ran inside and took over the aid for Ken from the officers. Ken was still unconscious and bleeding badly. Standing beside the ambulance was Stacy as Ken was lifted inside. Stacy was visibly shaken but was allowed to ride in the ambulance with Ken to the hospital.

Chapter 57
HOSPITAL EMERGENCY

The situation with Ken was critical. The short ride to the hospital was scary, with Ken's blood pressure getting down to seventy over forty. The bleeding hadn't stopped, and he'd lost a lot of blood. Upon reaching the hospital, the emergency room team swung into action. The paramedics had called ahead, and the doctors were prepared and waiting for Ken. He was given blood and taken to surgery within minutes.

Stacy called Stormy and Audria and told them to tell Ilene that Ken had been shot and was in the hospital. They weren't sure how to break the news to her. There was no easy way.

Audria and Stormy walked quickly to Ilene's condo. Audria knocked on the door. Ilene opened the door, and she could see the tears in both their eyes. "What's wrong?" Ilene asked almost immediately.

"Ilene, Ken's been shot. He's alive, but he's in intensive care at the hospital. We need to go there, now."

Ilene immediately looked shocked. She couldn't talk for a moment as both Audria and Stormy hugged her. Then suddenly, she started crying and said, "What happened?"

"They think it was another terrorist who came in at the docks as they were returning from the fishing trip. Ken and Stacy went after him. Ken got him, but got shot," said Stormy.

Ilene caught her breath and wiped the tears from her eyes. "Will one of you stay with David and Jan?"

"I will," replied Stormy. "Audria, you go with Ilene over to the hospital. Go, I'll handle it! Ya'll go now," demanded Stormy.

Newton and Captain Tim had heard the siren and made their way to the hospital after dealing with the murder at the dock. Everyone gathered in the waiting room outside the emergency room and waited. Stacy told of their effort to follow the killer and the heroic effort that Ken had made to prevent the killing of the Kents. Ilene was in tears and paced the floor. Audria would console her each time she'd break down.

After about thirty minutes, Duncan and Nellie Kent walked into the waiting room. They immediately went to Ilene and consoled her.

"We're so sorry this has happened. We're with you and wanting Ken to be okay. He did a brave thing by attacking an armed killer. He saved our lives. If there is anything we can do, just ask."

"Thank you," responded Ilene.

It seemed like hours had passed, and everyone continually paced or sat around the waiting room in anticipation of some word on the results of the surgery. It had been two hours since

Ken had gone into surgery, and no word. Duncan asked the ER nurse to see if she could find out how it was going. Within a minute, Dr. A. J. McDonald walked into the waiting room, still in his surgery scrubs, and asked for Ilene. Dr. McDonald knew Ilene from her work in Dr. Davis's office.

"Ilene, I want to give you an update on Ken," he said with a calm voice. Everyone immediately focused their attention on Dr. McDonald and held their breath.

"Ken came through the surgery very well. He's not awake yet but is being moved into the recovery room right now. We removed two bullets. One bullet had damaged his intestinal wall and lodged in his back. Fortunately, it didn't damage his spinal cord. There was a lot of damage, and we'll have to watch that wound damage for any internal infections.

"The second bullet had penetrated his left lung and stopped in his shoulder blade. His left lung is deflated and will take some time to mend. The current risk is blood clots. We had to give him two units of blood. He should be showing some improvement after a couple of days. He'll be in a lot of pain, and it will be difficult for him to breathe.

"We have him on oxygen to make that easier. Until then, we'll have him on intravenous antibiotics and painkillers. He has two tubes installed to drain any blood and fluids.

"If you'd like, Ilene, you can come into recovery and be with Ken when he wakes up. Since you're a nurse, you may stay as long as you like."

Ilene stepped up to Dr. McDonald; he put his arm around her shoulder and escorted her down the hall. As he walked Ilene down the hallway, he whispered, "My wife,

Salina, would be happy to help with your kids if you need her. I called her just before the surgery to let her know I would be late. She remembered keeping them for you back in Destin."

Duncan offered to have some food brought over if anyone wanted to continue waiting in the room, but everyone declined the food. Everyone in the waiting room except Duncan and Nellie slowly began to drift out and head toward home. It had been a tough day, and everyone was exhausted. Before they left the room, Duncan told everyone not to come in to work tomorrow.

Nellie and Duncan agreed they couldn't leave until after Ken woke up and they could see him and thank him. They waited another two hours and at midnight were allowed to see Ken. He was still quite groggy and weak, drifting in and out of sleep. Duncan stood next to Ken's bed and touched his right shoulder.

"Ken, I cannot say 'Thank you' enough for saving our lives today. You're going to get well. I want you to know that you don't need to worry about anything but getting well. I will personally see to it that your family is taken care of with anything they need."

Ken nodded but didn't say anything because of the oxygen mask on his face. As Duncan backed away, Nellie took his place next to Ken. With tears in her eyes, she leaned over and whispered in his ear. "Thank you so much for saving us. You're my hero and will be forever. Thank you, thank you, thank you!" Ken gave a small nod to acknowledge hearing her. Having been able to say "Thank you" and feeling better that Ken was stable, they left the room. Ilene was planning to stay overnight.

Duncan instructed the intensive care nurse supervisor to get a bed into the room for Ilene, so that she wouldn't have to sit in the small chair in the room, and to get her some food, just in case she decided to eat something.

Leaving the room, Nellie commented to Duncan, "Honey, with the bloody situation at home, let's spend the night at one of the office overnight suites. It's just down the street. It's definitely going to be a very restless night. That way we can be back here early to check on Ken and Ilene."

"I think that's a great idea. The room is stocked with everything we would need. I'll have the home cleaned up tomorrow, unless the sheriff has taped off our home as a crime scene," said Duncan.

Chapter 58
RECOVERY

Dawn came slowly for Ilene. She hadn't slept. Newton and Stormy had kept David and Jan at their house. Ken was barely awake when Duncan and Nellie were at the hospital the night before, he couldn't remember any of the details of their visit. Throughout the night, Ken would wake up for a few minutes and look around. Ilene was sitting by his bed and would grab his hand to let him know she was there. Then, he would drift back off to sleep. Morning in the hospital intensive care unit started early, with lots of noise as the nurses changed shifts.

Ken's blood pressure had improved over night, and he was able to talk once a nose tube replaced the oxygen mask. However, he was still very weak. With his IV still going, he had no appetite, but his breakfast was brought anyway. Ilene tried to feed him some, but he would only drink some of the milk. At 9, the day nurse came to get him up and have him walk some. Ilene knew that was necessary to help prevent pneumonia. Ken made the slow walk around the ward just fine, and then it was time for a bandage change. Ken started to complain that the nurses just wouldn't let him rest. That told Ilene he was going to be all right.

At 2 that afternoon, Audria and Stormy came in with David and Jan to visit. As they headed out, they pushed Ilene to take David and Jan and go home to get some rest. She reluctantly agreed.

Ken had visitors every day. Stacy, Newton, Audria, and Stormy took turns staying with him. Many of his coworkers would drop by to check on him. Duncan and Nellie had visited morning and evening every day. Security had brought in the New Zealand sheriff and gotten Ken's statement. They were amazed that Ken had managed to overtake the gun-wielding man and kill him with two kitchen knives. Ken explained that his marine training and service in the Middle East had honed his skills with a knife and he had actually been in hand-to-hand combat before.

The sheriff told Ken, "That was mighty brave of you, Mr. Wallace. What you did saved Mr. and Mrs. Kent. I know everyone here is proud of you. You're a real hero. And, I know you're going to be fully recovered soon."

Ken managed a slight smile and replied, "Thank you, sir. It had to be done, Sheriff, and there was no one else to do it. I got the job by default." Ilene, standing at Ken's side, was so proud of him.

After four days, Ken was ready to leave the hospital and go home. He felt he'd been in the bed about as long as he could stand. He was being released to go home but could not go back to work until he received a full okay to work from

Dr. McDonald, who suggested that it would likely be six weeks. Stacy and Newton dropped by to check on him early that morning. As they walked in the door, Ken looked very serious.

The two walked over to his bed and Ken asked, "All right, you assholes, I've been thinking. Did ya'll eat my share of the fish that we caught the other day or what? I haven't seen or heard a word, and I think ya'll might be holding out on me and taking advantage of me in my sad condition."

"Yep, we ate 'em all," said Newton.

"Well, ya'll better go back fishing, 'cause I want my share. I'm going home today, and I want my damn fish!" said Ken as he started to laugh.

"Well, Mr. Ninja Man, I can tell you are indeed getting well. And, I also want you to know that I thought I was in pretty good shape until you drug my ass for three miles up the ravine and through the damn peach orchard. I thought I was going to die," laughed Stacy.

"By the way, can we help you get ready to leave today? Can we get you a ride to the condo?" asked Newton.

"No thanks. Ilene is coming to get me around noon today. Thanks for checking on me. I'll see ya'll back at the condo. Now get out of here, and go find my fish. I want to grill some of those filets this evening when I get home."

"Yes sir, boss! We're going fish hunting. But, just for the record, it wasn't us but probably Captain Tim," said Stacy as they walked out of the room.

Later that evening, Stacy showed up at Ken's condo with seventy-five pounds of filleted, wrapped, and frozen tuna. Ilene barely had room in the freezer for it even after keeping four packages out for grilling. Stacy explained that Captain Tim had cleaned the fish, wrapped it up, and put it in his freezer.

"Captain Tim was still bitching about having to clean the fish. He said to tell you that you'd do anything to get out of cleaning fish. And that you owed him for all of the freezer paper he had to use, 'cause that was not part of the charter deal."

"We have got to come up with something to get him on real soon. It's our turn to retaliate," laughed Ken.

Chapter 59
ON THE MEND

Ken was feeling much better within a week of leaving the hospital, but it still hurt to move his left arm and he still had pain in his abdomen when he walked for more than a minute or two. He was able to move around the condo, but he was starting to get bored. He'd been back to see Dr. McDonald the day before, and tomorrow, he'd begin therapy to improve mobility in his shoulder. He'd have to do that daily for five more weeks and then, hopefully, he'd be allowed to go back to work.

Chapter 60
THE HOUSE CLEANING

With all of the authorities' investigations finally complete, the Kents were allowed back in their home. They chose to send in a cleaning crew before moving back from the management suite. It only took a day, and the home had been cleaned thoroughly when they arrived. Duncan and Nellie drove to Ken's condo and visited him before they moved back. They were happy to see that Ken was recovering nicely and was off of most of his pain medications.

Arriving home, they attempted to get back to normal, but each time they walked into the kitchen, they had uneasy feelings and flashbacks of the very traumatic event. At 5 o'clock, they settled into their den, and Duncan poured himself a tall glass of Jack and Coke. Nellie had a glass of tea that she'd just brewed. It was time to get back to normal. After a few sips on his drink, Duncan began to speak.

"Nellie, we have to do something for Ken and Ilene. Ken saved us from certain death. He's a brave man. I've been giving this some thought, and I want us to have them over for dinner when Ken is well."

Nellie added, "I think that's a wonderful idea. But, I think that Stacy, Newton, and Captain Tim and their wives should be invited also. All of them were a part of the heroic efforts that day."

"I agree. Let's do it," said Duncan.

Chapter 61
THE INVITATION

It had been eight weeks since Ken's injury. An invitation from the Kents arrived in Wednesday's mail. Ken had been making a good recovery and had returned to work two weeks earlier. It was so different here. With no insurance, the doctor didn't have to sign a release. He just had to say, "Go back to work." There were no bills and no co-pays to worry about. How different. How sweet.

Ilene picked up the mail at the town mail center right after grocery shopping. She opened the mail when she arrived at the condo. The invitation was in a fancy beige envelope with a raised emblem of a green kiwi bird standing on a bar of gold bullion. It was the colony emblem. Opening the envelope, she read:

On Saturday, September 20
At 6:00p.m.
Mr. and Mrs. Duncan Kent
at their home located at
No. 1 Secret Street
Request the presence of
Mr. and Mrs. Ken Wallace

For hors d'oeuvres
Refreshments
Dinner
and Conversation
RSVP

Ken had a follow-up appointment after work at the doctor's office and made it to the condo just ten minutes after Ilene had opened the invitation. Picking up the invitation on the dining table, he read it as Ilene told him what it was.

"Wow. This is nice, Ilene. The big man has invited us to his house," he said with a smile. "It's not like I haven't been there before. The last time I was there, I broke in and ruined their fried apple pies!" he laughed.

276

Ilene added, "I think this will be a bit more of a fun event. It sounds fancy, though, and I don't know what to wear."

"Why don't you call Nellie, confirm our attendance, and, while talking to her, find out the appropriate dress code?" said Ken.

"Good idea. It's only three days away, so we'd better get a sitter lined up. I think I'll call Stormy," said Ilene.

Ilene called Stormy and asked her if she would sit for her Saturday. Stormy answered, "I can't, Ilene—we got an invitation, too."

"Oh. Huh. I wonder if Audria got an invitation? I'll call her." Hanging up from the call to Stormy, Ilene phoned Audria. "Audria, did you get an invitation today?"

"Sure did," answered Audria. "We're all excited."

"We are too, and so is Stormy," replied Ilene.

"I wonder how many were invited?" asked Audria.

"I hope it isn't too many. I'd be happy with just us three couples," added Ilene.

"Me, too. Let me know if you hear more. I'll talk to you tomorrow," said Audria.

Chapter 62
THE DINNER

Saturday came quickly. The Wallaces began to get ready three hours before the scheduled start time of 6. Ken could never understand why women took so long to get ready. At most, he could be ready in forty-five minutes. Since Ken could get ready so fast, he'd been assigned the function of getting the kids prepared for the babysitter, who was coming over at 5. Ken dared not rush Ilene, as that would likely result in a fate worse than his recent bullet wounds.

Ilene had found out when she called Nellie that it was going to be on the dressy side. For men, a coat was appropriate, and ties were optional but recommended. It was nice to get dressed up for a change. Audria and Stormy were all excited, too, and all three had gone shopping and bought new dresses for the event. Ilene found that all of her current dresses were a bit tight. During Ilene's conversation with Nellie, she'd shared the guest list with her. She already knew that the Baltzegars and the Bakers would be there, but also on the guest list were other people involved in the events surrounding Jay Cameron's attack.

The list included Captain Tim, his wife Donna and Dr. A. J. McDonald and his wife, Salina. It was great that the Kents had invited Dr. McDonald since he'd been critical in saving Ken's life. Ken and Ilene knew Salina from the initial trip to Destin for their interview, and Ilene was eager to see her again. She'd seen Salina around town and in the school. Salina was always so busy with the children that getting any quality time with her was almost impossible. Ilene had heard so much about Captain Tim's adventures with the Gang of Three, as they now called themselves, that she couldn't wait to meet him and his wife. The main topic between the guys so far had been wondering what food and liquor would be there. Ilene thought, *They are such men.*

Finally, Ilene was ready. She looked beautiful in a strapped cherry-red, low-cut dress with the diamond necklace and earrings that Ken had bought for her birthday. Ken was wearing a blue sports coat, and he was actually wearing a tie. Ilene thought Ken looked so handsome when he dressed up. She'd bought the tie for him in town, and, fittingly, it was bright blue with the green colony kiwi bird standing on a bar of gold. It had been so long since Ken had worn a tie it took him ten minutes to get it tied right. They made a very attractive couple when they were all dressed up.

Their twelve-year-old babysitter, Catherine Lemoine, arrived right on time at 5. She lived in the same complex, so no real travel was necessary, and that made it nice. Ilene knew her mother, and she'd told Ilene she would check in on them from time to time. Catherine took David and Jan into the den and started playing one of their games with them.

Nellie told Ilene that they would have drivers pick up the attendees at the front of their particular buildings between 5:45 and 6:00. As they walked out to the entrance of their condo complex, they saw one of the colony's black GMCs waiting out front. The driver was dressed as a chauffeur, and she opened the rear car door for Ilene and Ken.

The nice, slow drive through the country club to the Kents' home was made without any talking. Perhaps it was the excitement or anticipation of the coming event. Past the golf course, they turned right onto Secret Street and drove to the end. As they arrived at the Kents', the home was lit from the outside with hidden floodlights in the flowerbeds shining up on the walls. All the trees in the yard had lights hidden near their base that shined upward, illuminating the trees. It was so very pretty.

Ilene finally spoke as they pulled under the *porte-cochère*. "Ken, I want a house like this."

"Sure, I'll start construction next week," laughed Ken.

After exiting the car, the driver drove away, perhaps to pick up another guest. They held hands as they walked across the slate driveway and stepped up to the front door. Ken rang the doorbell.

Through the frosted glass doors, they could see the figures of Duncan and Nellie as they approached the door. The door opened, and the Kents welcomed them to their home. They walked through the massive foyer as Duncan led them into the bar area, adjacent to the kitchen, where Duncan introduced them to Jon-Michael.

"Jon-Michael is our butler; he will be taking care of you tonight." Duncan already had some type of mixed drink in his hand, and Nellie had a glass of Chardonnay.

"What would you like, ma'am?" asked Jon-Michael.

"I'll have a glass of orange juice," answered Ilene.

Ken said, "What do you mean, Ilene? You know you like that good Colony Chardonnay," holding her glass into the air. "Come on—enjoy the night," pushed Ken.

Ilene looked over at Ken and sheepishly, smiled, shrugged her shoulders, and said, "Maybe later, sweetheart."

Nellie, the people person, was watching Ilene's every move. "Oh, my God, Ilene—you're pregnant," exclaimed Nellie.

"Uh . . . uh, well, yes, ma'am—I just found out yesterday. Dr. Carolyn confirmed it while I was at work with her," smiled Ilene.

"I'm so happy for you," replied Nellie.

Ken was standing there beside both ladies with his mouth open and a shocked look on his face. "You . . . you weren't going to tell me?" asked Ken with a shocked smile on his face.

"I thought this was as good a time as any," she said and continued with the big smile across her face. Ken gave Ilene a warm hug and a kiss on the cheek. Duncan couldn't resist the opportunity.

"Well, Ken, I thought you were all crippled up, and I was feeling sorry for you, but it looks like you've been getting in some additional physical therapy," grinned Duncan as he raised his glass for a toast. Then he said, "To Ilene and Ken's upcoming new addition."

Duncan loved to pick on folks he liked and couldn't let this opportunity pass to have some fun. Duncan laughed, as he patted Ken on the back.

"Ouch, watch the shoulder," exclaimed Ken. Ken figured he could dish it out, too. He was about to tell Duncan he was going to have to move into a four-bedroom condo, to accommodate the new addition. But, just then, the doorbell rang, and Duncan and Nellie left to greet the next guests. Ken asked Jon-Michael for a Jack and Coke in a tall glass. Then, as Jon-Michael started to pour, Ken said with a smile, "Better make that a double—it looks like I am drinking for two tonight."

Walking in were Captain Tim and Donna, as well as Newton and Stormy. As they came in and were escorted to the bar, another suv pulled up with Dr. McDonald, Salina, Stacy, and Audria. The dinner party was about to begin. Jon-Michael was busy filling drink glasses and tending to the hors d'oeuvres.

Everyone was dressed very nicely. The ladies had collaborated and looked quite stunning. They'd all been to the hair salon and visited Samantha Crowder. They used her not only for the great work she could do with their hair, but Samantha would always keep them in stitches laughing and carrying on about her vibrant life chasing those two hundred single men.

The Gang of Three had planned the day before on what they were going to do that night to get back at Captain Tim for the cowboy-boot trick.

"Hey, Captain Tim—I almost didn't recognize you without your normal fish cologne on," jabbed Newton.

Stacy drew fire next. "Man, what is going on? This must be an imposter. Donna, did you secretly replace Tim? This guy smells like a normal person. It just can't be Captain Tim."

Ken added, "Glad to meet you, Tim. You must work in the landscaping department, because you have that flowery smell still lingering from today's work."

They kept kidding him that he actually cleaned up pretty good and didn't have his usual fish smell and that they were having a hard time recognizing him without his "fish cologne" on. Donna had told Captain Tim that he had to be nice for the evening, so every time Tim would start to come back with a wisecrack, Donna would jab him in the side. Tim would wince and say with a smile, "I'm so sorry, dear. I know I promised to be good, but, it's just so hard with these low-life, dirty, rotten scumbags. I'll get you guys later!"

Donna was about five foot five with brown hair and quite petite. She was a real extrovert and always put her two cents in on almost every topic. While Tim was the captain of the boat, it was very clear that Donna was the captain of Tim!

"Donna, I remember your name. You were the personnel manager who sent us the letter to come to interview in Destin," said Ilene as they were introduced by Nellie.

"Oh, yes, I remember, too. But there were so many families being hired at the time, it does get a bit blurry. I'm so glad it worked out for you. Tim is always talking about the Gang of Three and how much fun he has fishing with them. And, what Ken did saving Duncan and Nellie was so brave. You should be so proud of him," said Donna.

"I'm very proud of him," answered Ilene.

Duncan enjoyed watching the guys pick at Tim and the fun they were all having at Tim's expense. He could't help but stir the coals a bit. He smiled as he told the guys as they huddled up and verbally attacked Tim, "Guys, I wanted us to have fish tonight so Tim wouldn't feel out of place."

Tim just turned red with embarrassment and said, "Now look guys—ya'll be nice tonight, 'cause I have to, or Donna will kill me."

A few steps away from the bar, Jon-Michael had set up a table that was covered with hors d'oeuvres circling a large fresh flower arrangement.

The conversation and drinks flowed for more than an hour. Salina, Audria, Stormy, and Nellie were all excited about Ilene's announcement. Everyone was surprised that Salina had just had her fourth child only three months before. She was well known around town as the one who loved children the most. She and A. J. planned to have more. They all gathered in typical women group fashion and talked about kids, clothes, and, of course, their husbands.

Duncan asked the guys to step out onto the back patio, where he had a nice firepit going. Jon-Michael would drift in and out, bringing trays of hors d'oeuvres and drinks to keep everyone refreshed. The beautiful patio was paved with flagstone pavers. Stone benches circled the crackling fire and were covered with soft, tan-colored sitting cushions. The lighting in the trees was just breathtaking. A slightly cool breeze was drifting in from the sea, and they could hear the waves breaking on the rocky coast below the homes on Secret Street.

"Duncan, you have a beautiful place here; thanks for inviting us here tonight," said Ken.

"Thanks, Ken. It's been a real challenge to build all of this in just three years. But, it's been lots of fun. I've been very happy to see all of my hard work helping people and building a complete community with nothing but opportunity for everyone," replied Duncan. "I've said this before, but I cannot thank all of you guys enough for your courageous efforts that ended up saving Nellie's and my lives. You're the kind of people I like to be around and why I started this project.

"In just a short time, we'll be reaching our three-year milestone. At that time, I plan to share with all of you more details about our project. I trust that you will want to continue on for your ten-year contract."

"We love it here," said Stacy.

"It's awesome here," said Tim.

Everyone raised their glasses and said, "To Duncan and Nellie. Thank you."

Upon finishing the toast, Duncan exclaimed, "Guys, it is almost 7:30 now, so let's go in, get another cocktail, and see if dinner is ready."

Just before walking into the house, Duncan gathered the men at the back door and said, "As you all probably know, this whole project has been funded by my personal resources. I have the unique ability to do just about anything if money can buy it. However, money cannot buy everything. My old saying is that the second-best things in life cost money. That implies that the first and best items are free. But, then the first and best things are indeed real, and I often wonder if it just might be possible to buy those things. Those things would include love, safety, security, independence, peace, life, and liberty, to name a few.

"The United States' founding fathers tried to figure that out and knew that it couldn't be guaranteed and inserted the word *pursuit* of happiness into the Constitution for that reason.

"Perhaps that question is the driving force in my efforts to build this place and to research whether there are any possible gains on the first and best items. I certainly hope there are.

"Oh, well, I didn't want to talk too much tonight, so let's go inside."

Dinner was indeed ready, and Duncan had spared no expense to show his appreciation to everyone over dinner. He had brought in the colony premier surf and turf restaurant to cook and serve dinner. The menu was a chef's salad followed by filet mignon and king crab legs with drawn butter. Along with the surf and turf, there were mashed potatoes and gravy, sautéed zucchini, and sautéed portabella mushrooms.

The conversations over dinner were light, with everyone talking about their activities and families. After the main course, the caterer brought in a dessert of strawberry shortcake and ice cream. Everyone was stuffed.

After dessert, Nellie excused herself and came back moments later with five wrapped and bowed gift boxes about six inches square. She said, "I have here a token of our appreciation for all of you and hope that you'll enjoy this for many years to come and remember that we do love you." She handed them out individually to each of the ladies. "Please open them."

Everyone began to unwrap the packages and open the box. Inside was a green glass kiwi standing on a real four-ounce block of pure gold. It was the colony symbol, but this was the first time they had ever seen one in three dimensions and especially standing on a real block of 24-karat gold. They were just beautiful.

Then, Duncan took control of the conversation and said, "Friends, I want to do something special for all of you as a token of our appreciation. If you're okay with it, I'd like to put each of you on the top of the list for a new home here in the country club. We're a little bit ahead of schedule, and you can be involved in the custom design and location of your new home. I'd expect you would be in your new home in about six months. All of our custom homes have a minimum of five bedrooms and five thousand square feet. Will that work for you?"

"Oh, yes," echoed everyone. Ken thought, *This is so awesome.* Everyone stood up and started hugging and thanking Duncan and Nellie. Audria, Stormy, Salina, and Donna were all crying with joy.

Salina said, "My hands are shaking. I'm so happy."

Once everyone was moving toward the door, Duncan thanked each couple for coming and wished them well for the evening. He gave all of the ladies a hug and shook hands with all of the men.

As Duncan shook hands with Ken, he quietly whispered to Ken, "I want you to come by the office and see me Monday morning at 9. I need to talk to you about something."

"Okay, I'll see you at nine o'clock," replied Ken. He wondered what this was about. Duncan had not mentioned this during the presence of the other guests, so Ken thought that it must be something personal.

Three chauffeured SUVs were waiting at the *porte-cochère* for everyone. They left with Duncan and Nellie waving them goodbye from their front door. Ken and Ilene were alone in one of the SUVs as they had been when they came. Driving back, they felt so happy. They were going to have another child, and they were going to have a brand-new, custom home for their growing family. Things had certainly changed for the better, and they were so thankful for Duncan and Nellie for making it all happen.

Ken whispered to Ilene, "Honey, I just don't think there's anything else that I could possibly need now. We struggled for so long before and were going nowhere, and now, just three years later, we're on top of the world with a bright future, or, should I say, on the bottom of the world?" They laughed, and then he gave her a long kiss.

After they arrived home, Ken decided to tell Ilene about the private comment Duncan had made.

"Ilene, Duncan asked me to come to his office Monday morning at 9:00, but he didn't say what it was about. I can't imagine what it is. I'm very curious. What could it be?"

Ilene thought for a moment. "Maybe it's some kind of bravery award, or maybe some type of promotion?"

"Well, if it's a promotion, that would usually come from my boss, Gene Winfree, so it must not be that. It could be a move to a different job here. I just don't know. My brain is overloaded trying to guess," said Ken.

"You'll find out soon, Ken, because it's now midnight, and we'd better get some sleep." With that, they retired for the night.

Chapter 63
THE MEETING
WITH DUNCAN

Morning came slowly as Ken had tossed and turned all night. Was it all the food and alcohol the night before, or was it his brain working overtime on his meeting with Duncan? He decided it was probably both.

It was Sunday, and Ilene was off work. He tiptoed around to let everyone sleep. He paced the floor, read the paper—anything to relieve his mind of what the meeting would be about. When everyone woke up, they decided to go out for breakfast and spend the day in the park. After what seemed like an eternity, the day was finally over, and it was time to get a good night's rest.

Ken awoke with a rush. Finally, it was Monday. Getting ready, he decided to dress in tan slacks, a long-sleeved maroon shirt, and a black sports coat. He wouldn't wear a tie, as that was never done in the colony except on special formal occasions, such as dinner with the Kents. He had coffee and buttered toast for breakfast; then he eased out of the condo at 8:30 and walked through the park into town.

It was another day of wonderful New Zealand weather. An early-morning fog had drifted in from the sea, giving the town an eerie look. People were out for their morning walks, and the fog made everyone appear as blurry creatures from some distant planet.

As Ken reached the bank building on Gold Circle, he couldn't help but wonder about the reason for the meeting. He liked his job at the power plant. His community-service work had been fun, too, as he got to wire homes that were being built and work on the project computers and servers. It was fun to do some hands-on work. What if Duncan offered him a different job? Would he really want that? Ken walked into the bank and directly to the elevator. He knew Duncan was on the top floor, but Ken had never been on any floor beyond the first. He didn't know what to expect.

The elevator stopped on the sixth floor, and Ken stepped into the lush office area. He walked to the receptionist and asked to see Duncan. She asked him to take a seat in the adjacent waiting area. There were three other people in the waiting area. Ken greeted them with a nod and soft "Hello." They were dressed in coat and ties, so they were most likely salesmen from some New Zealand companies trying to sell something to the project.

After ten minutes, Duncan's secretary, Debbie, walked into the waiting room and asked for Ken Wallace. She escorted Ken into Duncan's office, offered him coffee or water, and, after Ken declined, she left the room.

"Welcome, Ken—have a seat," said Duncan. Duncan motioned for him to go to the round table to the right of Duncan's desk. Duncan stood up with his cup of coffee and walked over to Ken, shook his hand, and took a seat at the table. Ken sat down directly across from Duncan.

Ken felt that he needed to say something. "Duncan, Ilene and I had a great time Saturday night. It was great to see your beautiful home, too."

Duncan replied, "Thank you, Ken, I think we all had a great time, and we had some good conversations. You guys and your wives are great people, and I'm proud to be your friend.

"Now, let's get down to business. Ken, anything that we say here today needs to be in strict confidence. If you talk to Ilene, she must also understand that. Do I have your word?"

"Yes, you do," answered Ken.

"Ken, we are nearing our three-year presentation, when we'll disclose more about the Research Project to everyone. It will be a big event. I want to share with you today an overview of what that presentation will reveal and why we're all here."

Duncan then began to go into great detail about his history and the real purpose of the Research Project. He explained the complete ten-year plan. Duncan went over the Board members' backgrounds and their management roles. By the time he'd finished, three hours had passed, and it was time for lunch. Duncan suggested that they eat at the management cafeteria, located on the third floor. Ken had no idea that a cafeteria was there.

They left the sixth floor and headed to the cafeteria. It was small, and the food was served in a buffet style. The food looked really good. Having skipped a full breakfast, Ken was hungry. He selected the grilled salmon, asparagus, a twice-baked potato, and a dessert of carrot cake. Duncan had the lamb chops with mixed vegetables. The hostess seated them in a private room.

Duncan restarted the conversation by saying, "Ken, I've given you a lot of information this morning that will soon be shared with everyone. I know, from your background file before coming here and from your work history here, that you're a smart and trustworthy person. I personally know that you are brave, with lots of courage. We're going to need to bring people up from our ranks to take on bigger roles here. Over time, we'll be adding a representative system into the management structure, but I'd like to offer to you an opportunity that will rarely come up. I've reviewed this with the Board and have their full approval.

"Ken, I'd like to offer to you a position as the eighth director of our management board. You have a good relationship with the feelings and issues of the team members of the Research Project. We need that relationship represented on our Board to help us make proper decisions going forward for the colony. This will help us in our upcoming three-year community meeting event to show that the folks here are becoming integrated into the management. I know you can do this, and I'd be proud to have you on the management team here.

"You'd have an office here on the sixth floor. You would be assigned an additional management role that will grow your management skills. That role is yet to be determined. As far as compensation, you now know the long-term benefits will far outweigh any current compensation, but we are currently paying Board members $1 million a year in gold. And, you can have your new home built on one of the vacant lots on the prestigious Secret Street that is reserved for our key leaders.

"So, Ken, what do you think?"

Ken had never expected to get such an offer. This was just unbelievable. He pinched himself to see if he was dreaming. Nope, he wasn't dreaming. His head felt heavy, and his mind jumped from thought to thought.

He thought of Ilene and their kids. He thought of the difficult life in Shreveport. He remembered his time fighting in the Middle East and how that had helped him save the Kents. He had to stay focused on the present. He suddenly realized that he was looking down at his plate of food and not at Duncan.

Ken quickly woke up from his flashbacks, raised his head, looked directly into Duncan's eyes, and said, "Duncan, I would be delighted to serve you in any capacity you feel is appropriate for me. I feel somewhat unworthy, to be a director with you and to be in management here. It would be an unimaginable opportunity for my family and me. I accept your offer!"

"Then, welcome to the Board, Ken. I had a feeling that you would accept," Duncan said with a smile. He continued, "Now, I want you to keep this confidential until we have our three-year event in six weeks. So continue with your present work position at the plant, and we'll announce your promotion at the event. It's going to be difficult to keep it quiet, but I know you can do it. Perhaps, after you talk to Ilene, you two could come over to our place, and we'll grill some hamburgers and have some discussion on what you might like for your new home."

"That sounds great," said Ken.

"Let's give you about two weeks to be thinking about your new home design before we get together. Perhaps you and Ilene could take a walk down Secret Street, check out the lots, and pick out one that you like," added Duncan.

"I can hardly wait to tell Ilene. She's going to be so excited," replied Ken.

"Okay then, let's call it a day," Duncan said as he stood, walked to the door, and held it open for Ken. As Ken and Duncan shook hands, Duncan asked, "By the way, Ken, what is your favorite color?"

"It's blue," answered Ken. He dared not ask why.

Chapter 64
TELLING ILENE

Ken made it home an hour before Ilene and the kids. He opened the refrigerator and poured himself a glass of Chardonnay. He walked out onto the patio and sat down. There was a lot to tell Ilene. He wondered how much to say that evening. Perhaps he would just tell her about the promotion. Yes, that would be enough for tonight.

Ken called Ilene and asked her to bring home dinner from the pizza place. When Ilene arrived, they had dinner, and the kids went out to play in the park. From the balcony, Ilene and Ken watched them play, and Ilene finally asked. "Well, so, are you going to tell me about your meeting today or not? You've had me on pins and needles for more than an hour now. Come on, Ken—give it up!"

Ken started, "You know, we talked about what this might be last night. I thought maybe I would get some promotion or something with my job at the power plant. But, Ilene, I think

I'm still in shock. Keep in mind that this is very confidential and cannot be shared with anyone until after January 1."

"Okay, okay—just tell me," said Ilene as she became more frustrated.

For some reason, the right words to tell Ilene seemed difficult for Ken. He just felt unworthy of such a position. "Okay then, here it is," he blurted out. "I've been given the new position as the eighth member of the board of directors for the colony."

"Ken, that's wonderful!" Ilene said with a smile coming over her face.

"And, it comes with our new house being built on the exclusive Secret Street. And, a new base salary of $1 million a year."

"Holy shit! Oh . . . excuse me. Uh, did I hear you say a million dollars?" asked Ilene.

"I know—I've been in shock all day. But we have to keep this quiet for now. If we don't, I don't get the job." Ken felt that he needed to make up the threat of not getting the job to make sure Ilene didn't spill her guts to her friends Audria, Stormy, and Salina and her nursing buddies. "Duncan and Nellie want us to come over in a couple of weeks for hamburgers on the grill, a kind of casual deal. Just us, though, and we'll talk about what our ideas are for the new house. I'm sure our house won't be on the same scale as Duncan and Nellie's, but maybe ten thousand square feet. He didn't say what size. But all of the other directors live on Secret Street, and their homes are large and look beautiful from the outside. There are about twenty lots on Secret Street, and he wants us to pick one out soon.

"Also, Duncan told me a lot more about the history and workings of the colony and the Research Project, but that would take hours, and you'll find out all of that stuff soon enough."

Ken stood up and shouted down for the kids to come in. It was getting dark. He knew Ilene would be fired up now and talking until midnight. But, he didn't care. He felt like he'd just won the big lottery.

Ken was going to the power plant the next day to continue with his old job. It would be hard to focus on the job with the upcoming change, but he could manage with a smile on his face.

A week later, Duncan called Ken and asked him to come to the office after hours, around 6. Ken arrived, Duncan met him at the front door of the bank, and they went directly to the sixth floor.

"Ken, I want to show you your new office," said Duncan with a smile. He led Ken about midway down the hallway and opened a door to one of the offices. Opening the door and holding it open, he motioned for Ken to enter first. The lights were already on, and the office took Ken's breath away. He immediately saw the beautiful deep-blue leather inlayed desktop. The blue leather was trimmed with a narrow strip of gold-colored trim. The wood was a beautifully grained cherry wood. Behind the desk was a gorgeous deep blue leather executive chair. The back of the room was full-length windows, and the view looked to the north across the park and toward the golf course. A light-blue curtain was drawn open and bunched at both ends of the windows. Ken walked around the desk and stood beside his new chair. A new computer was sitting on the desk. Ken looked to the right and saw a matching wood credenza with a cherry wood wainscot and beautiful beige wallpaper above. The left side of the room was similar, except a 6-foot-long wet bar was at the entry. Some pictures had been installed with beautiful golden frames for Ken to fill with his choice of pictures or photos.

"Well, what do you think?" asked Duncan.

"This is just amazing. It's beautiful. I love it and can't wait to be in here. Thank you, Duncan. I really appreciate this," replied Ken.

"Once you move in full-time, you can make it your own. We finished it yesterday. I wanted to get you in to see it today." Duncan reached into his pocket and handed a set of keys to Ken. "Here are the keys to your office, to the bank building front door, and to a new white Denali that you can pick up once we've announced your promotion."

Ken's head was spinning. He thought, and then said, "A high-level management position, a fine office, a new home, a new car, a safe place to raise a family, a beautiful and unpolluted country. It just couldn't get any better. Thank you so much, Duncan. You've been so kind to me and my family."

"You're welcome, Ken. Now, let's go home." They walked out of the building together, and Duncan gave Ken a ride to the condo. Duncan told Ken that a Board meeting was held at least each month. And he wanted Ken to start attending those meetings effective immediately. The next meeting would be held on December 15.

Chapter 65
CLOSING SOME INVESTMENTS

It was only one month away from the three year anniversary of the colony kick-off and Bruce Bills was at his desk again, checking the colony account as usual. The stock market was off more than 50 percent, and it was time to close out the account. He quickly placed buy-to-close orders on all his short sales and then checked the bottom line of cash in the account. The total was $34 billion, including the $10 billion that was initially deposited. The plan had worked! Bruce's next move was to use all of the cash to buy more gold coins for delivery to the Colony Bank.

Chapter 66
THE BOARD MEETING

Ken headed off for the 10 o'clock December Board meeting with Duncan, Nellie, Bruce, Tom, John, Bob, and Joe. He was anxious and decided to get there early.

Ken arrived at the bank building two hours before the scheduled Board meeting time. He entered the sixth floor and walked to his new office. While still keeping his new position confidential to the general population, he was careful to avoid being seen as much as possible. He closed the door behind him and proceeded to sit in his new chair. He fired up his new computer and logged onto his new, confidential email account as a Board member. The Board member email was a private system and was structured such that it could only be used internally by the eight Board members and Duncan's executive secretary.

The boardroom was another beautiful room. It was located on the same floor as the Board member offices. The entrance was glass double doors; each door had the colony green kiwi standing on a gold bar etched into the glass. The walls and trim along the sides of the room were Japanese rosewood with a large stone fireplace opposite the entry door. Oil paintings of each of the original seven Board members trimmed the wooden walls at eye level.

Debbie had placed board documents along with water on the table for each director. A side table had a tray of local fruit grown within the farm.

At exactly 10, Duncan called the meeting to order. "Gentlemen, welcome to the December Board meeting. We typically kick off our Board meetings by asking Debbie to read the minutes of the last meeting. But, before we do that, I want to recognize and welcome our newly elected Board member, Mr. Ken Wallace, to our group." The Board applauded their approval. Duncan added, "I've brought Ken fully up to speed on the history and the operations of our purpose and direction here. And now, I'd like to ask Debbie to read the minutes of the last Board meeting."

Debbie read the minutes, which included the Board's unanimous vote to add Ken to the Board. The Board approved the minutes as read. Duncan then asked Bruce to kick off the meeting with a financial review.

Bruce began, "For the review, I'll be using a rounded monthly average gold pricing of $1,500 per ounce for this first part. I want to report that we now have a total gold reserve in the safe deposit boxes and reserves for the five thousand Colony Team families of $7.2 billion and a Colony gold reserve of $91 billion, of which $24 billion came from the short sales, and $54 billion came from Duncan and Nellie's contribution after-tax sale of Grainteck three years ago. Thirteen billion is the balance of the original equity trust that Duncan and Nellie originally donated. Our Wall Street account currently has a cash balance of about $10 billion that could support further short sales. We've spent about $10 billion on infrastructure to build the colony. The Colony Bank also has a gold deposit of $5.6 billion in personal accounts of the seven Board members of the colony. The colony is currently 90 percent self-sufficient, considering our current exports and imports. This means our rate of spending from our treasury is only about $5 million per month on the Colony Cards, excluding the $2.4 billion per year in committed family salaries."

"Great report," said Duncan. "But, should we continue to short stocks?"

"I don't see why not. The world situation is deteriorating, and there's no end in sight," responded Bruce.

Duncan added, "Okay then, does everyone agree?"

Everyone nodded. "Okay then, I'll start tonight," replied Bruce.

"Bob, please give us an update on Security & Rescue," requested Duncan.

Bob began. "We currently have sixty-six full-time security personnel; twelve are covering the entrance 24/7; twelve are covering the marina 24/7; twelve are covering the island perimeter, mostly with monitor cameras; twenty are serving as roving security and rescue and fire protection; ten are in supervisory and back-up positions. We are augmenting our security and rescue department with our community service hours of one thousand hours per week, which includes training, cross training, and relief support. We've had only minor issues in the last thirty days."

"John, where are we from an operations standpoint?" asked Duncan.

John replied, "We're actively building homes for those wanting one. We've completed three hundred so far and have another twenty under construction. We have a waiting list of only two hundred and thirty-two. It seems that many of the residents really like the condo lifestyle. There are currently 182 families that are expecting a baby. This is causing some relocation needs to meet our one-bedroom-per-child policy. But, we're on top of that. Water and utilities are fine. Energy reserves are okay, as we've finished our natural gas pipeline. We're in the process of building an auxiliary pipeline from the north, just in case we have interruptions from the south. Food supplies are more than adequate, with plenty of cattle, hogs, chickens, fish, fruits, and vegetables, including corn, wheat, and rice. We've maintained our policy of absolutely no imports of grains of any kind. We're still importing some seafood, beef, and pork so that we can continue to expand our herds and fishing fleet. Farm and fisheries personnel are steady at three hundred and forty-seven people. We're still using some New Zealand contractors around the marina and industrial area and for repairing items that need more people than we currently have. They do all of their work either outside the colony or in the industrial area."

Duncan stood and began to walk around the boardroom and reported to the group on the medical issues. He stated, "The medical issues are all going well. We've had a total of two hundred and seventy-eight births in the first three years. We had seven pregnant women when they arrived and only eleven births in Year One. Year Two had one hundred and twelve births, and Year Three has seen one hundred and fifty-five births. We currently have 182 pregnancies, which is about 7.3 percent of the women here. Our pharmacy has plenty of medicines and supplies on hand. We've purchased adequate medicines to cover a minimum of five years of potential needs. Our drug-development team is continually geared up for the manufacture of all possible and reasonable drugs here and should be 100 percent self-sufficient in five years."

Duncan sat down and said, "Gentlemen, I want to report that all is going well here at the colony. However, the world situation has begun to deteriorate. You all get the news and Internet reports and know it's bad and getting worse, as we expected. The Colony Board knew when we started this project five years ago that, with limited supplies and expanding populations, only one major catalyst was likely needed to create global chaos. We just didn't know when a catalyst of sufficient size would occur. For that reason, we built this colony to isolate everyone here from as much world chaos as possible.

"Another volcanic eruption occurred in Iceland four months ago and now continues to cause ash to spread across the entire northern hemisphere. Damaged crops and water will continue for a minimum of two years. That has caused a failure of many crops and pastureland. Food supplies are being rationed in wealthier countries. Poorer countries are simply starving, looting, and killing. And now it's spreading to the wealthier countries.

"The war on terror continues to escalate. The Middle East is essentially in full-scale war. Terrorists are everywhere trying to blow themselves and others up in order to get their promised virgins. Muslim factions are fighting each other for their own specific interpretation of the Koran. Governments are failing and falling into anarchy. People are revolting. World oil supplies are being impacted.

"The global birth rate's rapid decline is forcing governments to scramble to try to figure out what's causing it. However, the ramifications of its effects are being felt in every business and social structure. If they do eventually find out the true cause, Blocked Canyon will be totally bankrupt immediately. Blocked Canyon's buyout of Grainteck took on all assets *and* liabilities. But who knows if anyone will ever truly figure out the cause? The government's focus is now on trying to stop the anarchy.

"Without any population growth, the stock market is continuing to decline, while the opposite of the 'Baby Boomer' effect is taking place. Wall Street is calling it the 'Baby Bust.'

"The various world government deficits have now come home to roost. They can no longer borrow money from other countries, as any source of loan money has simply dried up. Without borrowing, the countries are defaulting on their trillion-dollar loans. Inflation and interest rates are currently more than 10 percent in the United States and higher elsewhere and continue to rise as food and materials become scarcer. Most governments are simply printing more paper dollars to pay for their bills, and that's causing severe inflation.

"People are hoarding any foods or money they may have. No one wants to lend money. Gold prices are rising a little bit almost every day, as no one wants any government paper money.

"New Ebola outbreaks continue to wreak havoc and spread in Africa and the Middle East. With the wealthier countries suffering from financial failure and growing anarchy, they aren't providing the monetary and humanitarian aid that they once did.

"New Zealand is fortunate to be isolated from most of this chaos. With only four million people and plenty of land located in the southern hemisphere, their food supply is still adequate to support the population. The lack of a Muslim population results in essentially no terrorism, with the exception of our oil tanker event. However, New Zealanders are concerned about their rapid birth rate drop and are looking for solutions.

"New Zealand is a great location for us to be right now! We're paying our property taxes and buying lots of meat and supplies, which they appreciate very much. They're aware that this area is a Research Project and, thus, are pretty much leaving us alone. My only concern is someone, seeing all of the children being born here and recognizing that we're different from the rest of the world, will start some kind of investigation. We need to keep security tight.

"I think that with our three-year event planned for next month, *now* is the time to make our population aware of the whole plan. Only a dozen of the team members have indicated they would like to cash out and go back to the States. Our participants have seen their gold caches grow to almost $1.5 million in gold. Even with the 50 percent forfeiture for a three-year termination, it would still be a nice chunk for three years of time, but most everyone wants to keep the money growing and keep it all. I would guess that, once they know the whole story, they wouldn't want to go back home at all."

Everyone agreed that it was time to have the three-year event. With that, Duncan adjourned the Board meeting.

Chapter 67
THE THREE-YEAR EVENT

The event had been scheduled for New Years Day. It turned out to be another beautiful Saturday, with low humidity and a typical New Zealand summer high temperature of eighty degrees. Rumors had been circulating for weeks that this was going to be big. Everyone knew the three-year minimum commitment time would be over the following day. The entire colony was in a buzz.

Since the weather was going to be so nice, Duncan had decided to have a grand street party. The whole street was set up with various food-and-beverage stations spread out over a two block area. There were Italian, Mexican, barbecue, seafood, and hors d'oeuvre stations. Decorations and lights were on all the buildings, and it gave the street a nighttime Disney World look. It was quite beautiful.

Starting time for the outdoor event was 7 p.m., with the grand auditorium event starting an hour and a half later.

The grand auditorium had been prepared for the big event. Everyone older than eighteen was scheduled to attend, except for a limited critical-service team covering power, medical, security, and other services. Those who could not attend were watching through closed-circuit TV. Children aged fifteen to eighteen were scheduled to manage the children aged five to fifteen at the various entertainment venues. The younger children were in daycare, and the daycare volunteers were watching the closed-circuit TV.

Ken and Ilene dropped David and Jan at their scheduled drop-off locations in the park behind the condos. They saw Salina directing children and making sure everyone was in their proper groups. Walking on toward the auditorium, they met up with Newton and Stormy and Stacy and Audria. They all walked together toward the auditorium.

Speculation abounded. "What do you think we'll hear today?" asked Audria.

"I have no idea," replied Stormy.

Ilene commented, "I think it's going to be a shocker."

"You do, really?" responded Newton.

Ilene continued, "Oh yeah, this meeting had been planned before we all got here. It has to be big. There have been some very unusual things happening here, but I can't tell you what those things are, due to confidentiality with my nursing job."

"Oh come on, Ilene—you're among friends."

"Nope, ain't happening," said Ilene.

"Okay, just be that way," said Audria. The friends continued their walk to the town auditorium, as the traffic from the condos got quite heavy. The sidewalks and roadways were full.

Almost everyone arrived a few minutes early and began milling around and visiting with neighbors and friends outside, enjoying the food and drinks. The auditorium was scheduled to open for seating at 8. The presentation was scheduled to begin at 8:30 sharp.

Chapter 68
HEADED TO THE AUDITORIUM

The stage was set with a podium and microphone with a thirty-by-thirty-foot white screen that already had a slide on it showing the colony logo.

A long table to the right of the podium was set up for Duncan and the board of directors. It was covered with plain white cloth. Eight chairs were set up on the backside of the table so that everyone on the Board would be facing the audience.

At 8:25, Duncan, Nellie, Tom, John, Joe, Bob, and Bruce walked onto the stage and took their seats at the table. The men were all dressed in dark suits and ties. Nellie was wearing a black dress and was carrying a red jacket over her arm. The auditorium noise was abuzz until Tom Clark stepped up to the podium. Suddenly, it was so quiet you could hear a pin drop.

Tom began, "Welcome, everyone. Congratulations on the completion of your first three years of the ESCAPE Research Project. I trust you've all enjoyed your time here so far."

Everyone applauded loudly for a full minute. "As we start here today, I want to thank Duncan and Nellie Kent for creating this world-class green community. Their creative and imaginative ideas have solidified into a reality that is unique in the entire world. That reality is now providing all of us with a safe place to raise our families and enjoy the fruits of our labor. The Kents had a vision and supported that vision with their personal wealth. Nellie has told me many times that Duncan wanted a farm and she wanted her friends, so they compromised and developed this town on the farm and invited all of us here to live, to work, to raise our families, and share in their fortune. As for me, I'm very appreciative of their generosity and commitment to all of us here." Everyone in the auditorium stood and applauded loudly. Duncan and Nellie stood and acknowledged the accolades.

"Duncan promised the Board members that he would share with all of you the complete purpose of the Research Project. He's decided that now is the time. To do that, I want to bring on that very special person. While some of you have met him already, I'm here to introduce to you the president of the colony and leader of the ESCAPE Research Project . . . the person responsible for funding 100 percent of the complete ESCAPE Research Project. **And here now is Duncan Kent!**"

Chapter 69
DUNCAN'S TALK

The applause lasted for another full three minutes as Duncan slowly stood from his chair, kissed Nellie on the cheek, walked to the podium, shook Tom's hand, and looked over the standing crowd of people. Duncan attempted to get the applause stopped, and when it finally did, he began to speak. His strong baritone voice was amplified throughout the auditorium in order for everyone to hear.

"Ladies and Gentlemen, welcome. I am excited today to share with you the story behind the ESCAPE Project and what it means for all of us.

"But first, let me start by saying that you all had signed up for a ten-year minimum contract with an option to drop out after three years at a reduced compensation package. Now that the three-year milestone has been reached, we will need any of you wishing to drop out to simply let us know in writing at the Colony Bank no later than one week from today. I'm hopeful that all of you will stay with us for the full ten years and beyond.

"Now, let me share with you the full story of the ESCAPE Research Project:

"As the sole owners of Grainteck, Nellie and I were approached for several years to sell our company by Wall Street hedge funds. With the exception of the New Zealand plant, which we separated and fully retained, we sold 100 percent of Grainteck exactly three years ago. We no longer own any Grainteck shares.

"Joe Hawkins, my personal lawyer, updated our will three years ago. Joe is also our only lawyer. We decided to give 95 percent of all of our assets and money to the colony treasury. The sale of Grainteck alone was $76 billion. Our assets consisted of an initial funding to the colony of approximately $20 billion. So, you can see that the treasury is on sound footing today and for a very long time.

"Next, let me explain the word ESCAPE as used in the ESCAPE Research Project." Duncan paused as the large screen projected the word ESCAPE large enough for everyone to see. The next screen showed the word ESCAPE vertically with letter extensions showing the full meaning:

Environmentally

Secure

Country

And

Peaceful

Earth

"When you all came here, you knew about the world's many problems. There are unending wars, uncontained nuclear-bomb proliferation, terrorists, drugs, crime, gangs, religious zealots, bad government, excessive taxation, air and water pollution, crowding, food and water shortages, energy shortages, poverty, and disease just to mention a few. All of these problems were continuing to grow unabated.

"But, these were just the symptoms and effects of an overall very big single problem for the world. This big problem of unlimited population expansion has been ravaging the world. Much of this population growth has occurred within the lowest IQ and poorly educated populations. Efforts to help those by providing food and immunizations have only resulted in massive and uncontrolled breeding. That help has a backfiring effect that is causing poor, illiterate populations to grow and to spin out of control. This then diminishes the ability of the earth to support and feed everyone. This has led to continued escalation of starvation and human misery as well as the rapid destruction of the earth's natural resources and ability to support this growing population. With limited and declining resources on the planet and a world population of more than seventeen billion people and increasing rapidly, humankind could not and would not survive. It will simply be a matter of time before some major catastrophic events drive the people to anarchy. We're seeing that beginning to happen everywhere we look now, especially after the recent Iceland volcano eruption.

"On a personal note, I started Grainteck thirty-seven years ago. My career path has been extremely rewarding for me and my lovely wife, Nellie. It was rewarding for all of the Grainteck employees, too. Our business goal was simply to add to and improve the world food supply. That worked short-term, but the food-capacity addition was met with just more impoverished people consuming the added capacity. You see, the overriding problem was a population growth out of control and a world not willing to deal with the problem. With four of my dear friends, Tom Clark, John Earnest, Joe Hawkins and Bob Erickson, along with Nellie, we collaborated on how we could do something—anything—to solve the problem.

"That collaboration resulted in a strategic plan that we knew would take a lot of time and money to accomplish. But, time and money would not be enough." Duncan now raised his voice and exclaimed, "We need you! You are all hand-selected individuals and families with very high IQ levels . . . You are good, honest people . . . You are hard working and family oriented . . . You and your families all deserved more from life than you were getting . . . Your skills and training were the most important component for the ESCAPE Project to be successful.

"We established this community and brought you all in as a part of the team. We have more than five thousand families here. Our research shows that our culture has proven reasonably efficient and doesn't need the burdens present outside of our community. We have no need for military, insurance, license, taxes, religion, and political parties to argue and fight over.

No need for lawyers—except for Joe Hawkins, of course!" Duncan glanced at Joe as everyone laughed.

Duncan continued, "Our mutual support for the colony is through mandatory community service work time as a component part of each of your normal forty-hour work-weeks. Everyone contributes to the overall good versus some politicized tax and bureaucratic wasteful process. Our new governing process selects one representative per year for each five-year age group, beginning with age group twenty-five through twenty-nine years old. Each representative serves four years and cannot be re-selected for fifteen years. This way, after four years, you will end up with a total of twenty-four representatives. They're selected for their age group by the highest annual IQ score of a standard testing program. There are no popularity contests or politics or lobbying self-interests. Selected individuals serve as volunteers, as do all government positions utilizing their eight hours per week of community-service work allocation. I want to announce today your first six representatives." The giant screen projected the names and pictures as Duncan read them. "They are:

Kay Copeland	Medical Surgeon
Jerry Chang	Computer Systems
Penny Lyons	Massage Therapist
Stacy Baltzegar	Mechanical Engineer
Judy Jones	Medical Doctor
Dan Wilson	Logistics Scheduler

I want them all to stand, and let's give them a hand." The new representatives stood, and the auditorium erupted in applause once more. Once the applause stopped, Duncan began again: "I'm excited to have these individuals as part of the management structure.

"Next, I want you to know that, effective immediately, Ken Wallace has been elected to the Board of Directors. Ken is an electrical engineer with a United States Marine background and training. I'm sure you all know of the courageous event two months ago, where Ken courageously saved Nellie and me from a murderer slipping in here from the States.

"Ken, I'd like for you to come up and take a seat at the table with the other Board Members. Please stand and give Ken a hand." Everyone stood and applauded as Ken walked onto the stage. It was a standing ovation! The large screen showed a picture of Ken.

Duncan began again. "We now have a base structure for a new working country here at the colony. And, yes, you did hear me correctly; I did say *country*. There will be more to say on that in a moment." Duncan paused for a couple of deep breaths.

"So, now, I want to share with you a much bigger picture. And my friends and colleagues, it is big! Around fifteen years ago, through my genetic research, I developed a breakthrough in human genealogy. I have shared that technology and information with only eight people, all here today. You're all very smart people, so bear with me on a short technical journey as I share this information with you."

Slides began to show representative pictures of genes. "Telomeres are disposable buffers at the ends of chromosomes that are shortened during cell division; their presence protects the genes of the chromosome from being shortened. A good analogy would be much like your plastic shoelace ends protect your shoelaces from becoming frayed and unraveled. During chromosome replication to replace damaged body cells, the enzymes that duplicate DNA cannot continue their duplication all the way to the end of a chromosome. So, with each and every duplication, the telomeres of the chromosome become shorter and shorter. Over time, due to each cell division, which is critical to replace bad or damaged cells, the telomere ends become too short and, as such, after a finite number of cell divisions, one's cells simply fragment and break down, and this fragmented or imperfect gene leads to aging and ultimately death. I found out that I could lengthen human LIFESPANS to a total of approximately **two hundred and seventy years** by genetically modifying the **telomere** region at each end of the chromosome.

"The technology to implement this was initially through a single injection. Nellie and I took those first injections fifteen years ago when we were fifty-one and fifty-two years old. My five dear friends and their families received the injections four years ago. The life-lengthening process involves no real changes during the first twenty years of life or during the last twenty years, but slows down aging for the two hundred and thirty years in between. It merely stretches out the middle portion. Essentially then, one would reach midlife at age one hundred and thirty-five versus the normal age of forty-two.

"As a next step, the old saying 'you are what you eat' is really true. The technology I developed at Grainteck has now been implemented through our own R&D genetically modified seed plant. That provided the ability to imbed the genetic change in all of you through the corn, wheat, and rice you've been eating during the last three years. And now, all of you can reasonably expect to have a life expectancy of two hundred and seventy years versus eighty-five years! Childbirth should even be possible all the way to age one hundred and twenty for most normal healthy women and men. You now have a lot more time to make a difference for your family, your children, and to your society."

A gasp rolled through the crowd; slowly giving way to wild applause and yells as everyone realized what they'd just heard.

Duncan turned to the Board members seated to his right. "Nellie, will you join me at the podium, please?" Nellie rose from her chair and walked to Duncan. Duncan whispered into her ear and then turned to the audience exclaiming, "And for proof, as many of you may know, I will be seventy years old in two weeks. Nellie has allowed me to share with you that she will be sixty-nine years old in March. And now, with our new life expectancy, she is equivalent to the ripe old age structure of twenty-two years old! And, I'm announcing today that we are expecting our first child in June!" Everyone in the auditorium stood up and began shouting and applauding. The rest of the Board members stood up to show their excitement for Nellie and Duncan. When the applause stopped, Nellie returned to her chair and sat down.

Duncan turned back to the audience and said, "Thank you all for your kindness and excitement for us. Let me move forward and continue with my presentation. Because of this more efficient cell replacement, I believe most instances of cancer, heart disease, diabetes, and other age-related or genetic-triggered diseases will be substantially reduced at least through age two hundred and fifty.

"While we believe this is good for all of you here, it does nothing to address the big problem.

"And now, let me also share with you the resolution of the **BIG PROBLEM of just too many people in a small, limited world.** The world's population will soon grow to a point that the planet will not be able to support human life. We had no desire to see anyone currently alive have his or her life shortened, and that includes all the way from conception to the natural end of life. With that in mind, I realized the only solution was to deal with the **REPLICATION of the population.**

"Replication was actually the big problem that might actually be solvable. If the population would only control its rate of reproduction, then the population could be stopped from its current exponential growth. Obviously, any global slowing of replication was not happening, and ultimately that overpopulation was going to destroy the entire human species.

"That said, four years ago I began to develop and prepare for production at all of the Grainteck plants in the world a separate modified strain of genetically modified seeds with a different genetic modification from the one I just described. Grainteck did not implement any of these modifications. This modification would not extend or shorten people's lives in any way. But it did modify the human genetic sequence in such a way that the chromosome of the human sperm and the egg could no longer combine. The development objective was to make these grains available to governments that needed to humanely reduce their countries' populations in order to prevent the ultimate starvation of millions of people. However, Blocked Canyon, the company that purchased Grainteck, including all of its assets and liabilities, was unaware of the potential effect on human genes and failed to test the impact of the grains on humans. They were warned, but they neglected to pay any attention to the warning labels on computers and seed bags that they were not to use these seeds for human or animal food production due to possible physical modifications to the human genome. Blocked Canyon chose to ignore these warnings. They began selling these seeds on the world market three years ago. These genetically modified foods produced from these seeds made it onto the world's tables during the last two years. This has resulted in a dramatic drop in births throughout the world that ultimately will likely reach zero except for this protected population here.

"When I sold Grainteck, I was concerned this could happen, if not with Blocked Canyon, then potentially with some terrorist organizations with genetic-modification skills, so I instituted strict import restrictions on grains of any type into our community. We developed our own exclusive grain seed production company.

"And now, without any new births in the rest of the world, the world population will be dropping at a 3 percent annual rate. Over the next forty-five years or so, during the normal child-bearing ages of young women, the current world population, again excluding our community, will not be replicating itself. The world's current population will continue to age normally and ultimately pass away. That is except for you—members of the ESCAPE Project.

"This means that in one hundred years or less, there will be no risk of nuclear war, no risk of terrorism, no religious wars, no political wars. The future is now yours and yours alone! All of the assets of the world will belong to you and your children.

"We've been diligent in keeping the grains that would make you infertile away from the colony, and we will continue to do that. Anyone leaving the colony for now will surely end up consuming the genetically modified grains used in the world and become sterile, and that includes any of your children who accompany you. After the next ninety or so years, if you were to leave, there will be no infrastructure to support you and few if any people left. Those left in the rest of the world will be very old. With all of the world problems and anarchy we're seeing, we aren't sure that many people in the rest of the world will survive even the next thirty to forty years."

Duncan paused for a few seconds, looked over the crowd, and began his final comments, "My friends, you are the hope for humanity. What we have here today is simply a new beginning.

You can now redraft the rules in a manner of a single nation of the earth. In less than one hundred years, you will inherit all of the resources left on this planet. You'll have all of the gold, silver, other minerals, oil, food, water, natural gas, and all energy sources. The damaged and exploited land, sea, and air will be beginning to heal. You'll be able to go forth and destroy all nuclear and other weapons. In the history of man, this has never been possible until now. I know there will be problems and challenges for you to deal with. But, I challenge you as the best and brightest, with a renewed and longer adult life at your disposal, for your children and your generations to come, to look at the past and help create a governing structure and culture that will guide mankind and long endure. Our directors have provided you with a guideline, but we want you to play an active role in a new constitution soon to be established here. However, there will be no professional politicians allowed . . . ever.

"I want to thank all of you for your support of this project, and I hope you recognize today how lucky and empowered you are to seize the day and make a beautiful tomorrow.

"Good day, my friends!"

The audience rose to their feet and applauded loudly as Duncan walked to Nellie's chair and held out his hand. Nellie smiled and rose to take Duncan's hand.

As they walked offstage, Nellie said to Duncan, "You know we almost gave my pregnancy away ahead of time at the party. Your idea of having Jon-Michael fill up a secret Chardonnay bottle with apple juice worked well." They held hands as they walked from the stage along with the other Board members.

Nellie kept smiling at Duncan as they left the room, and she whispered in Duncan's ear as she patted her tummy.

"I want ten children, you know, and *Charlie* is going to want some brothers and sisters, so you'd better get busy, old man."

"It just has to be the water here," replied Duncan with a big grin. He kissed Nellie on the cheek as they walked away.

Chapter 70
THE WALK HOME

Ken and Ilene walked home from the meeting slowly through the park. At first, they said nothing. Then, as her thoughts continued to build, Ilene asked, "Well, Ken—what do you think?"

Ken answered with the same question, "What do *you* think?" Neither wanted to answer first.

Finally, Ilene answered, "I think the world is falling apart. It was falling apart long before we came here. We're lucky . . . just plain lucky to have been selected for this. I never want to go back. But, I feel much sorrow for the people back home in the States and the world and yet . . . I realize that no one's life has been shortened."

They continued to walk as Ken said, "Ilene, you're the love of my life, and we both want to raise our children in peace and safety with the most security that we can give them. Peace and safety doesn't exist anywhere in the world outside of this place. I believe that the Kents are right and have done the earth and mankind a true service when no one else could or would."

Ilene responded, "Ken, let's go home . . . to our condo and the rest of our lives. We have new plans to make!"

Ken laughed and smiled.

"By the way, sweetheart, you're looking a lot younger!"

NOT THE END
But the beginning!

EPILOGUE
AUCKLAND AIRPORT

The private jet landed at noon, and FBI agents Ben Norwood and Tony Doster exited the plane. It had been a long flight from Virginia to New Zealand. They'd get a good night's rest before their planned meeting with the New Zealand police investigators. This was a preliminary courtesy, as their main purpose was the ongoing investigation into the death of Jay Cameron and Blocked Canyon. A surprise visit to the Tapora Research Project was planned for the following day.

Made in the USA
Lexington, KY
17 October 2017